SHATTERED
CITY

Noël F. Caraccio

BELLASTORIA PRESS

Stories from the heart

ISBN: 978-1-942209-47-8

Shattered City

Cover design by Wicked Smart Designs

BELLASTORIA PRESS
P.O. Box 60341
Longmeadow, Massachusetts 01116

"Let us pray not to be sheltered from dangers but to be fearless when facing them."

Rabindranath Tagore

Acknowledgments

Very special thanks to Richard Lavsky for all his help with the computer issues. Without his help, who knows what would have been lost in cyberspace? I also appreciate his patience in proofreading the manuscript both for content and errors.

Thanks to Sandy Schoeneman for reading the manuscript and giving me her perspective on the story from a New Yorker's viewpoint, but especially for her always astute insights and counsel on life's problems.

Chapter 1

VALERIE

Valerie didn't exactly hate flying. She hated all the trappings of getting to the airport on time. She hated having the limo waiting in the driveway while she threw the last few items into her suitcase. She hated checking for her ticket and wallet in her purse a few thousand times. She hated dragging all the stuff to the door, with Todd standing in the front hallway with a bemused smile on his face, since this was always the pattern. She hated the thought of going through security at LAX, of having to take off her shoes, open her laptop, put her phone in the bin, and then try to get it all back in the right place in twelve seconds so as to not hold up the rest of the line behind her.

Valerie knew this was all a smokescreen. It was true that she hated all of these things related to flying, but what was underlying all the agitation was the fact that she was leaving Todd, her home and all that was familiar and precious to her. It was such a great opportunity to be asked to be the lead attorney on this huge case pending in federal court in New York, that she couldn't pass it up, much as the little voice inside was telling her not to go. Was that little voice the last holdover from when she was a kid and was always shy and afraid of any new thing? Right now the little voice was screaming inside her that this was all a mistake that they were picking the wrong person. That there were other people better qualified and better suited to this monstrous task. One part of her felt that she was really just a kid faking it in a business suit and heels, and not even a real grown up while the other part of her knew Valerie Wilkinson was a talented and experienced attorney well beyond her years.

The yellow shirt she was wearing looked good against her honey-colored hair and fair complexion, which was right now a copper shade of tan. The yellow in the shirt was a softer color than she usually wore to work. At work, she wore power colors like bright reds and brilliant blues to make a statement to her clients and to the courts. Her hair was pulled back in a ponytail, and as she continued to gaze at herself in the mirror, she hardly looked formidable. She could have been mistaken for a history professor in a liberal arts college, or perhaps a promising architect.

The doorbell shocked her out of her reverie; it was the limo driver. "Hey, Val, the limo's here," Todd added redundantly, as if someone else was going to be ringing the doorbell at this precise time of the morning. Now came the hard part. She had to say goodbye to Todd. Sure they had talked about it. Sure they knew it was the greatest compliment that the client wanted her in New York to take the lead on a major commercial case. Sure they promised her carte blanche on resources and accommodations, but now that the time had come to "shuffle off to Buffalo," she was trying hard not to cry.

Todd came to the bedroom door. "What can I carry out to the limo for you?"

As Val turned around to look at him, the tears welled up and stung her eyes. Todd came all the way into the bedroom in response to that look, and drew her to him.

"C'mon, Val, we talked about this. This is a chance of a lifetime for your career. You will be able to write your ticket anywhere after this. You are so good and you don't even give yourself enough credit. This is a huge corporation which could have picked any law firm and any attorney it wanted. They picked you. They picked you over all the attorneys in the New York office. What could be a better vote of confidence? You should be thrilled and proud. Now is not the time to cry. You can cry when you lose the case." Val punched him in the arm at the joke.

"See, that's the combative lawyer I know and love. Punch me again; you'll feel better. You'll feel like you're at work," Todd laughed.

He wiped the tear off her cheek with a tenderness she loved. The mere thought of that made her well up again. Todd tried another tack.

"The limo driver is going to think I'm beating you in here if you go out there with your eyes all red. Then I'll get arrested for domestic violence and my lawyer will be on a plane to New York. I'll never get bail and I'll rot in jail." Val now had some semblance of a smirk on her face.

"I'll be out to see you in New York in a few weeks, courtesy of The Fleming Corp. Hell, you could ask for a Porsche to take you back and forth to work and they'll give it to you. Just come pick me up from the airport in it." Todd moved her purposefully in the direction of the door. "C'mon, no more tears. I'll talk to you tonight when you get there."

As the limo pulled on the freeway, Val continued to stare out the window. She hadn't said much of anything to the driver. She was afraid he'd hear the tremor in her voice. If she was this upset at leaving Todd, why was it that they had been together for three years, and yet they weren't doing anything in the way of getting married? Every so often her biological clock began to tick louder.

Right now she tamped those thoughts down. No need to make herself more upset than she already was.

Chapter 2

PAUL

Paul Bennett hung up the phone and jabbed his hand up in the air to signify victory. He jumped up so fast from his desk that he knocked his desk chair into the wall. He didn't care if anyone heard it and he didn't care if he put a hole in the wall. He took a few big strides to the door and closed it with a little more ferocity then he planned. The door banged with even more noise than the desk chair. Now that the door to his office was closed, and he was alone, he let out a few more war whoops and a few more jabs into the air.

Whom should he call? The voice in his head screamed, "Everyone." Everyone he ever knew throughout his whole life. Everyone he competed with in college and business school. Everyone he beat out for jobs. Everyone who beat him out for jobs. All his buddies at the club. All the assholes at the club who wanted to beat him at golf.

After a few seconds the rush of adrenaline began to subside, and he realized how fast his heart was still beating. He forced himself to walk up and down in his office slowly in an attempt to get his breathing under control. Okay, okay, there will still be plenty of time for celebrating, and even gloating. For now, he needed to think about what to do and how best to proceed.

He didn't hate his job at the public relations firm, and it paid well. The problem was it was so plain vanilla. When he joined the firm located in Denver three years ago, they had a good client roster and he saw the firm as a stepping stone, but the two owners were getting old. Paul thought they were bridging to retirement. He didn't see them going after exciting new accounts. They were content to service the clients they had. When Paul signed on, he thought the firm was the right size to be taken seriously by bigger clients and a chance for him to be on the team going after the new clients. He envisioned himself being noticed by the two owners, and because of how well he did, eventually becoming one of the owners himself. It didn't work out that way at all because the firm was tired and in a rut. Paul was ready, yes, ready for this new challenge and new adventure.

Now that his heart rate had slowed down, Paul had to figure out his exit strategy. This wasn't a business in which to burn bridges. He had learned already that karma is a bitch. He had seen it with other people and learned the lesson once himself early in his career. What goes around comes around, and when that happens, you have to be very careful that it doesn't hit you square in the face. Maybe he'd even offer to throw this firm some business.

Okay, back to whom he should call. Debby first. Then he would go see Kevin. No, Kevin first and then Debby. Paul picked up his coffee mug, which at the present moment, was still about a third full. He had to be careful; this had to look casual, but Paul needed to share this with Kevin. Debby would be happy, but wouldn't understand the full import of what this meant.

Paul opened his door and as casually as he could, looked down the long corridor. He fingered the piece of paper in his pocket on which he had just scribbled a few words. Everything seemed to be as it should. The typical office noises of phones ringing, copiers whirring away and the incessant tapping of computer keys. No one seemed to have noticed the noises coming from his office. As he walked toward the kitchen and the coffee makers, Paul nodded hello to two administrative assistants and one young account exec.

In the kitchen, Paul willed himself to rinse out his coffee mug, and then pour himself some coffee. All deliberate actions. Chuck Walker appeared at the kitchen door as Paul turned to leave. Paul groaned inwardly. Chuck was one of the middle-level guys who would always be a middle-level guy. He was the plainest vanilla of the plain vanilla. The guy hadn't had an original idea in the last two years. If you let him corner you, the next thing you knew, you had wasted twenty minutes, learned nothing, and most probably given Chuck the only original idea he ever had for a project.

"How's it going, Chuck?"

"Okay, you see the game last night?" Chuck asked, almost as one word.

Although Paul was an avid sports fan, Chuck could monopolize a conversation about sports better than anyone else. "Nope, I wasn't home; I missed it."

Paul made a point of looking at his watch. "I gotta run. I have a conference call."

Chuck didn't budge from the doorway for an awkward few seconds. It was almost as if Chuck didn't believe that Paul hadn't seen the game. Paul took three steps toward Chuck before he finally moved. Paul had no idea what that was about.

Fortunately, Kevin's office was in the same direction as Paul's, but just farther down the hallway, so as far as Chuck was concerned, Paul was headed in the correct direction. Again, Paul had to keep his pace from looking hurried or frantic. It needed to look like two colleagues having a conversation. When Paul got to Kevin's office, Kevin was on the phone, but waved Paul into the office. Paul gave Kevin the sign with his finger across his neck, meaning cut. Kevin got it right away and said, "Listen, I've got to wrap this up now, I'm late for a meeting. Talk to you tomorrow."

Kevin looked up at Paul expectantly, and Paul pulled the piece of paper out of his pocket and handed it to Kevin. The message read, "Don't react or say anything. I GOT IT! You're coming with me."

Kevin flushed, and a big smile spread across his face.

Before Kevin could say anything, Paul jumped in. "Want to have lunch today? How about I come by just after noon?" All Kevin could do was nod.

This was going to be a blow to the firm, because Paul and Kevin were two of the best people and did bring in new business, almost in spite of the way the firm was run. Just not the mega clients that Paul wanted to go for.

Now Paul was ready to call Debby. She would like the idea of a new job and the big salary, but he wasn't so sure how she would react to his going to New York. Without her.

Chapter 3

TOM

Thomas Amendola looked out the picture window of his den at home at the tennis court in his back yard. It had certainly been an extravagance, but he loved tennis so much. Despite the fact that he had precious little time, he still played three or four times a week, even if he played at ungodly hours. Past the fencing of the tennis court was beautiful green lawn and some gorgeous flower beds. He would miss this, but the offer was for one year, with either side having the option to call it quits thereafter. After all, he didn't have to sell this place, and he planned to fly back here to Atlanta every other weekend. Maybe it was time to change things up now that Laurie had passed.

He hadn't told his hospital yet until the offer was finalized. The phone conversation he just finished, cemented it. He should see an e-mail Monday morning with the offer. Matthews Memorial Hospital had been more than accommodating to everything he wanted for the transplant program, since his name would be a huge factor in getting NIH and foundation grants.

Two of his kids were already out of college and the youngest was at Yale, which looked to be about eighty miles from New York City, where he would be. She could come to visit him once in a while for the weekend whenever she wanted, and the lures were the shows on Broadway as well as professional baseball, football and basketball teams. It was less than a two-hour drive, certainly far less time than New Haven to Atlanta.

Paula was going to be another story. While Tom had been "transplanted" to Atlanta, to use a bad pun, he was originally from Delaware. He had learned to love the South, and it surprised him how much it now felt like home. Paula, on the other hand, was born in Georgia, and was a dyed-in-the-wool Southerner. They were starting to spend more time together, and Tom liked that, but he was ambivalent about how far he wanted this relationship to go. He still dwelt on the long battle with cancer, which he and Laurie had waged together and which they'd lost. Because Laurie had been sick for a long time before her death, Tom felt as if he had been alone for ages.

Paula was a good sport and full of life. That had been a refreshing change for him and he liked that. But he wasn't at all sure how Paula was going to react to the news that he was going to New York for a year at least. He also wasn't sure if Paula would ever adjust to life in the North, much less New York City. He wasn't sure if she would even want to try. If he was going to be honest with himself, he hadn't even really consulted her on this decision. So there was going to be the double whammy of not consulting her about the offer and not consulting her before making the decision.

The truth of the matter was that once the preliminary feelers had gone out to him from Matthews Memorial and he replied that he had more than a little interest, the train had left the station. It just remained to be seen how far the train was going to go, and it seemed like it was headed to New York City.

Tom had been walking through the house as he was trying to think things through. He paused for a second to look at himself in the mirror in the dining room.

Even though his hair was salt and pepper, at least he still had almost a full head of hair. He was tall and trim. Not bad looking. Maybe there would be some interesting women in New York.

Tom actually laughed out loud at himself at that thought. He really didn't know anyone in New York, so he wasn't exactly expecting an active social life. More important, even though the transplant program was already in existence, his research would probably take the program to a much higher level. That was going to require a lot of his time. His research was so exciting and held such promise for patients who needed a transplant. That's what he needed to focus on, and not this foolishness about meeting women. Still, it did offer him something to think about, even if he couldn't say this out loud. After all, he was still a successful doctor. And he was unattached, sort of.

Chapter 4

PAUL

Paul buzzed Kevin on the intercom. "Ready to go?" he asked Kevin without further conversation.

"Yep, all set."

"I'll meet you in the lobby in five minutes." With that, Paul hung up and grabbed his suit jacket from the hook on the back of his door and left the office. He headed for the elevator and hoped he wouldn't be waylaid by anyone who needed something from him before he could get out of the office.

Fortunately, the elevator cooperated and arrived shortly after he pushed the button. He was on the "local" and the car stopped on every floor on the way down. Paul was tapping his foot the whole way down. When the elevator door opened, Paul took a fast look around and was pleased to see Kevin already in the lobby, leaning against a pillar.

"Hey, Paul, the usual place?" asked Kevin.

"No, let's head over to Clifford's. I know it's a walk, but I want to be away from anyone we know or any other nosy diners."

They walked briskly and arrived in about ten minutes. Even though Clifford's was busy, there were still a few open tables and Paul and Kevin grabbed the last available booth. The waiter brought over the menus and left with their drink order.

"Tell me what's going on; I've been losing my mind waiting for lunchtime to get out of the office."

Paul took one more look around to make sure there was no one they knew anywhere near them in the restaurant, and then he began.

"I got the call this morning, as you know. They want me! They agreed to my number for the salary and they'll pay for my housing and car. I'll be based in New York, but there will be a fair amount of travelling. Everyone but the campaign manager and David's "personal counselor," as he calls him, will report to me. The "personal counselor" is a friend of David's from college, so they go way back. His name is Andrew Dustin. I guess David wants someone he's known forever and feels he can absolutely trust.

"The guy is phenomenally successful. He's made mega millions in the pharmaceutical industry, so in addition to being an old friend, the guy has a boatload of dollars he can donate to David's war chest.

"David wants me to fly to Florida to meet Andrew Dustin. From the way he's talking, unless I spit at Andrew or sleep with his wife, I have the job. Our areas of responsibility aren't going to overlap. Andrew is going to be with David most of the time on the campaign trail, and I will mostly be in New York. They will be doing policy and I'll be doing fundraising. When they need me to be with David, then I fly to wherever he is at that time."

"I assume you have Googled him and know everything about him." Kevin said that as a statement of fact, and not as a question.

"Of course I have. But that's not enough. I've made a few calls once I knew I was seriously in the running. I need all the non-public information I can get my hands on. I've gotten a lot of inside info with those calls.

"I had a client with a big job in pharma from my job two firms ago. I've been waiting to call him until I knew I had the job. I just didn't want to show my hand too early in case I didn't get the job. You never know who knows who and something gets out before you have the job in the bag. I could have been screwed both ways. Suppose I didn't get the job and then somehow it gets back here that I was seriously looking. That's the stuff nightmares are made of."

Paul was about to continue on about himself, when finally, Kevin couldn't contain himself any longer.

"What about me? Where do I fit in?" Kevin almost seemed like a little kid asking if he could play with the big kids. Paul thought the remark probably came out more of a plea than Kevin had wanted it to sound.

"I told you, man, you're coming with me."

"I got that, but what am I doing?"

"I get a staff, and I told David I need at least one person that I know personally and can rely on. Not quite sure how big my staff is going to be. I think he liked that idea. I pitched it so that it came out that's it's the kind of relationship that he has with Andrew. You don't know all the people who are going to be working on a campaign, so it's important that the people at the top are known quantities.

"We'll get to the number of people later once he shows me a budget. I may get to handpick a few more people to bring with us from the beginning. It remains to be seen right now.

"Aren't you going to ask me about salary? You know you want to." Paul grinned.

Kevin smiled back. "I knew from what you said this morning that is was going to be great or you wouldn't have been that excited. Okay, I'll bite. What's the salary?"

"Take your current salary and add one hundred thousand to it. Sounds pretty good, right?"

"Are we good for the year of the pre-campaign stuff and then the campaign itself?"

"We definitely are."

Chapter 5

VALERIE

Valerie got out of the limo and looked around. So here she was in New York. Not her first time here, but her first time seeing New York in a whole different light. It was late September and the City was still hot. She would probably be here for eight to ten months at a minimum, so she would see a few changes of seasons. Valerie was the lead attorney for the plaintiff in a complex commercial case involving multiple claims of breach of contract in the building of a new luxury condominium project, Letters of Credit and guarantees.

At least the neighborhood looked very upscale and they had passed three or four great looking bistros within two blocks on the cross streets. Not that she anticipated going out for dinner very much, but she did know that every place delivered in New York. Especially if she came home late from the office, which was pretty much a given based on what would go on with this lawsuit. The limo driver handed her suitcase to the doorman. Valerie thanked the driver and shook his hand with some money in hers, which transferred neatly to his hand.

"I do a lot of work for your firm, ma'am. If you want, you can ask for me by name. My name is Louis. I'll be more than happy to drive for you anytime. Just remember, Louis."

Valerie laughed. "Okay, Louis, I will remember your name and remember to ask for you."

Valerie turned to the doorman, who smiled at her as he held the door open and motioned her to go ahead of him. Valerie introduced herself to the doorman and said she was a new tenant. As they moved through the door, the doorman deftly moved ahead of Valerie and guided her to the desk of the concierge. Valerie introduced herself again, this time to the concierge. He was a short, balding man of about fifty years old in a dark suit that had not been bought off the rack. In another situation, he would not have been memorable, but there was something pleasant about his smile.

"Ms. Wilkinson, we've been expecting you. Your luggage arrived two days ago and is already in your apartment. If you need help unpacking or getting settled, I can send someone up to help you. We want to do everything possible to make your stay here a success. Would you like me to have someone bring your suitcase upstairs now?"

Valerie said she could roll it behind her to the elevator. The concierge handed her the keys and again reiterated that he was more than happy to help in any way. Valerie thought to herself that the patter, if recited by someone else, would have made her think that he was a complete suck up, but maybe it was real. She would have to wait and see. She certainly wanted him to like her. He would be very useful during her stay in New York. Valerie made a mental note to tip him sooner rather than later.

As she came off the elevator on the fourth floor, she noted the fresh flowers in a vase on a small table in the hallway. As she walked to her right down the hall, she also noticed that the walls looked to be freshly painted and she could see the marks from the vacuum cleaner on the rug. So far, so good. The plane had been on time, there had been no turbulence in the air, the limo driver was waiting for her with a sign with her name on it in baggage claim, the concierge seemed more than willing to please and the building looked to be well maintained. If her apartment was this good, then maybe all these things were good omens for her stay in New York.

Valerie opened the door to the apartment and a bright apartment greeted her. The living room was large and the furniture was modern, but not minimalist. There was a good-sized couch, with a coffee table, two end tables with lamps, a love seat and an armchair in a conversation grouping. All nicely appointed and all neutral. The splash of color was a huge abstract painting over the couch, with red, black and yellow as the predominant colors. Valerie wouldn't necessarily have bought this painting, but it did provide the necessary color so that the rest of the room wouldn't be considered boring.

As Valerie headed toward what she presumed was the bedroom, she stopped momentarily because she thought she heard a gushing sound. As she approached the bedroom, the sound became noticeably louder. She walked into the bedroom and what moments before had merely been a sound, now became a reality. The sound was rushing water, never a good sound in a house or apartment. As she approached the bathroom, the rug underfoot felt mushy and wet. Her mind knew even before she actually saw it with her eyes.

The bathroom floor was completely underwater, and a large section of the ceiling had collapsed onto the tile floor. Valerie gasped, and took four steps backward. So much for all the good omens up until this moment. It took her a few seconds for the shock to wear off and her mind to process what she had just seen. As her intellect took over, she realized that this was not her house and she didn't have to call and pay for the plumber, and most certainly, a contractor.

She had another moment of panic about where she would stay tonight. Hell, this is New York City, with a million hotel rooms, she thought. This was going to be the management company's problem, not hers, if as the concierge had said earlier, her "stay was going to be a success."

Valerie backed out of the bathroom and went to retrieve her cell phone from her purse in the living room. "Shit, I have no idea of the concierge's phone number," she said out loud to no one in particular. As she was about to grab the keys and go back down to the lobby, she saw a phone on the wall in the hallway between the kitchen and the bedroom, which mercifully said "House phone."

She picked up the phone and dialed 50 as the instructions said. She heard one ring and the voice at the other end said, "Concierge, how may I help you?"

"John, this is Valerie Wilkinson. I just checked in a few moments ago. The bathroom is flooded and a large part of the bathroom ceiling is now lying on the bathroom floor."

"Oh, my!" came the response at the other end of the phone. "I will be right up. Don't worry."

Valerie returned the phone to its carriage and went to sit on the couch in the living room. All of a sudden, all the travelling and anticipation caught up with her, and she was very tired. It seemed she had just about sat down when the doorbell rang. Okay, so he's the proverbial Johnny on the Spot. *How the hell did he get up here this fast?* She thought.

As she opened the door, before she could say hello, John started apologizing profusely. "Ms. Wilkinson, I am so very sorry that this was your introduction to The

Austin. We pride ourselves on making our guests' stay very enjoyable. This introduction may be memorable, but hardly enjoyable."

"John, it's okay, I know that these things happen. In fact, I was going to make the obvious pun on your name of being Johnny on the Spot since you came up here so fast." Valerie's attempt at humor seemed to be lost on John for the moment, based on the anguished look on his face. Seeing that, she motioned him into the bathroom.

They had just walked into the bathroom when the doorbell rang again. Valerie looked surprised, but John quickly interjected, "It's the plumber. I don't know what took him so long."

Valerie did a double take on John and realized that he wasn't kidding. John was already on his way to answer the door. John returned with a young man in his mid-thirties, in a light blue uniform shirt and dark blue uniform pants.

"Hello, ma'am, sorry about this," the young man said as his eyes quickly surveyed the situation. "We'll have to take a look in the apartment directly above this one. Has anyone else called to report any problem?" the plumber asked John. John shook his head in dismay.

John turned to Valerie and said, "Would you be kind enough to give me a few minutes to go call the guest above you and if he doesn't answer, then I'll go up with the master key. I hope nothing has happened to him. He is elderly, but I don't mean to burden you with this."

Valerie almost laughed out loud at the groveling going on before her eyes. "Please, go see what's going on and if the guest is okay. This is not a tragedy if no one is ill or has fallen upstairs."

John nodded in thanks, and then continued. "We have a few empty apartments and I will have the staff come and move all your luggage immediately, so that you are not further inconvenienced. I know you have had a long plane trip and you must be exhausted."

"That would be great, John. I just realized how tired I really am."

"I assure you, Ms. Wilkinson, that the apartment we give you will be even nicer than this one."

"Okay, John, take care of the problem upstairs first and then someone can move me to the new apartment."

Little did Valerie know that her earlier thoughts about a good omen might be coming to fruition with this change of apartments.

Chapter 6

TOM

Tom Amendola called Paula on his cell from the car. "I'll be at your house in five minutes. Do you just want to come outside, so we're not late?" Paula said yes, she was ready and she would come outside to meet him.

The ride to their friends' house for dinner was about twenty minutes. He hadn't really thought about it until tonight, but the opportunity presented itself, and if he explained it properly, maybe Paula wouldn't be too upset about his move to New York. He had to present it as a great opportunity that he couldn't pass up both for his career and for research in transplants. He had to stress that New York was only a short plane ride and that he planned to come back to Atlanta at least once a month and maybe more. Paula could certainly come to New York any weekend she wanted to. The trump card was that he was going to tell her that he had no intention of selling his house in Atlanta, since this was probably only going to be a one-year deal. In his own mind, he knew that was probably a lie, since if he really liked the program, he would probably stay in New York for several years. This provided him with a unique opportunity to make even more of a name for himself in the field. With success in the program in New York, he could write his ticket to anywhere he wanted to go. The research dollars would continue to pour in and he could take those dollars to whatever program he wanted, wherever he wanted.

There were huge hospitals in Atlanta that would drool for him to come back with his expertise, his prestige and his research dollars. Tom also marveled at the salary that was coming with this job. He wished that his parents were still alive to see this, because they had sacrificed mightily to put him through college and medical school. He was happy that he had been able to help them financially when they needed help toward the end of their lives and do a little to repay them.

Tom's mind clicked back to Paula, and a mild sense of dread came over him. He knew that however he sugar coated it, Paula was going to be unhappy. At least he could contain her upset for right now to the twenty-minute drive. Tom also counted on the fact that Paula was too much of a Southern and genteel woman with impeccable manners, to walk into a house full of people with red eyes or a scowl on her face. After that he was hoping that she would have time to mull over what he said and maybe come to terms with it. He also knew that he had to include her in the news sooner rather than later, or that would create yet another set of problems.

As he pulled into the driveway and beeped the horn, Paula sort of "swished" out the front door with what Tom called an outfit with "flouncy" things on the top. In truth, she looked great in the hot pink top and white pants, and if nothing else, made you look twice. Or maybe more than twice. Paula seemed to have a perpetual tan and her arms glowed against the sleeveless top. She had on a long necklace, also in a bright white, providing contrast against the hot pink. As she leaned over to kiss him once she was in the car, the necklace gave him a smack in the cheekbone with a resounding thwack.

"Oh, Lordy, I am so sorry. Did I catch you in the eye, sugar?" asked Paula in her pleasantly Southern drawl.

"No, just in the cheek. It's okay, I'll live. We'll just tell everyone at dinner that you hauled off and belted me. I was just too much of a gentleman to hit you back." He laughed. The thought flashed through Tom's mind that later on she might actually haul off and belt him one, once he told her his news.

They made small talk for the first few minutes of the drive. Traffic was a little heavier than normal, so it was going to take them longer than twenty minutes to get there.

After several miles of start and stop traffic, they were only going about thirty-five miles an hour, so Tom figured the time was right. "Paula, I had a very interesting call yesterday from a hospital in New York City. One of the doctors in their transplant team has called me several times over the past few months with questions about some of our procedures and how we handle things. A real nice guy; his name is Tim McAndrews. We've gotten on great on the phone and we're pretty much on the same wavelength on some of the most difficult cases.

"Anyway, they have a very good chance of getting some mega grants for research on transplants. They also have a position open there for the chief of that service. Tim would like me to go to New York and speak to them about taking the job for a year. The chief would have a lot of latitude and a lot of grant money. He thinks with my reputation with transplants, plus the money that the hospital is willing to put into the program, would almost definitely guarantee them the grants."

Tom stopped to take a breath and cast a sideways glance at Paula to see her reaction. At first, she was still staring straight ahead. Tom looked back at the road and then at Paula again. By the time of the second look, Paula had turned ninety degrees to look at Tom.

Paula opened her mouth as if to speak, and then closed it again. Those few seconds of silence in the car after Tom stopped speaking seemed like hours. He didn't know whether to jump in or keep quiet. Since as a doctor and as a surgeon he was used to being in charge, he took charge.

"Great opportunity, don't you think? They recognize my work and want to take it further. It's quite a compliment to me." He decided to put the best possible spin on it.

The response from Paula was short; in fact, very short. "New York City? For a year?"

"Yeah, that's how long the grant would be."

"But New York? What about your work here?"

"Well, as I said, this will be a continuation of my work, and a chance to take it to new levels."

"What about me? What about us?" Paula's voice had taken on quite a plaintive tone, and Tom thought he heard a quiver in her voice as well.

Now they were getting to the heart of the matter, as he knew they would. "Paula, it's only for a year and I plan to come home once a month or maybe even every other weekend. You can come up to New York for the weekend. You've never been to New York. There's so much for you to see and do. We could see shows on Broadway and they have so many great museums. You've never seen the Statue of Liberty, the Brooklyn Bridge or the famous lions in front of the New York Public Library. There are a million restaurants with every kind of food imaginable. Think of it as a great adventure for us."

All Paula could manage was a miserable, "I don't know."

"Look, I know this is a lot to digest right now, but I am excited about this opportunity. I need to go up to New York and talk to several people in person. Nothing is written in stone. It's just very intriguing, and I wanted you to be a part of it."

Mercifully, they arrived at their friends' house and the conversation would have to come to an end, just as Tom had hoped it would.

The seven-year-old Tom was saying very loudly in his mind, "Liar, liar, pants on fire." Yes, Tom was going to New York to talk to the team, but what he hadn't told Paula was that he had, in fact, already accepted the job.

Chapter 7

PAUL

Paul stepped off the plane into the jet way, and even though the jet way was covered, it didn't make a perfect seal with the side of the airplane. Therefore, the hot and oppressive air hit him in the face. So this was going to be summer in Florida. He was eager to get into the terminal, where at least the air conditioning would envelop him again. He pulled his rolling carry-on suitcase behind him and threw his navy blue blazer over his shoulder as he walked toward baggage claim.

He sincerely doubted he was going to need the blazer, but in case David wanted to go someplace nice for dinner, Paul didn't want to be caught short and look like an idiot. He had even thrown a tie in his suitcase, just in case, although he was virtually certain that nothing was that formal in Florida any more. He didn't want to mess up because of some small detail and look like he couldn't multi-task. He'd heard his share of horror stories about people losing important jobs over what seemed like an inconsequential detail.

The baggage arrived on the carousel relatively quickly, and mercifully, his suitcase was among them. David had wanted to send a car service for Paul, but Paul managed to talk his way out of that, so at least he'd have the freedom of his own car and didn't have to rely totally on David and his minions for his every move. Since he was going to be in Florida for a short time, he expected he'd be in meetings for most of the time, but the car gave him a small measure of independence in case there was some down time.

He used his Hertz Gold Club membership, and his name was on the board when he got to the car rental. At this rate, maybe he'd have time for a quick workout or swim before meeting David. It wasn't a long ride from the airport to the hotel, and Paul decided to wait until he was checked in and was in his room before calling David. Maybe he would have time for that swim, if he didn't have to go to David's house early. Doing some exercise was a good way for him to calm his nerves and clear his head. It had been tough to free his calendar in the office on short notice and finish the work he absolutely needed to get done to get away. He had to use the excuse of a family emergency to take time off on such short notice.

Assuming that this trip went well and Paul definitely had the job, he would resign from the firm, but not before then. Even though Paul felt confident that all his discussions with David had gone well, he wanted it to be a thousand per cent that he had the job before he resigned. David had even said he would give Paul a written contract for a year with an option for another year, so that he could have his campaign in high gear, as soon as he wanted to formally announce. Despite himself, Paul could feel some butterflies in his stomach. This was a huge move and if it went well, Paul would be playing on the national stage now in David's presidential campaign, and this would hopefully punch his ticket for the future.

Once Paul was in the hotel room, he called David. David picked up his cell on the third ring, and sounded like a happy kid at a birthday party. "Paul, so good to hear from you." Paul thought it was somewhat of a strange remark from David since it wasn't like Paul's call was being made at random. They had prearranged that Paul would call once he was in Florida.

"Thanks, David. I just got to the hotel."

"Well, I hope you had a splendid trip. Now you're in the Sunshine State, and it's such a wonderful place to be." Now David sounded like the head of tourism for Florida.

Paul decided he better play along. "Yes, it is wonderful. Lots of sun, and of course, heat."

David laughed. "You'll get used to it. It's very different from what you're accustomed to. Why don't you come to my house at 6 pm? I thought we'd have dinner here so we can talk freely and no one can overhear our conversation. You and I can talk for a while and then Andrew Dustin will join us a little later."

"That's fine, David. I'm looking forward to meeting Andrew in person."

"I'll tell you tonight, but I have a lot of meetings set up in the next few days. There are quite a number of people I want you to meet. It's better that you all get acquainted sooner rather than later."

"Great, David, I'm looking forward to it."

"Paul, this is a casual dinner at my house. I know you think you are being interviewed tonight, but you don't need to show up in a shirt and tie. A golf shirt is fine. See you at 6 pm."

Chapter 8

VALERIE

It seemed as if John, the concierge, had indeed been true to his word. The new apartment had two bedrooms instead of the one in the original apartment and a better view. He said he would put her in a better place for her inconvenience. It seemed as if the fairy godmother had somehow whisked all her suitcases to the new apartment, while Valerie had gone down to the restaurant for a few minutes. There was also a fruit and cheese basket waiting for her in the refrigerator, again as a peace offering.

John had also been quick to explain that the apartments on this floor had been newly renovated. "It should be very quiet here, Ms. Wilkinson. Since we just finished the renovation, these apartments are all still empty. It will be as if you have this entire wing to yourself for a while. Most of the building is empty as we renovate."

"Thanks, John; this is very nice of you. I know that it wasn't your fault about the flood in the other apartment. You have been more than diligent in taking care of this situation and getting me settled in this new apartment. Is everything okay with the tenant who was above me in the other apartment?"

John coughed meaningfully into his hand, not just to clear his throat, but to buy himself time. "Ah, we have a little problem with that gentleman."

Valerie nodded. "I don't need the particulars, but I was just wondering if he was okay physically or if he had to be taken to the hospital."

John was trying to find a polite way of answering her and yet not answering her. It reminded her of some attorneys she had dealt with in the past.

"He's fine physically. No need for EMS or the hospital. We have been in touch with his son already about the situation. He's an elderly widower. Sometimes he gets lonely and likes his red wine. Things 'flow' from there, if you understand my meaning." John had used the quotation marks in the air to emphasize the word "flow" to make his point and Valerie got it.

"Well, if there's nothing else I can do for you, Ms. Wilkinson, I will leave you to settle in. Please don't ever hesitate to call me if you need anything. I am here to assist you in any way possible."

"Thanks so much, John, you have been wonderful. I really am tired after the trip and I'll start to get settled in."

John nodded, backed himself out the door and was gone in one move. Although John wasn't English, nor did he have an English accent, he reminded her of Anthony Hopkins as the butler in the movie, *The Remains of the Day*.

All of a sudden, the anticipation and stress of leaving, the plane trip and the all the brouhaha of changing apartments caught up with her.

She spent about a half hour unpacking and then sat down on the couch to call Todd. She had called him earlier from the restaurant to tell him about the fiasco with the apartment.

"Hey, babe, it's me. I'm in the new apartment."

"So how is it? Did John come through on his promise to make your stay a success?"

"I'll say. The new apartment has two bedrooms instead of one for starters. The view is much better. The cool thing is that the apartments on this floor have been newly renovated. Everything is brand new. All the carpeting is brand new; it's got that smell that says it's new. I think the whole place has also been freshly painted."

"Wow, sounds terrific."

"Since this portion of the floor has just been renovated, there's no one else living around me. It should be totally quiet. That's so great, since I'm not used to living in an apartment. I won't have to worry about noise from other tenants."

"Boy, it seems that your client kept his word that if you came to New York, everything they did for you would be first class."

"Yeah, you're right. I think you are going to like this place when you come here. Listen, I just wanted to tell you that everything was working out okay with the apartment. All of a sudden, I'm really tired. It's been a long day. I'm going to go to bed. Love you. Talk to you in the morning. Bye."

Chapter 9

VALERIE

Valerie spent Sunday unpacking and making the apartment look a little more like home. With the time change, her body clock was off, but she was in no particular rush to get moving. Her plan was to explore the neighborhood and see what was near the apartment and do some food shopping. On the plane trip, she had decided that she needed to do an attitude adjustment. She was going to live in New York City, perhaps the greatest city in the world, and she should take full advantage of it.

She knew she was a talented attorney and this case in New York would be wonderful for her career, but she had yet to come to terms with her own anxiety about having all these people report to her and her client's own very large expectations. She had won a similar case in California against heavy odds, so she was considered quite an expert, but this was still a huge undertaking. Again, she had made up her mind that she was going to change her attitude, dive in, enjoy New York and win her case.

Instead of waiting until Monday morning to go into the office, Valerie decided to make a short trip to the office on Sunday afternoon. She would bring in a few personal items, set up her desk and maybe settle in a little. It was a way of getting a jump on things, checking out her office and possibly getting over her jitters. She e-mailed one of the associates Sunday morning and asked if he could call security at the front desk to get her into the building, but Valerie needed keys to actually get into the front door of the office. The associate practically had a heart attack hearing that Valerie wanted to go into the office on the Sunday before she was due to start, because that meant that he should probably go in to the office too. Valerie laughed to herself, because this was the closest you could come to hearing panic in an e-mail.

Valerie assured him that all she wanted to do was bring some personal things into the office and get the lay of the land. He was not needed. Mark, the associate, said he would check with a few people to see who, if anyone, would actually be working in the office on Sunday and could open the door for her. Barring that, he said he would drop off his keys at the front desk with Security. Within less than a half hour, Mark was back to her with the names and cell phone numbers of two associates who said they would be in the office starting about noon. Was that early enough?

Valerie assured him that would be fine, and no, he really didn't need to come into the office himself. It hadn't escaped Valerie's attention that as least two of the associates would be working on a Sunday afternoon. Was the New York office that much of a sweatshop? She guessed she would find out soon enough.

As Valerie was about to end the exchange of e-mails, she realized that she didn't know where her new office was located. Mark gave her directions, and said her name was already on the door. Okay, so she was over the first three hurdles of getting into the building and past security, into the locked outer office and could even find her own office.

A few hours later, Valerie stepped out of the cab in front of the office building and looked up at a massive building with a vast glass front. In this sunlight, the building had a green hue to it. There was actually a glare off the glass as she looked up at the behemoth that would become a large part of her life for probably close to a year. She wasn't sure if she liked this look, but it really didn't matter. For the vast majority of her time, she would be swallowed up by this building and would be on the inside looking out. Compared to the few minutes it took to get inside the building versus the amount of time she would be inside it, she figured that it would be a ratio heavily in favor of the interior.

She also hoped she would have a window. God, what would she do if she was walled in on all four sides? That would be so horrible compared to what she was used to. There was a very real possibility that she might not have an office with a window. Even though she was a partner in the firm, and partner offices always had windows, she was essentially "on loan" to the New York office. If they didn't have a partner-sized office available, she might well be stuck with an associate-sized office and maybe no window. This was New York City, with a huge price per square foot, so they probably wouldn't have an office just lying around and vacant. Okay, Valerie, get a grip. This is not a tragedy of any magnitude at all; someone who had a partner-sized office could leave and an office would open up. Stop torturing yourself over every detail, when nothing has happened—yet.

As she said hello to the security guard at the front desk, it was apparent that he'd been briefed about her early arrival on a Sunday. He told her tomorrow she would be issued a permanent ID pass with her picture on it, but he was quick to point out with a bit of a sheepish grin that the person in charge of taking the pic-

tures and issuing the passes didn't work on the weekends.

Valerie caught his meaning and grinned back at
him. She said simply, "I'm just here to put some of my
personal items in my office, not to do any work here
today. I hope I won't be here on the weekends much
either, but you never know." Valerie hoped she wasn't
lying to him, but perhaps she was. With her laptop, she
could very well be working on the weekends, but not
necessarily from the office. *We shall see,* she thought.

The guard pointed her in the direction of the elevators and told her the firm was on the tenth floor. He
said he would like to carry up her two tote bags, but
said he couldn't leave the front desk. As the elevator
door pinged open on the tenth floor, Valerie saw double
wooden doors with the firm name on them. Not terribly
ostentatious, and perhaps a tad understated. The firm
had the entire tenth floor. She would soon know what
lay behind those doors. As she had been instructed
when she called Julie, the associate who was working
this afternoon, she rang the doorbell on the left side of
the double doors. A few seconds later, a breathless Julie opened one of the doors.

She held out her hand to shake Valerie's and then
realized that Valerie had no free hands. Both of them
smiled at the other and Julie grinned and reached for
one of the tote bags. "Hi, I'm Julie Willett," said a dark
haired young woman in jeans and a lavender sweater.
She had her hair pulled back in a ponytail, and
no makeup. She looked about sixteen years old, but
Valerie knew that Julie had to be at least twenty-
four or twenty-five years old at a minimum, if she
had gone to law school immediately after graduation
from college.

"Glad to meet you, Julie, I'm Valerie Wilkinson.
Thanks for helping me get into the office."

"Nice to meet you, Ms. Wilkinson. I'm glad I was here to help you out. Mark told me they were expecting you tomorrow."

"First of all, it's Valerie. No need to be so formal. Ms. Wilkinson is my mother." Valerie knew that at most she was probably ten to twelve years older than Julie. Julie nodded.

"So do you know where my office is?"

"Sure, follow me. It's a little bit of a maze, but you'll get used to it. As far as I know, we haven't lost anyone in the office in years. You can always drop a few breadcrumbs until you learn your way."

They did make a few right and left hand turns as they wove their way toward the back of the office. In law firm terms, the farther away you were from the front desk, the higher up you were in the pecking order in the firm and the more prestige, and ultimately the more dollars you were given. Judging by the fact that they were making a few twists and turns to get to Valerie's office, it appeared to be going well. As they traipsed down the hall, Julie pointed out conference rooms and small kitchens, and other "points of interest."

Just as Julie was slowing down and reading names on the individual offices to find Valerie's, Julie launched into what could be called nothing more than a blatant sales pitch for herself. "I know you're here for the Fleming litigation, and I'm in one of the litigation groups with Mr. Whiteman. But we're finishing up with a big case now, and if you need some associates to help you staff up, I'd be available and very willing."

Valerie was a little taken aback by the blind ambition, but she did give Julie credit for being bold and opportunistic in the very few minutes since they had met.

Valerie had no idea how the New York office determined staffing on any particular matter. She presumed that she would discuss this with one of her partners in the litigation department as to who was available and who had the appropriate expertise to work with her on the case. Valerie also wanted to interview the associates and see whom she wanted to pick. The associates didn't make a sales pitch to the partners in the L.A. office where Valerie had been, but this was New York and maybe they did things differently here. Valerie didn't want to obligate herself and commit the faux pas of the century, before the office even opened on Monday morning.

"Thanks for the offer, Julie, and I will keep it in mind. I have to see how they arrange the staffing here before I can make any commitments." All of a sudden Valerie felt she was on the defensive. The door to her office couldn't have come at a better time. Julie didn't appear to be deterred by Valerie having been noncommittal.

"Well, here we are," said Julie as she opened the door to Valerie's office. Since she had been leading Valerie in the trek from the front desk through the maze of offices and conference rooms, she walked into the office ahead of Valerie. Valerie took a deep breath and walked into the office. Her new home actually, because she thought she would spend more time here than in her apartment.

Before she had a chance to take in the whole of the office, she noticed with a great sigh of relief that the office had not only one, but two big windows. Before she could say anything else, Julie almost bounced out of the office, with the final plea.

"As I said, Valerie, I am available and would very much like to work with you. Again, my name is Julie

Willett. I better get back to work. I'm sure I'll see you tomorrow." With that, Julie closed the door and disappeared. Valerie stopped a minute and surveyed her new office. She still wasn't sure what she thought about the blatant sales pitch.

Chapter 10

DB Minus 21 Days

TOM

The plane from Atlanta touched down at John F. Kennedy International Airport and Tom counted at least three signs telling him which airport he was in and what city. Were the New Yorkers that stupid that they had to be reminded of both every few minutes? He hoped not.

Surprisingly, it hadn't taken all that long to get his suitcase, and the hospital had arranged a car service to pick him up and take him into Manhattan. It was a gorgeous day, the kind that you saw in pictures of New York. The sky was very blue with big cumulus clouds, and the view as they headed toward the Midtown Tunnel was beautiful with a body of water in the distance, which Tom knew wasn't the Atlantic Ocean, but wasn't sure if it was Flushing Bay or the East River. He made a mental note to check on that, so that he wasn't geographically illiterate. He also thought they could have come up with a better name than Flushing.

Once they were in Manhattan, the view of the East River really was something. The river had a few large sailboats moving along at a good clip, so there must have been wind whipping the sails. He also saw two tugboats about a mile apart, both moving barges down the river.

The Manhattan skyline was always breathtaking to Tom on the other occasions he had been in New York. As the car made its way north on the East River Drive, or FDR as it was called, he remembered the first time he had seen NYU Hospital around Thirty-first street, and encompassing a few blocks right off First Avenue, just south of where they were now.

Tom remembered reading that at the turn of the century into the nineteen hundreds, the doctors at NYU had started to realize that cleanliness was important to patients undergoing surgery to try to avoid infection, and so they did some operations outside near the East River. Now the idea seemed almost primitive, but then it was revolutionary.

They had done reasonably well on the FDR, but now that they were on the local streets in Manhattan, traffic had slowed to a crawl. Tom watched in dismay as the light on First Avenue turned red twice and the car wasn't even at the intersection yet. One entire lane was blocked in various places with Fed Ex trucks, UPS trucks, and various other box trucks. All had their lights flashing to indicate that their parking there was temporary, but they were blocking traffic nonetheless and reducing crosstown traffic to an enraging one lane on a busy Friday afternoon.

Tom saw a man in a traffic enforcement uniform strolling toward them. Strolling was the operative word. The man looked like he was out for a bird watching session, because he clearly was looking anywhere and everywhere but at the snarled traffic and standing delivery trucks. Tom had the urge to open the window and yell at the man, but stopped himself, knowing it would do no good. *I better get used to this if I'm going to live in New York City.*

I'm going to have to take this horrible traffic into account when I look at places to live. I don't want to be too far from the hospital. The list of possible rentals was tucked into his carry-on. Tom didn't have the patience or the room in the back of the car to start rummaging around for it. Finally, and mercifully, the car stopped in front of the Excelsior Hotel and the crawl was over.

As he walked into the lobby and saw the high ceilings and the huge chandeliers, Tom wanted to pinch himself. For some inexplicable reason, the hospital would not pay for his stay in New York City for this meeting. He guessed that they expected him to come and go in one day. He decided to stay at the Excelsior and treat himself for the few days in New York City, even though this place was ridiculously expensive.

The kid from humble beginnings, whose parents worked hard and believed in the American Dream, was now standing in the lobby of a hotel for seven hundred fifty dollars a night, and not really giving it much of a second thought. Tom's parents had seen that he was a very bright kid whose energies needed to be channeled into something productive and lucrative. They were very middle class, and wanted more, much more, for their son. His parents used every opportunity to instill that work ethic and drilled the American Dream into him. He could still see the expression on his mother's face the day the acceptance letter came from medical school. The envelope had been sitting prominently on the dining room table, in the middle of a maroon placemat, so the white envelope stood out vividly against the dark background. She had been dying to open that envelope all day since the mail came, but somehow managed to control herself until Tom came home and opened it for himself.

A female voice pulled him out of his reverie. It was the woman behind the desk wanting to check him in to the hotel. "May I help you, sir?"

After he was checked in and was solidly ensconced in his room, he took a quick shower and flicked on the

TV to catch up on the news and see what was going on in New York sports. Seeing some live sporting events in New York was high up on his list. He wanted to see the stadiums as much as he wanted to see the teams play. He hadn't been to New York since the new Yankee Stadium or Citifield had been built, and he was more than eager to see games at both places. Even though he thought he should be making some appointments with real estate agents to look at apartments, he decided to call his daughter, Amy, at Yale and go see her on Sunday if she was free. He had checked his GPS before he left home, and if he rented a car in New York for the day, he figured if the traffic wasn't too bad on a Sunday, he could be in New Haven in not much more than an hour and a half.

Chapter 11

MOHAMMED AND AKRAM

Although there were five boroughs in New York City and they were legally all one city, in reality, there were like five separate cities. Each had its own geographic peculiarities, each had its own crimes and, most importantly, each had its own ethnic makeup. The ethnic makeup largely defined the language or languages heard on the streets, the games played and the kind of food found in the local stores and restaurants. The five boroughs might only have been a few miles from each other, but in many respects they were light years apart. Travel a few miles in a different direction in New York City and everything changed. Sometimes it changed for the better and sometimes not.

The police in New York City could describe it best, because they dealt with it every day, twenty-four hours a day, three hundred sixty-five days a year, with an extra day in leap years. It was a difficult tightrope to walk, trying to respect so many cultures and customs, with the ever-present threat of terrorism. Everything changed on 9/11 and nothing stayed the same. What looked innocent might well be, or it might not be. The police and its counter-terrorism units had to be right one hundred per cent of the time. Difficult, if not impossible odds. They had been right so far, but could they continue to be perfect all the time?

Mohammed and Akram lived in Queens together in a small, nondescript apartment. They were cousins, but essentially had been raised as brothers. They were the same age and had grown up in Saudi Arabia three blocks from each other.

Mohammed was the third child of five, and was truly the middle child in all respects. All the clichés about the middle child seemed to have played out perfectly in his family. The first child in the family was a son, which pleased Mohammed's father to no end. He was bright and outgoing and did all the things which a first-born Muslim son was supposed to do. He attended the mosque with his father and went into the family business. That would have been enough for Mohammed's father. The second child was a girl, which mattered not to his father, since he already had the first-born son, and a star at that. Azirra was the girl her mother always wanted. She was stunning, with thick black hair and beautiful, full long eyelashes.

There was a break of four years between Azirra and Mohammed, almost as if their parents had the perfect family of four people, with a son and a daughter. Just twenty months after Mohammed was born, the fourth child arrived, another son, followed by the fifth child, another son. The last three children arrived in such rapid succession, that it was if they were one large child, all needing to be fed, bathed and put to bed at the same time. The two youngest boys were extremely good athletes and seemed headed for careers in professional soccer.

Mohammed was the middle child, who truly seemed stuck in the middle of everything. He was of average height and build and average looking. He was a good student, but not at the top of the class. The two things where he was clearly above average were in science and the study of the Koran. Both skills were ultimately going to prove very useful to him as an adult.

Akram was the same age as Mohammed, and the two went to the same school in the same grade and went to the same Mosque. Akram came from a much larger family of eight children, who overwhelmed their beleaguered mother, so Akram and Mohammed often just fared for themselves as they got older.

It was Akram's idea to go to the United States. He would never have gone unless Mohammed would agree to go with him. Together they could function quite well; alone each would flounder in the real world. Since Mohammed was proficient in science, he often did Akram's chemistry and mechanical engineering homework for him, while Akram was much better in languages and history, so he did the homework in those subjects for both of them. Their teachers never quite caught on why each boy did wonderful homework assignments and take-home papers, but only fared moderately well on school exams.

It was Akram's skill in languages that made him think that he spoke English well enough for them to go to America and make a new life for both of them. It didn't take a lot of convincing for Mohammed to agree that this would be the place for a new start and a wonderful adventure for both of them. Once Akram saw that Mohammed was beginning to be interested, he started tutoring him in English. Akram knew that the pictures of the blond girls in bikinis he showed Mohammed would be the final push needed to win him over.

To the shock and surprise of both young men, both sets of parents were adamantly opposed to the idea. The parents, who seemed indifferent to the two young men for most of their lives, were now digging their heels in that the "boys" not go. Mohammed was starting to cave in under the pressure and even the bikini pictures did not seem to be enough to keep him moving on the path to America. Akram was still eager to pursue this path, especially since it was his idea.

Akram was getting desperate not to lose this opportunity and his nerve. He simply could not go without Mohammed. He didn't want to admit it to himself, but he knew he would fail in a strange country without Mohammed, essentially his other half. It wasn't going to be easy to get into the United States, especially from a predominantly Muslim country, so Akram had to find a way.

One day toward the end of their last semester in school, the teacher announced that Saudi Arabia was sponsoring a new program for young Saudis to go to the United States for further education. The Saudi government would pay for round-trip airfare and one year's worth of tuition, if the student could get into an American college. The program was renewable each year if the student maintained at least a 3.0 cumulative average. Akram saw this as yet another opportunity to fulfill his plan and perhaps even bring both sets of parents around to the idea.

Akram started researching colleges furiously once he heard about this program. He quickly realized that it was too late to get into the premier colleges in the U.S., because the American colleges had started accepting students the preceding fall. They were now well into the following spring. When their teacher announced the program, he mentioned the names of four American colleges with whom the Saudi government had made a deal. One was in Maine, one in South Dakota, one in Mississippi and one in New York City. These were small colleges without much of a reputation and struggling financially for their existence. The Saudi government, in addition to paying the tuition, was also making a healthy payment to each college's endowment fund for every one of its students accepted. Akram dismissed the first colleges automatically, since he couldn't visualize himself and Mohammed buried under mountains of snow. He had to Google exactly where South Dakota was located. The college in Mississippi looked to be in the middle of nowhere. He also didn't think that two young Muslims with dark skin would be welcome in a very small town in the South. New York City was always the place of his dreams in going to the U.S.

Akram's plan was to use this college admission and student visa as his ticket to the U.S., which he would not otherwise have in this political climate. Both sets of parents were still reluctant to let the boys go so far away. They said if the Saudi government wanted to pay for all this, that was okay with them, but they were not going to pay for rent and food. They were hoping that this last roadblock might still deter the boys.

By chance one day, Akram was discussing his plan with a friend. He was boasting about their new life and the great adventure, because for the first time, people were interested in what he had to say. His dream was to get away from his boring existence. The friend mentioned casually that he had a cousin who lived in New York City and that Akram should look him up when he got to New York.

All of a sudden the wheels in Akram's head began turning and turning fast. Akram became very interested in the cousin. After a few questions, Akram had ascertained that the cousin belonged to a mosque in Queens. From there, Akram started e-mailing the cousin about places to live and job opportunities to help pay the rent. Most importantly, Akram found out as much as he could about the mosque in Queens.

Armed with the college admission, and a fistful of e-mails from the "New York cousin," Akram was able to convince his parents and his aunt and uncle that the "New York cousin" was already forwarding want ads for jobs in New York City and apartments close to where the cousin lived and the college. The clincher was that Akram and Mohammed started e-mailing the imam at the mosque, who was very pleased indeed that two young Muslims coming to America wanted to become affiliated with his mosque before they even arrived in America. When Mohammed and Akram showed their respective parents the e-mails back and forth to the imam, and their promise that they would immediately become members and stay members of that mosque, the four parents relented and said they could go to America. And so a chain of events was set in motion that none of the six people involved in Saudi Arabia could have foreseen from their side of the world.

Chapter 12

PAUL

Paul rolled through the impressive-looking gates to David Collins' Florida estate in Palm Beach after he was checked in with a guard manning the post. Two small bronze lions guarded the entrance, reminiscent of the two lions outside the New York City Public Library. Admittedly, these two lions were a good deal smaller than the Public Library ones, but still large enough to make one take notice. The guard was more than polite to Paul, but as the guard turned back to open the gate, Paul thought he caught a glimpse of a gun on his belt. However, since Paul's senses seemed to be hypersensitive from the time he pulled up to the gates, he was also aware of some high-tech security measures. Those were the ones he could see; he wondered how many more were not that visible. The presumption was that if certain security measures were visible, those in and of themselves were a deterrent to the less sophisticated criminals, with the hope that others intending harm would realize that there were other less visible and possibly more potent measures.

The driveway was long and surfaced with expensive paving stones, so the house was necessarily set far back from the street. The shrubbery and lawns were impeccably manicured. No bush or hedge looked to have a shoot out of place or an inch higher than its neighbor. Paul wondered if there were one or more gardeners at the ready in case some rogue bush grew at a rate faster than it was supposed to.

The beds of impatiens were gorgeous and seemingly endless. The gardeners had mixed bright reds with bright whites, pinks, violets and blues in such a way as to make it seem that the colors blended seamlessly one into the other, and the effect was almost breathtaking.

The house itself was something to behold. It was three stories and impressive, with a slate roof clearly standing out against the blue sky. It was massive, by anyone's standards, but even more so in Florida, where property on the water was at a premium, both in terms of space and sales price. Just from the outside, the place reeked of money, and old money at that. Based on what he had seen so far, Paul couldn't wait to see the inside of the house. He knew David Collins was wealthy, and Paul had certainly done as much research as he could on the man and his finances, but seeing this house in the flesh, drove it "home." Paul chuckled to himself at the unspoken pun in his head.

As Paul approached the house, a young man dressed in a neat white golf shirt with the two lions as a logo above the left breast pocket, pressed black pants and reflective sunglasses, met him in the driveway. Paul wondered if this was the "Florida uniform," but usually it was khaki pants in the Florida heat. He opened the car door and with a winning smile which actually seemed genuine said, "Good evening, Mr. Bennett. Mr. Collins is expecting you. Welcome. I'll be happy to park your car for you."

"Thank you. Am I the first to arrive tonight?"

Paul looked around and didn't see a car in sight, although David had said there would be other people coming to the house this evening.

"No, sir, you are not. There are several other people already here. Since it's such a great night, I believe you are going to be sitting out of the patio. Just go to the front door and Robert will show you where to go."

Again, Paul was impressed with this young man. He seemed to be just the right mix of being polite with not being an automaton. Paul also noticed the wire and ear bud as part of the young man's attire. The small detail of telling Paul that they would be out on the patio seemed to indicate that everyone was involved in the evening. Paul hesitated a moment trying to decide if he should take his black leather case with him to the house. He might need to take some notes and this case contained his tablet, pen and business cards. He decided to take it with him, even if he had to leave it in the front hallway.

As Paul got out of the car and thanked the young man for his help, he noticed a small handgun and holster the same color as the man's black pants. Not very obvious, but there nonetheless. Now Paul understood why the young man was not wearing khaki pants. The black holster and gun would have been too obvious. This was more security than Paul had ever been exposed to in his whole life at anyone's private residence. He didn't know whether he should feel incredibly safe, or freaked out of his mind.

The irony of the situation was that David was not supposed to be the money guy for the campaign. It was supposed to be his friend, Andrew Dustin. Based on what Paul had seen so far, and this was only the outside of the house, Paul was wildly impressed.

As if on cue in a stage performance, Robert opened the front door before Paul even knocked or rang the doorbell. The knocker on the front door, of course, had two lions on it. Paul assumed the young man with the wire in his ear and who was now parking his car, had called into the house. When Robert opened the front door, Paul had all he could do not to burst out laughing, whether from nerves or watching too many old TV sit-coms. Robert really looked like the butler, Lurch, on *The Addams Family*. If the guy opened his mouth and said, "You rang?" Paul figured he would hightail it out of there immediately.

"Lurch" said in a deep voice, but certainly not as deep as the real Lurch, "Good evening. Mr. Bennett. Welcome to Lions Lookout. Mr. Collins and the guests are on the patio. Please follow me and I'll show you the way."

The front foyer had a cathedral ceiling with a gigan-tic chandelier. Lurch turned and walked briskly toward the back of the house, but before they reached the back of the house, they had to walk through several more rooms. Paul wanted Lurch to walk a little more slowly so he could get a better look at all of these rooms. Paul decided that he would have to make several bathroom trips tonight, so that he could see as much as he could of the house himself.

In the past, Paul could remember Debbie going to a friend's new house and asking for the grand tour. He wished Debbie were here with him tonight, but she had just taken a new job less than a month before this op-portunity presented itself for him. She couldn't just walk out on her new job. Paul thought if anyone could pull off asking to see the house without it seeming too gauche, it was Debbie. Debbie had a way of getting people to do what she wanted, and having them think it was their idea. It seemed to be some innate skill, which he often wished he had, especially in this new job, which was going to involve a lot of fundraising.

The two rooms they passed through to get to the pa-tio were what looked to be a huge dining room and a family room. Paul couldn't count fast enough how many chairs were around the dining room table, but there certainly were more than twelve. It looked like a very formal dining room, almost like something to be used for state dinners with visiting heads of state. David must have felt this dining room was a precursor to the formal dining rooms in the White House.

The second room they walked through was a family room of sorts, with a massive flat screen TV mounted on the wall and a sand-colored sectional couch and various easy chairs. The couch had at least seven sections, which Paul saw in the quick pass through. There were striking turquoise pillows on the couch, which provided wonderful contrast to the pale color of the upholstery. There was a wet bar in the corner of the room and a rack with a ton of glasses hanging over the bar, like you'd see in a restaurant. This room intrigued Paul more than the formal dining room, and he definitely wanted a second and better look around.

And then they came to the door which led to the enclosed porch, the patio and the view of the ocean. "Oh my God!"

Lurch turned around. "Excuse me, sir, did you say something?"

Paul pretended to cough into his hand. "No, sorry, just coughing."

Chapter 13

TOM

The choices were to go looking for an apartment, wander around New York City and soak up the local color or rent a car and go see his daughter, Amy, at Yale. The pragmatic choice would be to look at apartments and get that job out of the way. Tom was definitely leaning toward the second and third choices. He'd have plenty of time to look for apartments, and if need be, he could stay a little longer at the hotel.

He called Amy and asked if he could come up and see her and take her to brunch. Amy was quite pleased that he wanted to drive to New Haven. She was the youngest of the three kids, and there was a four-year gap between her and her brother, Steve. In reality, her mother's death hit Amy the hardest because she was the youngest. Amy had never really been totally honest with her father that she felt lost without her mother because Tom was busy with his practice.

She loved Yale and had made some really close friends, maybe out of necessity. Somehow Atlanta just seemed too far away from New Haven, and Tom didn't fly up to see her except for Parents' Weekend. While Amy had been happy to see him, it was a bittersweet experience for her. No matter what they did over Parents' Weekend, Amy felt that there was a huge hole in her heart because her mother wasn't there to share it with them.

She knew that her father was more than happy to fly her home to Atlanta for vacations, but it was a hassle to go to Atlanta for a weekend, so she didn't ask to come home and neither did he. Amy seemed happy on the face of things, and Tom didn't probe below the surface. Amy was never sure why that was what happened. Maybe it was just easier for him. Maybe he didn't notice or maybe he didn't want to notice. One thing was certain in Amy's mind, and that was if her mother had still been alive, things would have been very different. So the fact that her father called her the first day he was in New York and wanted to come up to Yale to see her, was a very pleasant surprise.

Tom enjoyed the ride to Yale. He went up the Hutchinson River Parkway in New York, which turned into the Merritt Parkway. No trucks were allowed on these roads. The traffic was fairly light on a Sunday morning and he had a chance to take in the trees, which were beginning to turn color now that it was the fall. Not as much of the fall foliage thing in Atlanta. He had never quite understood people going gaga over fall foliage, nor could he understand spending weekends driving around endlessly looking at leaves. However, this ride might be changing his opinion a little, but he still doubted that he'd spend a weekend doing this. Tom preferred to be more active than sitting in a car or a bus for hours, no matter what you were looking at.

Since Tom had made such good time getting to New Haven, and since Amy lived off campus, he took a fast drive through the campus itself. If a set director wanted a location for a movie on a university campus, Tom thought that Yale had to rank among the top five in the Northeast. Maybe even in the top two with Harvard. The Gothic buildings were stately and seemed ready to accept the students and inspire learning.

As Tom drove onto the campus, he felt the proverbial tug at his heart strings. It didn't seem that long ago that he, Amy and Laurie first drove onto the campus in the spring of Amy's junior year in high school. It was hard for him to believe that was four years ago and Amy was now a junior in college. None of them had ever been to Yale before, and the word that struck Tom that day as they looked around the campus, was majestic. *So much has happened to me and my family in what seemed like such a short space of time*, he thought, and he verbalized the words, "So much."

The most prominent thing in his mind was the loss of Laurie. He thought of her often, but it was at times like this that the memories were so vivid, and left the tears stinging his eyes. Most of the times when he thought of Laurie, he tried to move away from the memory and focus on his work. He knew that wasn't the best thing to do, but he was also afraid if he allowed the grief to bubble up, that he would be swallowed up by it.

He knew the kids all missed her too, but Tom was imprisoned in his own private misery about Laurie's death. He was a doctor, for God's sake. He was supposed to save his family, not let them die. His transplant work had saved hundreds, if not thousands of people. Many of those he had treated, he remembered their faces. He now had the pictures to prove it.

Early on in his transplant work, one of his patients had been a teenage girl named Cara. She had been at death's door, but despite bad odds and a host of other complications, this kid refused to give up. The more she fought, the more she inspired Tom and everyone else on his team to fight for her, even when the situation was looking very bad. Cara was interested in photography, and her parents brought some of her work into the hospital for everyone to see and to be displayed in her room to encourage her recovery. Her work was better than good; it was exceptional.

During her last week in the hospital before her discharge, her energy level had improved enough that she had her mother wheel her around the transplant unit in a wheelchair, while Cara took pictures of everyone and everything. This included the potted plants, the clock above the nurses' station, and all the doctors, nurses and residents who worked on her. She took pictures of each person alone and then each person with her.

The day that she was to be discharged, she refused to leave until Tom came into her room to see her. When he arrived, she was fully dressed and packed, but steadfastly stayed put until Tom came to see her. She presented him with the "selfie" of her and Tom, long before it was even known as a "selfie." The picture of the two of them was in a five by eight picture frame. More importantly, she had her parents bring one of the other cameras she loved to the hospital. It wasn't a new camera and it wasn't the most expensive camera, but it was a prized possession of Cara's. She told Tom the only way she would give him the camera, was if he gave her his "solemn word" as she phrased it, that he would take a picture of every one of his patients who lived and went home from the hospital. Tom gave her his solemn word and because of Cara, a new tradition was born in the hospital that continued to date. The other tradition that continued with Cara was that she faithfully sent him photographs of important events in her marriage, her kids and her life, as well as some of her best photography.

Cara was now a renowned photographer, and Tom was more than a little surprised when he Googled her and saw some of her works. Over the years, Cara had given Tom a few very valuable pieces of her work. He had offered repeatedly to pay her for her work, but she refused, graciously saying that she wouldn't be around to do anything if it hadn't been for Tom. At least once a year, she and her husband would call Tom, come to Atlanta for a visit, and Tom and Laurie would take them to dinner, as a small thank you. There was something special about that kid, who had grown into a wonderful human being. She now lived in Connecticut, and Tom was pretty damn sure once she found out he was going to be in New York City, that he would see her more than a few times.

Every time they had dinner, she asked about the number of patients in his "life journal," which somehow increased almost miraculously. Tom would tell his patients Cara's story, and for many of them, to be in the life journal provided added incentive for them. In all the years since Cara had been a patient, he only had one person refuse to be in the life journal. Almost every patient who heard Cara's story wanted to see a picture of her. Tom was able to oblige, not only with the original picture of Cara as a teenager, but with more recent photos.

Cara was thrilled that her story and pictures provided an incentive to the current patients. Many of Tom's patients wanted not only their pictures in the life journal, but also wanted Tom to send their pictures to Cara. The life journal network was growing by leaps and bounds. Tom was definitely going to expand the life journal network to his new hospital in New York. Now that Cara was only in Westport, Connecticut, he was thinking of asking her to come speak to his patients in New York City, proving once again to Tom, that as a doctor, you had to treat the whole person. In Tom's mind it also clearly showed the interconnectedness of the psyche and the soma. It also proved the other old adage that God cures the patient and the doctor takes the fee.

Many more people whom Tom had never met had been saved in other hospitals, and essentially had been given back their lives, because of Tom's innovative techniques in cardiac transplants. But Laurie had died of cancer. Despite the best treatments, the physician friends and colleagues who made super-human efforts, they lost the battle. Even though Tom didn't treat Laurie himself, he took it as a profes-sional as well as personal loss. He knew it was illogi-cal, but somehow he felt it was his fault that HE did not save her.

Tom snapped out of his thoughts and his reminisc-ing, and called Amy on his cell to say he was close to her apartment. Should he park the car and come in, or did she want to come out?

Tom did not tell her about his stroll down memory lane. He wasn't sure what, if anything, it meant, but somehow today, the mental stroll seemed very power-ful.

Chapter 14

MOHAMMED AND AKRAM

It had now been three months since Mohammed and Akram flew into John F. Kennedy International Airport. Akram liked the sound of that. An international airport. Sounded pretty important to a kid from halfway around the world, who never thought he'd get out of his own way, much less get out of his own country.

The first two and a half months had been a big struggle for Mohammed and Akram. None of their potential job possibilities had panned out. Even though they were living frugally, their money was running out, faster than their hopes of a better life. Akram was determined that even if he had to eat dog food, that he was not going home, and more importantly, going home a failure. He was worried that Mohammed's resolve was not as strong as his. Akram considered the very real possibility that Mohammed might just give up and bolt for home. He was not as strong in his desire to stay in the United States, as Akram was, especially since the idea to come here had been his and he was not giving up without a huge fight.

Both young men had taken part-time jobs, but they were not going to be enough to pay the rent and allow them to eat, without supplementing from their small savings. Akram had pushed the issue before they left for America, insisting to Mohammed that the two of them had to work overtime, and make and squirrel away as much money as they possibly could before their trip. Akram now thanked Allah for giving him the foresight or things would have turned out much worse for them. He was working part-time in a deli, and even though he hated it and it bored him to death, it had turned out to be their salvation.

Akram took every hour offered to him by the owner to work. Akram's English was a little stilted at first, but the owner noticed that Akram's English had improved over the past few weeks. This was partly from working in the deli and partly from taking courses at the college in English. There were people who came into the deli who had lived in Queens for years, whose English was nowhere near as good as Akram's. He wasn't afraid to work, and he never complained about working the late shift, and occasionally helping out on the opening shift, if one of the more experienced guys was sick or drunk. In truth, Akram liked working the late shift by himself. He knew where the security cameras were located, and he was able to help himself to some of the cold cuts and some staples. These were tiding Akram and Mohammed over with food. It seemed as long as Akram was careful and didn't take too much, it wasn't obvious that anything was missing. The late shift was quiet and Akram was able to do his course work without much interruption.

Akram wasn't too fond of the beef jerky, but he had grown to like sea salt potato chips, stale blueberry muffins, Hershey chocolate bars, Milky Ways, Fritos and Lean Cuisine. Akram varied what he ate on the sly, so that it was not obvious that a lot of one item was missing. He was still planning on tasting Twinkies, since he had heard some very wild things about them. Did they really have a shelf life of one thousand years, as he had been led to believe? The deli sold a fair number of them, but Akram thought they were an odd color.

Although Akram had no idea it was called inventory control, the owner of this deli had no idea about it either. He walked around the store with a notepad and pen, making notes of what products looked low on the shelves and what he should order.

Akram asked the owner if Mohammed could work in the deli as well. Anything to keep Mohammed engaged and bringing in a few bucks. The owner said he had enough help, but he had a friend who had a trucking business, and perhaps his friend needed someone to help out. Even though Akram had been trying to tutor Mohammed in American English, Mohammed wasn't making much progress. Mohammed was shy and wasn't speaking to anyone consistently in English, even in his college classes. Two of the classes were large lecture classes where he didn't need to say anything, but one class was in American Lit and the other was in European History, which only had about twenty students each. He never spoke up in class and hurried out of the classroom as soon as class was over.

One night when they were at the mosque, Akram thought that Allah gave him a wonderful idea. The imam knew tons of people in the community, and they all seemed to want to be on his good side. When prayer was over, Akram told Mohammed that he had been inspired by Allah. Mohammed did a double take, and then saw that Akram was serious. He asked Mohammed to wait outside for him. Bewildered at what he had just heard come out of Akram's mouth, Mohammed merely nodded and shuffled toward the door with everyone else.

Akram pretended he had to use the bathroom downstairs. He took his good sweet time walking down the stairs to the bathroom, dawdled on the lower level reading signs and a few ads posted on the bulletin board.

When he thought he had killed enough time, he went back upstairs as slowly as possible. Just as he arrived on the main floor, the last two men were saying good-bye to the imam. As Akram walked toward the imam, the floorboards creaked and the imam turned quickly toward Akram, having been startled.

Akram tried to be as polite and self-effacing as possible. "I apologize if I startled you, imam. I needed to go downstairs to use the men's room. I have never been formally introduced to you. My name is Akram Saleem. I recently arrived in the United States and have been coming faithfully to the mosque to express my thanks to Allah for granting me a safe trip and bringing me to a new stage in my life." This was the carefully rehearsed speech he had been thinking about all night since he had the idea.

The imam eyed Akram up and down. Akram looked younger than he really was. The imam was a tall thin man of about sixty-five. "So, Akram, how have you been finding America and the new stage in your life?" turning Akram's words back on him.

"So far, I like it very much, but I feel I have to be careful not to lose the essential values of Islam, in a land which regards money as its god. I want to strike the right balance between Islam and yet being able to make a decent living and support my family."

"Are you married?"

"No, not yet, but I am looking for the right woman to be my wife and bring children into the world and into the faith. I feel though that I must be able to earn a good living before I marry. I want to better myself. I am also enrolled in my first semester in college."

"That's very admirable. It seems like a good plan," the imam countered, with a trace of a smile on his face.

Akram realized that now was the time to make his move. "Would it be too forward on my part to ask if there is anyone you know who might be willing to help me in my endeavor? Who might be willing to offer me a job?"

"Do you have a job now?"

Akram nodded and waved his hand in the air as if to dismiss the job completely. "It is only a part-time job, but I am seeking full-time employment in a job which will lead to a career."

Again, the imam smiled, but this time more openly. There was something boyish and almost endearing about this young man, trying to pursue the American Dream and balancing that with his Islamic values. "What field are you prepared to work in?"

"I am very good with people. I would like to work in computers, or human resources in a company, but I am willing to learn any field. It is too early for me to have to choose a major in college, but it might be computer science. I am a quick study."

The imam thought Akram was a little too old to be this naive, yet he dismissed the thought saying to himself that he just might be naive about how American culture worked. "I think that I may have someone who could be very helpful in getting you a job or he may hire you for one of his companies. Call me here next Wednesday after I speak to him. He will want to meet you in person. Write down my phone number and call me."

Akram felt tears well up in his eyes. This was not part of the act. He was so grateful! The imam saw the tears, and thought that this was going to work out well for all three sides, since he was including himself as one of the sides.

"I cannot thank you enough for your generosity. The brothers speak of you as a wise and caring leader. Now I am better able to understand why."

"Thank you for your kind words. I am always happy to help a deserving person. Make Allah proud by your actions as you go forward in life. There will come a time when I may ask you to return the favor and do something for someone else. Do not forget this day."

"Of course, I am at your disposal. You can feel assured you can call on me."

Akram had no idea how soon he was going to be asked to return the favor.

Chapter 15

TOM

A little after three A.M. Tom woke out of a deep sleep with chills, a sore throat and a fever. Just to add to his misery, he also had a splitting headache and shortly thereafter, he began vomiting. "Great, now I have every symptom in the book," he groaned out loud, even though he was all alone in the apartment. It was a long three and a half hours until seven a.m., when he called the hospital and spoke to the resident in charge.

The resident said all had been quiet during his shift and that Tom's patients had been holding their own. Tom told the resident of his symptoms and said he was not coming in to work, especially because his patients were immunocompromised and most certainly didn't need to be around anyone who was overtly manifesting symptoms. He gave the resident his cell phone number and told him to call if they needed him. He then left a message on the voice mail of his executive assistant, Sue, asking her to call him when she came in to work later that morning, that he was too sick to come in to the hospital, and that she was going to have to cancel appointments and meetings for him.

By about eleven a.m., he was still alternating between fever and chills, but the chills had lessened to a large degree and his headache was gone, but the vomiting had continued unabated. Tom called downstairs to John at the main desk, and explained to him that he was sick. He asked if someone could deliver a twelve-pack of ginger ale and twelve bottles of Gatorade. Ever the master of unnecessary details, John wanted to know what brand of ginger ale Tom wanted and what flavor of Gatorade. Since Tom was almost never sick, and even then it was usually only a cold, Tom was more than grumpy when he was sick. His response to John was "surprise me," and he hung up the phone.

About a half hour later, the doorbell rang and a young man was standing there with all the requested liquid. It took a considerable amount of effort to get out of bed to get to the door, so the doorbell rang a second time before Tom was able to get there.

"Dr. Amendola, here's what you asked for. Should I bring it in to the kitchen for you?"

"Nah, I got it. Thanks for getting this to me so fast." In one fell swoop, Tom took the two bags and handed a twenty-dollar bill to the young man.

"This is for you. I assume they will bill me for the ginger ale and the Gatorade."

The young man looked at the twenty-dollar bill in total surprise. "Well, thank you very much, sir. Please don't hesitate to call if you need anything else from us. I can even drive you to the doctor's office, if need be. We have a car and a van available for our residents." He glanced again at the twenty-dollar bill.

"Thanks, I will let you know if I need anything else and I thank you again for getting this to me so fast." As Tom closed the door, he laughed a little to himself. He hadn't actually meant to give the young man a twenty, but when he opened his wallet, he realized that he only had twenties. He hoped the kid enjoyed it and took his girlfriend out for a drink.

By the following morning, the ugliest symptoms had mostly passed, but Tom still had a fever of 101.5 degrees. He was still in bed, but at least he was sitting up, as opposed to yesterday, when he was totally prone, except for the horrible trips to the bathroom. Amy had spent the weekend with him, so called her to make sure she was okay and that she hadn't caught whatever it was he had. When he called in to the hospital this morning, his mind didn't seem to be in as much of a haze as it had been all day yesterday. He was even contemplating taking a shower, but for now that seemed like a lot of effort.

Fortunately for Tom, there had been no crises with his patients over the weekend when Amy was with him, and all day Monday and now Tuesday morning had been relatively quiet. The fellows and residents had not disappointed him, and Dr. Compton, who was on call over the past weekend, had apparently stepped in yesterday and helped the fellow with two issues on two different patients. Tom liked that, and made a mental note to give Dr. Compton a call to thank him.

Tom nodded off a few times during the afternoon, and when he woke up from the last nap, he noticed it was getting dark. At this time of year, it was getting dark earlier each day. His fever was down to 100.5 degrees, but it was fever nonetheless. He wanted chicken soup, and this was the first time he had wanted anything to eat since Sunday night and it was now late Tuesday.

He called down to the front desk again, and asked if they could send up a quart of chicken soup and a few hard rolls from the restaurant in the building. John was finally off duty, but the night manager, who was equally nice as John, and whose name Tom could not remember, said that the soup would be delivered within a half hour. Tom had filled the kitchen with all kinds of food which he thought Amy might like. Despite that, there was no chicken soup, and that was what he was craving. True to form, in a half hour, the doorbell rang, and a different young man had a bag in hand. Since yesterday, Tom had managed to find a five-dollar bill in his pants pocket, instead of having to tip another twenty dollars.

Tom went back to lie on the bed, and he turned the television back on. He had turned it off a few hours ago when the same stories had looped several times in an apparently slow news cycle. He also couldn't stand the soap operas and the talk shows, yet he didn't have enough concentration to read any of his medical journals or even a novel.

At least the five o'clock news was on, which was better than nothing. The news hadn't been on for more than a few minutes when the Breaking News banner flashed across the screen. The two anchors came back on the screen, both visibly shaken. Then an alert flashed in red on the screen.

New York City had several dirty bombs go off, and officials were telling people to shelter in place, wherever they were, and not to go outside. The alert repeated that people should stay inside office buildings, homes, stores and restaurants. Those outside were directed to get off the streets as quickly as possible and get inside to shelter. People were told to keep windows closed and to shut open windows and doors.

The anchors on the major television stations were asking the public to stay calm, follow instructions from NYPD and the mayor's office, until the situation could be assessed and appropriate action taken. The normally cheery and chatty anchors seemed grim and upset, and they had no other information at this moment to report to their viewers. Social media erupted as people were panic stricken and not knowing what to do. Social media actually provided more information than anything else.

Tom's stomach wrenched, but this time it was not from the stomach bug. Tom sat bolt upright in the bed and flipped around the TV stations, but the information seemed sketchy at best. Tom grabbed his cell phone and checked to see what the "Twitterverse" was saying. He virtually never used Twitter, and only checked it when Amy texted him that there was something he should see. Twitter was ablaze with information already. It seemed that so far several dirty bombs had gone off in Manhattan. Much of the information was conflicting, but there were a number of people who were confirming the same thing. Some sort of bomb had gone off near the United Nations on the east side of Manhattan, and two more near the World Trade Center and Penn Station. Tom was praying that no bombs had gone off in the subways or actually on the trains. If this information was correct, it appeared that the terrorists were looking for places where there were lots of people, especially since this was rush hour and these were transportation hubs.

Tom tried using his cell phone to make a call, but now he kept getting a message that all circuits were busy. Thank God, I'm old enough to have wanted a land line. Here was the perfect reason to have a back-up. Tom grabbed the land line near his night stand, and called Sue. She answered the phone on the first ring, and she clearly sounded rattled.

"Oh my God, Dr. A., this is awful. Just awful. What are we going to do?" Then she started to sob.

"Sue, it's okay, stay where you are. The hospital has a lot of resources, including backup generators. Has the hospital gone into the Disaster Plan?"

Sue didn't answer him and then went into a tirade about how she had to get home to her family. Tom was surprised that Sue was unraveling on the phone, because his view of her had been cool, calm and collected. Tom broke into the tirade and raised his voice with her.

"Sue, listen to me. You are not going anywhere. The hospital is one of the safest places you can be. You are going to stay inside the hospital as the police have said to do. Use the land line that we're speaking on. I'm going to hang up and you are going to call your husband and see that he's okay. Then I'm going to call you back in a few minutes. Do you have a job to do in the hospital's Disaster Plan?"

Apparently, Tom's tone of voice brought her back to reality and calmed her down a little. "Okay, let me call Ron. I just hope he hasn't left the office. He usually doesn't leave the office this early."

"Good, do that and you'll feel better. Has the hospital declared a disaster yet? I just asked you if you have a job to do in the hospital's Disaster Plan."

"Yes, the Hospital has declared a disaster. I'm in the Second Tier. I'm supposed to stay in my office until they call for the Second Tier, which is to help the ER and Admissions and log in patients."

"Okay, have they called the Second Tier to come down to the ER yet?"

"No, not yet."

"Then transfer me to the "T" unit, call Ron, and be ready to go help when they need you. The ER is probably going to be swamped. Sue, this is going to be all hands on deck, so be ready to go down to the ER. Don't forget to lock the office when you leave to go downstairs to help and remind everyone else on the floor to do the same. You can do this."

Tom was transferred to the nurses' station in the "T" or transplant unit. Betty Crowley was the head nurse who answered the phone and Tom could hear the edge in her voice. In the short time that Tom had been at the hospital, he had come to have great respect for Betty. She was smart, savvy and a first-rate nurse. They were lucky to have her. Tom had spoken to her many times since his arrival at the hospital, and they had been candid with each other, but with the understanding that what was said, remained between them.

"Betty, who is on today?" meaning what residents and fellows. Betty gave him the names, but before Tom could say anything, she said, "But the residents and fellows were called down to the ER as part of the Disaster Plan."

Tom was afraid of that. The last thing he needed was to have no coverage in the "T" unit when he had some very sick patients fighting for their lives.

"Have all the doctors been called down to the ER?" Tom's headache had abated earlier in the day, but now with the news of the dirty bombs, Susan's meltdown on the phone and this information that the unit was going to be woefully understaffed, his headache had returned with a vengeance. Tom held his breath, waiting for an answer.

Betty let out a heavy sigh. "No, they left one resident here."

"Who is it?" Based on the heavy sigh, Tom was afraid to hear the answer. "It's Haynes."

"Who the hell is Haynes?" Tom thought he knew all the residents and this name was not ringing any bells with him.

"He's a second year. You wouldn't know him because, to be candid, Dr. A., we think he's deaf and he's definitely dumb."

"How the hell did he get on this service?"

"Well, he somehow managed to squeak through his first year, and he was already in his second year before you arrived."

"So there's someone who's his guardian angel?"

"Yes, sir. He's Dr. Royce's nephew. His mother and Dr. Royce are brother and sister, so he has a different last name from Dr. Royce."

"Great, just great. Betty, if this Haynes even so much as deviates one fraction of an inch from the care plan for each patient, I want you to tackle him and tie him to the nurses' station. Why did they leave him in the unit?"

"Maybe they think he could do more damage to patients when he had to make snap decisions in the ER."

"Look, this would be difficult for any resident to handle alone, so please get your nurses following him around so he can't do anything stupid. I haven't been in because I have a virus with the full boat of symptoms, and I still have a fever. Now I can't leave my apartment. Here's my cell phone number and the house phone. The cell doesn't seem to be working. Call me with anything you need. Do you think you can get Haynes to call me so I can impress on him that he is not to deviate in any way from the care plans and that if anything comes up, he is to call me immediately?"

"Sure can, Dr. A. It will be my pleasure to call you and put you and Dr. Haynes on the speaker phone."

VALERIE

Valerie was just gathering her possessions to get out of the cab, when the alert from NBC News went off on her phone. This was an early night for Valerie after a meeting with an architect in his office who would be an expert witness on the case. She just didn't feel like going back to the office. She could answer her e-mails and do some more work from home tonight.

What a pain, she thought. Another water main break or massive five-car pile up to report. It was a never ending stream of bad news. Just as she opened the door of the cab, someone raced by and hit into the door, almost slamming it shut on her foot. Then she noticed that there were people running on the sidewalk. She managed to wiggle her way out of the cab with her purse and briefcase.

The other strange thing she noticed was that there was no doorman standing in front of the building. Even on the rainiest days, there was a doorman, who might be standing under the canopy, but he was still standing outside. Valerie's brain had not quite processed all these bits of information into a coherent whole. As she approached the front door, she saw the doorman inside the building, which was very strange. It was only as she walked right up to the front door that he opened the door for her from the inside. His expression was nothing short of pained.

"What's going on?" she asked the doorman.

"Haven't you heard? Dirty bombs have gone off in the city! We don't know much, but they want everyone to stay inside."

"No, I was in the cab and my cell phone had an alert go off, but I didn't check it. Oh my God, I can't believe this has actually happened!"

"I've been told to stay inside and keep the front door locked. We don't know what's going to happen. It's better that you stay inside and go up to your apartment where you'll be safe. There doesn't seem to be much real information and a lot of wild speculation. We want to prevent any looting and keep out anyone who isn't supposed to be here."

Valerie nodded and saw the fear in Joel's eyes. "Are you going to stay here, Joel?"

"I don't know, ma'am. We're supposed to stay inside and not be out in the contaminated air, but I want to get home to my family. My wife is home with our son, and they're safe for now. I'm scared that they're home alone without me. I don't know if the subways are running or if I should even be on the subway now. This is horrible."

Now the fear was beginning to sink in to Valerie as well. She felt that an awful pall was beginning to envelope her, and she shivered. "I understand, Joel, that you want to get home to your family. It may not be safe for you to be on the streets or the subway right now. I would think the subway is a big potential target. Can you keep in touch with your wife on the phone?"

"Yeah, the landline works, but the cell towers must be all jammed up. The cell service is spotty."

"Will you let us know if you're going to leave?"

"Yes, ma'am, I will."

"Are you seeing a lot of people going by on the street?"

"At first, yes, but now it seems to have quieted down. I don't know what's going to happen when it gets dark. Who knows what people will do? Could become the Wild West out there."

"Let's hope not. I'm going to go upstairs and see what's being reported on TV and the internet. Is there a night doorman who is supposed to come on duty later?"

"Yes, but I don't know if he'll come in to work."

"Okay, but you will let us know if you're going to leave?" She checked again.

"Yes, ma'am. I will."

"Stay safe, Joel. Hope this is not going to be a long night, but something tells me it is."

As she turned toward the elevator, something caught her attention out of the corner of her eye. Joel saw it and he turned as well. It was Paul and he was running full tilt from the sidewalk toward the front door. Joel recognized him and opened the front door just as Paul was about to throw himself against the glass of the front door.

Paul squeezed through the partially opened front door, and leaned forward hands on his knees, gasping for breath. Joel and Valerie looked at each other, and then back at Paul. "Are you okay, Paul?" Valerie asked. Paul shook his head in what appeared to be a yes and a no almost at the same time. He stood up and tried to talk, but he was so out of breath that he couldn't get too many words out of his mouth.

Finally, he said, "I was about ten or so blocks from here when the alert went off on my phone. They said to get inside right away, but every place closed up really fast, and no one would let me in an office building or an apartment without some ID. I tried a few places, and when that didn't work, I figured my best chance was to make a run for it here.

"It's already a jungle out there. I tripped and fell as I was running. I don't know if the guy tripped over me or landed on top of me purposely. He was a huge guy and he had me pinned down on the ground. The son of a bitch grabbed my arm and twisted it behind me and took my watch. I thought he was going to dislocate my elbow. The guy was up in a flash and took off. I got up as fast as I could before someone else fell on top of me. That's when I decided I had to get here as fast as possible before something else happened. I was maybe half a mile from here. What the hell would I have done if I had been on an appointment downtown?"

"Your cheek is cut. It doesn't look like too deep a cut and it looks like the bleeding has stopped. You should come on upstairs and wash it off," Valerie said.

"Do you guys know what is happening with this dirty bomb crap?"

"I just got here myself and I was about to head upstairs to my apartment to turn on the TV when you made your very dramatic entry." Valerie gave Paul what she hoped was a friendly smile, but at this moment, Valerie was not too sure of her own emotions.

"Let's go upstairs and see what we can find out." As Valerie and Paul headed toward the elevator, Valerie's cell phone rang and startled her. The caller ID said Brendan Stewart. Brendan was one of her partners in the firm and a character to say the least.

"Hello, Brendan."

"Thank God, I reached you, Valerie. The cell service is really spotty. I think I'm only I'm a few blocks from your apartment. I don't know if you're home, but I was hoping that you could tell your doorman to let me in. I'm stuck out in the street and no one will let me in. I'm freaking out to be outside after the dirty bombs went off when they've said we're supposed to get inside."

The panic was apparent in Brendan's voice. He sounded frantic and on the verge of tears.

"Brendan, I had just come home when the alerts went off. I'm in the lobby of the building. I'll tell the doorman to let you in and you can come up to my apartment."

"Thanks, Valerie, thanks so much. I'll be there in a couple of minutes."

Valerie told Joel what Brendan looked like and to let him into the building and then send him up to her apartment.

As Valerie and Paul arrived on the third floor and stepped off the elevator, Valerie said to Paul, "See you later. Go clean off that cut on your face."

Paul nodded and said, "I heard you say to the doorman to let you know if he's not going to stay. That would just make matters worse with no doorman."

"God, yes. Do you think any of this is going to cause power outages?"

"I wouldn't think, but hey, what do I know? Here's my card with my cell phone number. Give me yours."

Valerie said that the doorman told her that the cell phones weren't working all that well.

"Shit, that may be the real problem, with the networks being inundated."

VALERIE AND BRENDAN

A few minutes after Brendan had initially called Valerie, Joel called Valerie on the house phone to tell her that Brendan was on his way up in the elevator. This had given her time to turn on the TV to try to find out what updates there were and to change out of her work clothes and into a pair of jeans and a sweater. When the doorbell rang, Valerie opened the door, but certainly was not expecting to see the vision that was Brendan Stewart.

Even in the best of times, Brendan often looked like an unmade bed. Valerie had seen the dry cleaner deliver fresh shirts on hangers and pressed suits in plastic bags to the office. Yet despite that, Brendan often looked as if he had slept in his clothes. Valerie vividly recalled the first time he had come to introduce himself to her on her first day in the office. There has been a whole fiasco with his spilling the Dunkin' Donuts coffee on her desk and the ensuing futile efforts to mop up the coffee. Subsequently, Valerie had been surprised to learn that there was indeed a Mrs. Brendan Stewart. Valerie wondered to herself on several occasions if his wife saw him leave the house in the morning. If so, did he look okay when he left the house or did he somehow manage to become that disheveled on the way to work on Metro-North?

Brendan looked like a crazy, homeless person, so it was no surprise that doormen were turning him away.

His hair had been blown in all directions by the wind, probably by his running. Some of his hair was standing straight up in the air. His camel colored trench coat had a huge smear of mud down the front.

One leg of his suit pants had a rip in the knee. His tie was open and had apparently been blown across his shoulder and was lying across his trench coat. One shoe had been badly scuffed, while the other still held a shine.

"Jesus, Brendan, what the hell happened to you? You're a complete mess. Come on in."

Brendan entered the apartment as Valerie stood aside to let him in.

"It's like civilization as we know it has gone to hell. This dirty bomb only went off about an hour ago and people are acting like savages. It was like something out of *Lord of the Flies*."

"Take off that trench coat. It's filthy. What happened?"

"I tripped and fell and did a face plant. Some guy helped me up, but the mud was all over my coat. People were running like lunatics in every direction. When the cell phones told people what had happened and that they were supposed to get inside, that made people frantic. Buildings were locking their doors instead of letting people in, which just made the frenzy worse. This could really get much worse unless the authorities get this under control fast. There could be rioting, looting and people getting killed."

"I think that is precisely what happened. Those in control of the buildings, be they residential or commercial, were afraid of who they were possibly letting in to the buildings, so they just refused to let anyone in who didn't have ID for that building. When I pulled up in the cab, the doorman was inside the lobby instead of standing outside. He had been told to lock the front door and not let in anyone he didn't know, and management was afraid of looting."

"What are they saying on TV?" He motioned toward the flat screen.

"The mayor has been on TV saying that there were three dirty bombs set off and they are working to contain the spread of the chemicals and the radiation. He's asking for calm and saying that all the New York City hospitals on are on alert for anyone who was near the sites and feels ill. They have decontamination units already set up as part of the emergency procedures at the hospitals. The hospitals in the boroughs are also ready to accept people, if need be, as are the hospitals in Westchester and New Jersey.

"The good news is that there is almost no wind blowing right now, so they are hoping that nothing will be blown outside of Manhattan. He's stressed that it's very important for people to shelter in place and stay inside. I don't think they have a handle on the fact that there are many people who can't get inside. I'm hoping those people will think to go to places like Madison Square Garden, subway stations or the New York Public Library, where at least they will be inside. They've played this clip by the mayor a number of times already, and he promised to keep coming on TV to give updates."

"Sounds bad. We don't know how much they really know or how much they are telling us. I suppose that they are trying to tell the general public enough to prevent mass panic. I really hope it works, because from the little I saw, it was so bad."

"Right now we are probably a hell of a lot better off than most people in New York City. We're safe, we're in a luxury high rise, and we have food and running water. I was thinking that in addition to the bottled water I have, maybe we should fill up one of the bathtubs with water in case we lose power."

"Good idea. I would never have thought of that."

Valerie handed Brendan a hanger and told him to hang his trench coat in the shower as she led him into the bathroom. "Go get yourself cleaned up, and then we'll figure out what to do. I can make us some dinner. I think you are stuck here for tonight at least. Todd has some clothes here, but I'm not sure you two are even remotely close in size. Do you want to call your wife?"

"I tried calling her but I couldn't get through. Kept getting busy signals. I can't thank you enough for this, Valerie."

"I actually even have a landline. It's in the bedroom. Why don't you call her and tell her you're okay? I'm sure by now she's frantic as to where you are. You live out in Westchester, right?"

"Yes, in Pelham Manor. I have no idea if Metro-North is even running. Did the mayor say anything about Metro-North?"

"No, he didn't say anything about that. I remember reading about 9/11 that they wanted to get people out of New York City as fast as possible, so they used what they called 'load and go' on the railroads. Maybe with a dirty bomb, they won't do that because they don't know who has been exposed and who may be sick."

Valerie walked into the kitchen to see what she would make for dinner and to give Brendan some privacy on the phone with his wife. After a few minutes, he came into the kitchen and said softly, "Thank you so much again, Valerie. My wife was crying on the phone when she heard my voice. She, of course, had feared the worst for me. Let me go get cleaned up."

As Brendan looked at himself in the hall mirror, even Brendan, the master of disheveled, was taken aback. "Oh my Lord and Taylor, I am a sight to behold."

"You are, Brendan. You are. I'm hoping that in the near future, we will look back on this night and laugh about it."

However, there was a voice nagging at her saying that this was not going to be quick or easy and that it was probably going to be an ordeal. Valerie knew that it was certainly the right thing to take Brendan in, but she had never spent any lengthy amount of time with him. It could prove to be hilarious or it could be an unmitigated disaster.

Chapter 18

PAUL

The meeting in Florida went extremely well. Paul was amazed, after having seen David Collins' mansion and surrounding estate in Palm Beach, that David was not the "money man." How much more money could David's friend and personal counselor, Andrew Dustin, have? Andrew was a remarkably charming and friendly man. If Paul had not known something of Andrew's background in business, and his incredible successes, he would never have known it by the words from Andrew's own mouth. Andrew seemed to have no need to tell anyone how great he was, how much money he had, or how everyone should be in awe of his business acumen.

After their dinner together, Paul came away thinking that he almost liked Andrew more than David. It was obvious that David had been successful, yet he seemed almost naive about certain political situations and unaware that many people were motivated by greed. He couldn't have made this much money if he didn't understand how the world, and business, worked. David was somewhat of a newcomer and outsider to Washington politics, and he intended to use that to his advantage. He wasn't tainted by the sins of the politicians in Washington, and perhaps more importantly, he wasn't part of the logjam in Congress where nothing ever seemed to be accomplished.

David had been governor of Florida and only served two terms, and then walked away from politics for four years while he started slowly and methodically to set up his political machine. He was a moderate and had been on the fiscally conservative side. He balanced the budget in Florida, but in a tightrope walk that made even some of his enemies marvel, seemed fair in his cutting the budget so as not to make any one group bear the whole burden. As the state rebounded financially, he also restored the programs in an even-handed manner.

The three of them talked for almost an hour and a half over drinks and hors d'oeuvres, and then as if someone had sent a signal through the ether, David and Andrew's wives magically appeared on the patio. The hour and a half passed very quickly, because even though they talked solely about preparations for the upcoming campaign, and if indeed it was an interview, it didn't seem that way to Paul. David talked about Paul's role as if it were a fait accompli. It seemed as if David just wanted Paul and Andrew to meet in person and make sure they got on well.

By the time that David's and Andrew's wives appeared on the patio to collect the three men, apparently a few more guests had arrived and were in the house, having their own hors d'oeuvres and drinks. As Paul thought about it, the meeting about the upcoming campaign seemed to be coming to a close at just the time when the two women came down to the patio. Was this mere coincidence or impeccable timing? David stood up and stretched. "Sitting too long in a chair will kill you. Wish we had time for a swim or a massage before dinner. But will sitting too long in public office kill you as well?" He winked at his own joke.

Paul wanted to be a good sport, so his retort was, "I think sitting in the Oval Office for eight years would be quite good for you, David. Then we'll make the health assessment."

"I like a man with a good sense of humor." He then clapped Paul on the back. "Good thing my hair is already gray. Look what happened to Bill Clinton, George Bush and Barack Obama. All of them had dark hair when they were elected, and by the time they left office, their hair was very gray. No question it's a tough job. You just don't know what crisis each day is going to bring to the Presidency. Even with all that stress and how difficult it is, I still think I can do that job."

Andrew said in a quiet voice as if he were telling them a secret. "You're up to the challenge. America needs you, buddy."

Andrew said those two short sentences in such a definitive way that for the first time, Paul felt that he might be signing on to something great and not merely a job. For much of their preliminary discussions, Paul had looked at this new job as an opportunity to catapult himself onto the national stage. In their meeting tonight, Paul had looked beyond the campaign and saw only a win/win for himself. If David won the election, there would surely be a big job in Washington on the horizon for Paul. If David lost, Paul could see that he might make a good enough impression on Andrew that there could be a big job in one of Andrew's many and varied enterprises.

Andrew and David had known each other since college, a lot of years ago. Andrew seemed more astute to Paul than David, so if Andrew felt that way about David, Paul felt that he owed it to David to take a much harder second look.

Chapter 19

VALERIE

Valerie took one last deep breath before she turned the knob on the highly polished mahogany door of McAllister, Russo and Douglas. It was 7:30 AM on Monday morning, and although she half expected to be greeted by the receptionist, no one was as the front desk. Okay, the receptionist works nine to five.

Since she had been in the office yesterday afternoon, she was able to navigate her way to her office without getting lost. Good first sign of the day. Interestingly, although she passed a number of partner and associate offices on the way to her own office, all were dark and empty. Somewhere in the back of her mind she remembered hearing that New York City law firms tended to start working about 9:30 AM. That starting time had never really been an issue for her while she was in California. Even if she called someone in the New York office at eight o'clock in the morning in California, of course it was already eleven o'clock in New York.

This might turn out to be a great thing since she could get in an hour and half or two hours of work before anyone interrupted her. Shortly after 8:15 a.m., a tall and somewhat portly man of about fifty years old knocked lightly on the office door and stepped in holding a huge cup emblazoned with the words, Dunkin' Donuts.

"Valerie, I'm Brendan Stewart," he said, with one hand extended, and the other balancing the coffee and a crumpled white bag, which also said Dunkin' Donuts.

"Brendan, so nice to finally meet you in person. I think I was on vacation the last time you were in the L.A. office. Sorry I missed you." Valerie motioned to Brendan to sit in one of the client chairs. As he did, the lid of the coffee cup popped off and the coffee sloshed out and onto the top of her desk.

"Oh, so sorry. Let me clean this up." Before Valerie could react, Brendan had yanked brown paper napkins from the Dunkin' Donuts bag and proceeded to wipe the desk. The only problem was that the sloshing coffee had also soaked through the bag, so the napkins were already wet. Brendan dragged the already soggy napkins across the desk, which did nothing to remedy the situation, and in fact, probably made it worse as the coffee and milk smeared on the top of the desk.

Brendan stared at the mess on the desktop as if it were an alien creature. "Well, that didn't help matters at all," he declared as if he was making a papal proclamation. He jumped out of the chair and walked out of the office. Valerie stood there somewhat bewildered, not knowing if Brendan was abandoning ship or planning on some other cleaning activity.

He returned in a few seconds brandishing a wad of tissues, which he probably grabbed off the secretary's desk. Valerie didn't want to burst his bubble and tell him that tissues weren't all that absorbent with liquids, but Brendan seemed intent on effecting a cleanup. He smeared the liquid a second time across the edge of the desk and pronounced that it was much better. By this point, Valerie had all to do not to burst out laughing.

Not quite knowing what to do with the soggy wad of tissues, Brendan looked up at Valerie for some answer. She saw the wastepaper basket across the room and obliged Brendan. After unceremoniously dropping the tissues into the wastepaper basket, Brendan dropped himself back into the chair. He pulled two powdered sugar doughnuts out of the coffee-soaked bag, shook the coffee off the doughnuts and offered her one. Valerie declined.

The next act of the farce was about to begin. Brendan took a big bite out of the doughnut, and the powdered sugar flew off the doughnut as if it had a life of its own. It hit the lapel of Brendan's navy blue suit jacket, as well as the top of the still damp desk top. Of course, it stuck to his nose and cheek. Once again, Valerie didn't know how she was going to keep a straight face. There were no more dry napkins or tissues and Valerie couldn't think of a thing to do or say to remedy this powdered sugar "crisis."

Brendan had a good reputation as a trial attorney, but he was also the stereotype of the absent-minded professor. The stories about him were legendary, and after a few brief moments, Valerie was much more inclined to believe them. Valerie had heard that there was usually an associate assigned to Brendan for a deposition or trial, to make sure he got to court on time and with all his documents. He had been variously described as a buffoon or a clown. He once fell up the stairs to the courthouse and broke his foot on the way to a trial. EMS carted him off in an ambulance, while the associate stood there with several briefcases and files, but no lead trial attorney.

There was another story that Brendan once sat on the edge of the jury box and fell in. Not only was everyone in the courtroom laughing, but the court officers couldn't get him out because his foot was stuck. The jury had to be escorted out of the courtroom, but not before everyone, including the judge, was guffawing. Brendan kept yelling, "I'm fine, no I'm not fine. I'm fine, no, I'm not fine." There was some talk that Brendan fell into the jury box purposely to stall for time, since one of his witnesses was missing.

Perhaps the most famous Brendan story was that he and opposing counsel were at the bench for a sidebar conference with the judge during the trial. Brendan was gesticulating with a pen in his hand, when the fountain pen opened, spraying the judge, opposing counsel and Brendan with ink. As a result, the three of them looked as if they had a case of measles, but the biggest problem was that the pen flew up onto the bench and hit the Judge in the eye scratching his cornea. Court had to be adjourned for several days while the judge's cornea healed.

After spending only a few minutes with Brendan this morning, Valerie believed that these and a host of other stories that circulated about him were true. He was brilliant, but he was also a walking biohazard. Valerie didn't want to be one of these casualties. Despite these foibles, Valerie liked him. He seemed totally unpretentious, and Valerie couldn't yet tell if he was unaware of his comedic presentation. She could see how a jury might sympathize with his bumbling. He was "Everyman" in a navy blue suit, and the fickle finger of fate seemed to keep pointing directly at him.

Seemingly oblivious to the powdered sugar every-where, especially on his face, Brendan continued in a completely serious tone.

"I'm sure our partners will drop by today to introduce themselves to you, so perhaps this afternoon, you and I can meet to start going over the case. I have some recommendations of associates to work with us on the case, but I want you to meet with each of them to see who you like. I'll have

Marian, my paralegal, e-mail you their curriculum vitae, so you have some background on each of them before you meet them in person."

Brendan got up to leave the office and smiled warmly at her. "I'm looking forward to working with you on this case."

"I'm looking forward to it as well, Brendan. Thanks for stopping by first thing this morning."

Brendan was halfway out the door when Valerie called to him that he forgot his briefcase. He still had the half empty coffee cup and soggy bag in his hand.

"Yeah, I thought I came in here with more things in my hand." He reached for his briefcase and turned to leave a second time, but this time he tripped on his way out. He banged his hand against the filing cabinet, which made a huge bang.

Brendan never turned back to Valerie, but waved to her over his head. Valerie laughed and wondered if this was going to be one of the "I'm fine, or I'm not fine" times. She made a mental note never to go ahead of him down a flight of stairs or an escalator.

Chapter 20

TOM

The trip to see Amy and to see Yale again had gone very well yesterday. As he showered and shaved, he did something that he hadn't done in a long time. He spoke out loud to Laurie. Shortly after her death, Tom found himself saying out loud the things he was thinking in his head. It somehow made him feel that she was still close to him and could hear what he was saying. Although he didn't want to admit it to anyone, he inexplicably felt that Laurie was going to answer him from the other side. He wasn't quite sure how long he kept up the soliloquy, but there finally came a time when he gave up, because she never answered him. That threw him into a deeper sense of grief, but he felt he had lost her yet again.

Somehow the day spent with Amy energized him and he wanted to "share" it with Laurie. "Hey, kid, we, well mostly you, did such a good job with Amy. She is a wonderful kid. I loved being with her and the afternoon flew by. She's all excited about coming down to spend the weekend with me in New York. Actually, so am I. She wants to see some Broadway shows and she wants to see the Yankees, the Mets and the Knicks. I'm really looking forward to it. I don't think she was just bullshitting me about coming down either.

"I have to tell you though, honey, that I think I really fell down on the job after you died. I was drowning in my own grief and guilt over not being able to do more to save you. As a result, I threw myself into my work, but I don't think I did enough for the kids to help them cope with their loss. I sometimes had to act like it never happened in order to get through the day. You know that I never want to give my patients less than one hundred percent, so I had to push a lot into the background. By doing that for me, I think I did it to the kids, too.

"As the youngest, I now realize that Amy took it the hardest, and I wasn't there enough for her emotionally. I've begun to feel really guilty that in a sense she lost both of her parents. That's my fault. Maybe with this new job and my being in New York, I'll be able to spend time with her. I can't make up for what we lost, but I can do better going forward. The other thing I realized yesterday was that I never really spent time with Amy alone. I took "the kids" to places, but with my schedule being what it was, I took them all together. She's a special kid and I want to get to know her better.

"You know, honey, that I always wanted to make you proud of me. I think I've done that with my work, but now I'm going to do it with each kid, starting with Amy. Maybe you had something to do with my taking this new job, so that I could be closer to Amy. Until yesterday, I never really focused on how far Atlanta is from New Haven. Yeah, we all say hop on a plane, but I didn't do that for her, and so she didn't do it either.

"I love you and I miss you. You will always be the love of my life. You'll see, I'll do better with the kids. I'll make you proud."

Tom looked at the man looking back at him in the mirror. He was surprised to find that the man in the mirror had tears in his eyes.

Laurie still didn't answer him, but yet he felt she had heard him nonetheless.

He finished dressing and sat down to eat a quick breakfast after retrieving the newspaper left by the front door of the hotel room. That was one of the features he liked about this hotel. He had a small kitchenette where he could make breakfast and not have to be bothered with having to go somewhere to eat in the morning. He certainly didn't want to have to go out for his morning cup of coffee or if he wanted a snack or a drink at night once he was back in his room.

Tom's meeting at the hospital was at eight o'clock, presumably so that his colleagues could make rounds and then go to the office thereafter. He would meet with the other transplant surgeons as their surgery schedules allowed. The hospital administrator, Karen Gallagher, and Tim McAndrews, who was the surgeon who was primarily responsible for luring Tom to New York in the first place, were going to meet, hash out the details of Tom's employment and areas of responsibilities, and take Tom on a tour of the facility, but with the main focus on the transplant wing.

Matthews Memorial Hospital was a good twenty-minute walk from the hotel. He decided not to take a cab, but to walk instead. The traffic in New York City was already an irritation to him, and he knew he had to change his attitude and try to ignore the snail's pace of traffic. Walking also had a wonderful way of clearing his mind, and he could focus better after a walk. This was another reason for finding an apartment within walking distance of the hospital, and because his hours could be erratic at times, especially if a patient wasn't doing well after surgery.

Until Tom got a better handle on how capable the residents and fellows were on the transplant teams and how much trust he could place in them, he thought that he would probably come back to the hospital many nights to check on problems with patients post op. It was almost like a dance routine. The residents and fellows needed to get the appropriate sense of when Tom needed to be called for a post op problem. Some residents and fellows thought they should never call the attending physician about a problem with a patient, because they thought the attending physician would either be annoyed at being called in the middle of the night or the attending physician would not think the resident or fellow was knowledgeable enough. Once they all got how the "dance steps" were to go, then Tom would feel better about not having to check on everything himself.

Many doctors and surgeons tried to distance themselves from their patients. It was the classic defense mechanism, about not getting too close to a patient in case things went badly. This was especially true with surgeons in risky or particularly difficult surgeries. Tom felt that it was a choice that each doctor made early on. You could choose to distance yourself or you could choose to take the extra step and be more involved with the patient's struggle to live.

At first, Tom tried to distance himself, so as to blunt the pain. That choice didn't last very long for him. Tom knew it would be more painful personally to be involved, especially if the patient didn't make it. Tom had had his fair share of losses with patients and he took it personally. He wanted to take it personally. That drove him to do better each day and it drove him to innovate. When something failed or didn't go well, he wanted to find a way to improve, even in the smallest details. In Tom's mind, he could be a mechanic or he could be a surgeon and healer. He chose the latter.

He had repeated that metaphor many times to his residents. If he felt that a resident had overlooked something or didn't care enough to make the extra effort, then his question to the resident was, "Do you just want to be a mechanic?"

For most of them, he had only had to ask that question once, and the resident got it. If Tom had to ask the question three times of the same resident, then Tom didn't want that resident on his service working with his patients.

Chapter 21

TOM

Matthews Memorial was an impressive campus on the east side of Manhattan. Despite the fact that it was situated on some of the most valuable pieces of real estate in New York City, its early administrators had enough foresight to realize that the value of real estate was only going to appreciate exponentially, and they had literally begged and borrowed money to buy up the surrounding properties. There were four huge buildings which comprised the campus, an extraordinary feat for a hospital located in the heart of a city as densely populated as New York City.

The view of the East River from two of the buildings was breathtaking, even on miserable rainy days. On a blustery and rainy day, there were whitecaps on the River, and the tugboats and barges had to navigate the choppy river. The view on a sunny day was picture perfect. The river was a blue, the color you saw in books. The sailboats were out, and the view of the Fifty- Ninth Street Bridge was majestic against the backdrops of the river and the sky.

Tom entered the lobby of the building where the administration wing was located. He gave his name to the guard at the desk, who issued him an electronic visitor pass and instructions to the location of the elevator and the floor number where he was going. As the elevator door opened to the fifth floor, Tom walked to his right and down to the end of the hallway, where he saw the sign on the door which said Hospital Administration.

He swiped his pass to open the door, and as he walked in, a young woman in her early thirties greeted him. "Good morning, Dr. Amendola. Dr. Gallagher is expecting you." Tom must have registered a look of surprise, to which the young receptionist said, "The security guard downstairs gave you an electronic visitor pass which registered on my computer to say you were on the way up here. We have implemented lots of security measures in the past few years. Some are very visible and some are not. Please give me a minute to tell Dr. Gallagher that you're here."

As Tom looked at the various plaques on the wall, the door opened and a very attractive brunette said, "Tom, I'm Karen Gallagher. So nice to meet you in person."

"Nice to meet you too, Karen. I'm reading the very impressive list of awards."

"Thank you. We really do pride ourselves on striving for excellence. Please come in to my office. Would you like some coffee or tea? I'm about to have my second cup of coffee, so you can join me, if you want."

"Yes, I'd like a cup of coffee, with some milk."

Karen nodded to the receptionist, and motioned for Tom to follow her. "Leslie will bring us the coffee in my office. Do you ever wonder what people did before they opened each meeting with coffee? Somehow it works well as an icebreaker."

"Maybe it's an icebreaker or maybe it's an eye opener. It's liquid comfort food, but that caffeine kick is necessary to get you through some mind-numbing meetings," he countered with a smile.

They chatted about Tom's trip to New York and Karen asked him where he was currently staying while in New York, and where he thought he might like to live. He told Karen about his trip to Yale to see Amy and their plans to explore the city together. Karen was surprisingly easy to talk to, and they sipped the coffee as if they were old friends. Within a few minutes, Tom found himself asking Karen how she got into hospital administration and how she liked it.

"In addition to my medical degree, I also have an MBA in Hospital Administration. I do miss practicing medicine full time, but I team teach two courses to the medical students just to keep my hand in it. I have to admit that I am surprised by how much I like administration. There are the real boring and tedious parts of the job, but I like to solve problems and every hospital has a host of problems that need tackling, if not solving.

"I, of course, am not wild about dealing with the finances, but I have good people in finance who take a lot of the burden off me. It's the proverbial necessary evil. I have a supportive Board of Governors, and I have doctors who are very good at what they do. For the most part, they are not prima donnas, but every so often one of them acts like one and then I have another problem to solve. I should have done my residency in psychiatry, because sometimes I think there are a lot of people who could use some therapy." The last part of her remarks elicited a smile from both Karen and Tom.

"I'm sure you've been asked this a hundred times, but how do the large male egos do with you?"

Karen laughed a little and said, "It was a struggle at the beginning. Not only was I a woman, but I was also younger than many of the older doctors. There were a few tug-of-war battles and a few arm wrestling matches, but they found out I'm tenacious and not easily intimidated. Once that word got out, the frontal assaults stopped. Then there were a couple of passive-aggressive people who thought they were smarter than I, but I beat them at their own game. All of that was pretty much over after the first two years, and now I think people know that I am open to suggestions and they just come and talk to me. We obviously are receptive to innovation, and since that is known, people come up with all sorts of interesting concepts.

"This, of course, brings us full circle back to finances. We cull through the ideas and see which of the innovations we can bring to fruition. It also leads us directly back to why you are here. Innovation, excellence and finances." Karen's grin had now developed into a full-blown smile.

In the short space of time that they had been talking, Tom really liked Karen. She was smart, articulate and seemed very genuine. She had survived, and apparently thrived, in a very male-dominated world. Tom liked that she was very direct with him. In all the research Tom had done on her, the reports were very positive. Her reputation was that she was tough, but fair. For a brief moment, all the unreasonable hospital administrators flashed through his mind.

Karen was looking at him, waiting for a response. "I'm sorry, Karen, for a moment I had post-traumatic stress disorder about all the small-minded administrators I've dealt with who thought 'bean-counting' was synonymous with good medicine. That doesn't seem to be your style."

"Thank you. Would you like me to show you around the transplant wing? I know Tim McAndrews is a big fan of yours and he's eager to meet with you. He has a case in the OR today, but he assures me he thinks he will be free by the middle of the afternoon. If by some miracle, he's finished by the time we're ready for lunch, he'd like to join us. Peter Savage, who is the Vice Chair of the Board, is also going to join us for lunch.

"It's no secret that you are coming to the hospital today, so I will be able to introduce you to a lot of people. The grapevine has been alive and well about your visit, and maybe it's better that way, so you can feel free to speak to people and ask questions. I thought it would be very awkward if you had to walk through the transplant wing with a paper bag on your head.

"As you would expect, many of the surgeons are in the OR this morning and afternoon, but as you know, they don't all operate on the same day, nor do they have the same number of cases today. Our colleagues are trying to make themselves available today to meet you in person. Come on, let's take a walk over there."

"I am disappointed that I can't wear the paper bag I brought with me. I used Magic Marker on it and I cut out the holes for the eyes."

"Another time, Tom. We'll find a day when you can use it. Follow me."

Tom had also noticed that Karen had referred to the other doctors as "our colleagues." He liked that. Maybe he was getting too old for petty politics and if Karen was any indication of how things were run here, he already had a favorable indication. Sure there would be some doctors who would be jealous or self-absorbed, but Karen did not seem like Pollyanna, and she was painting a good picture of this hospital, where excellence in medicine and innovation were the focus.

Chapter 22

TOM

After two long, grueling days at Matthews Memorial, Tom had a dull headache behind his eyes. He never realized how exhausting it was to be chatty, polite and interesting. Tom had lots of questions about the transplant teams, and in turn, they had a million questions for him. The residents and fellows were particularly excited to meet him and to have an opportunity to ask him some questions. The more senior residents and the fellows were all jockeying to get a chance to speak to him, because they were the ones who would be working the most closely with him. Karen was going to cut short some of the discussions with the residents, but Tom told her to let them go forward.

It did bring him back to when he was a resident in what seemed to be a very long time ago, and he was young, eager and anxious to be noticed. Tom learned that sometimes the best surgeon was not the one who was the most surgically adept. It was the surgeon who took some extra time with the patients, who checked and double-checked the information about the patient and who was willing to impart his knowledge to his younger colleagues. By the end of the second day, Tom had opened his collar and pulled down his tie. His suit jacket was sitting on another chair. He almost floated away in the conference room from all the coffee, water and Diet Coke he drank while speaking to people.

He had met about three-quarters of the surgeons, but there were still a few who were tied up in surgery. Tom knew that feeling. Sometimes what looked to be a somewhat routine surgery at the beginning, didn't end up being routine at all. Sometimes the four-hour surgery turned out to be seven hours, and you came out of the OR mentally and physically drained. He hoped that tomorrow he would end up meeting the rest of his fellow surgeons. There was a late plane back to Atlanta that he was hoping to make, but he still had a reservation on an early flight Thursday morning.

On the second morning, Tom spent a good deal of it going over the points to be incorporated into his contract, which would be drafted shortly and sent to his attorney. Then they worked on the issues that were important to Tom in the transplant program, as well as the grant money to be applied for. It was no surprise that with his reputation, Tom could shake loose a lot of grant money.

Since Tom had seen the apartment at The Austin once before, along with two others in other buildings, he returned tonight to speak to John, the concierge, and to see the apartment one final time. He had pretty much made up his mind that he liked this apartment and was going to sign a lease. Tom also liked the fact that the building had been newly renovated and hopefully this floor would be on the quiet side. Tom knew he needed to get a good night's sleep before any surgery the following day.

As Tom and John got in the elevator, a female voice called out, "Hold the elevator, please." John put his hand on the elevator door, and it stopped and opened. It was Valerie, carrying a briefcase in each hand, and her purse slung over her shoulder. The purse slid off her shoulder and as she tried to shrug it back on. She dropped one briefcase with a resounding thud on the floor of the elevator. John lunged to try to grab the purse and briefcase, but it was too late. The purse hit

John in the shin on its way down, and the metal buckle caught him flush. A small yelp escaped John's lips, even as he tried to maintain his composure and his ever-present smile.

"Oh my God, John, I am so sorry. Are you okay?"

"Fine, fine, Ms. Wilkinson," John said through clenched teeth.

"You don't look okay to me. You can apply for Worker's Comp." This was Valerie's attempt at humor, and it failed miserably. When there was no reaction from John other than a grimace, Valerie said, "Sorry, that was a bad attempt at a joke."

Ever the polite gentleman, John said, "Ms. Wilkinson, allow me to introduce you to Dr. Amendola. He will be taking the apartment next door to yours and he just wants to see it one more time. Dr. Amendola, this is Ms. Wilkinson, your neighbor."

Instead of trying to shake Valerie's hand, Tom made a gesture about taking one of the briefcases from Valerie and she nodded her assent. With her now free hand, she extended it to Tom, and said, "Nice to meet you. Please call me Valerie."

"I'm Tom. That was my first name long before it was Doctor."

Valerie smiled and replied, "Yeah, I think Doctor would have been an awfully formal first name to give a baby. I'm happy to hear that I'm going to have a neighbor. It's very quiet up here, perhaps a little too quiet."

By now the elevator door opened, and Tom and John gestured for Valerie to precede them.

"I'm okay with quiet, since my days are filled with noise and interruptions. I also need to get sleep the night before my operations."

"So you're a surgeon. Where do you practice?"

"I'm about to join the staff at Matthews Memorial. I'm moving up from Atlanta."

"What field are you in?"

"I do cardiac transplants."

"Impressive. I bet it's exciting work."

"The research is exciting and it's rewarding work. We just don't want any particular case to be 'exciting' because then it means it didn't go according to plan, and we're having problems."

"Got it, but it still sounds exciting. You're giving people a second chance to live that they would never have had otherwise."

Tom cracked a big smile. "That part is the best. It makes everything else worthwhile."

"So when are you moving in?"

"I'll be back and forth between here and Atlanta for a while. I have some things to finish up there, and I have some patients I want to make sure get out of the hospital and go home, before I leave. You never know what great words those are to a patient who's been in the hospital for a long time. I say 'You can go home' and their faces light up."

"I'm sure that's true."

Tom and Valerie had been standing and chatting outside Valerie's apartment door with John standing behind Tom as if he were invisible. Finally, Valerie caught herself and said, "I'm sorry, I'm holding you up." She fumbled in her big purse for the keys, while Tom stood there bemused. "You can just put that down and I'm fine."

"I'm in no particular rush. My plane isn't until tomorrow morning, so I have time to kill. Would it be a big imposition for me to take a look at your apartment, while John is still here? I'd like to see how it differs from mine, if that's okay."

"Sure, come on in." Valerie now handed her second briefcase to Tom, and fished around in earnest in her black hole of a purse for a few more seconds for her keys. Based on this brief encounter in the elevator and at the apartment door, Tom was expecting the apartment to be a bomb. It was quite the contrary. Everything in the apartment was neat. The second bedroom, which Valerie used as an office, had piles of paper next to her laptop, but it looked as if the files were well organized. The master bedroom had no clothes draped over chairs and the bed was made.

"That's quite an impressive number of files in your office."

Valerie groaned. "I'm an attorney and I'm the lead attorney on a very large commercial case. The files seem to grow exponentially. This is just part of it; the rest are in the office. I'm here temporarily from L.A. for the case."

"And how do you like New York City?"

"I've only been here a short time. I do want to take advantage of being in New York, but right now, I need to get the associates up to speed on the case, so I can't say I've been able to explore or enjoy the Big Apple."

"Do you miss L.A.?"

"Yeah, a little. I miss my friends, and I miss that everything is done outside in L.A. I miss the ocean."

"You know that there is another ocean on this coast?" Tom said with a smirk.

"I do, but I have yet to get a glimpse of it."

"Maybe when I get here, you and I could take a drive to Long Island or the Jersey shore before it gets too cold to enjoy the ocean." To his surprise, Valerie said yes she would like it.

Throughout this whole tour of Valerie's apartment and the interchange between them, John had remained completely silent. John knew that Valerie's apartment and Tom's new apartment were exactly the same. John's facial expression remained completely pleasant and nondescript. He stayed in the living room while Valerie showed Tom around the remainder of the apartment. Neither Tom nor Valerie saw John roll his eyes.

Chapter 23

PAUL

Paul's entry into The Austin was anticlimactic in one way and unbelievable in another. Andrew Dustin's contacts were many and varied. Through one of his many connections, Andrew knew one of the owners of The Austin. He found out that The Austin was having difficulty renting its newly renovated apartments, proving that even in New York City, there was a limit on what people would pay. With Westchester and Fairfield Counties claiming some of the most beautiful suburbs and well-known public schools, people also had numerous living choices while being only a short train ride away on Metro-North. Admittedly, that limit on what people would pay was much higher in New York City than practically anywhere else in the United States, but there were other luxury apartments with many of the same amenities as The Austin, but for far less money.

Andrew made a deal to rent at least three of the apartments for the higher echelon people in the campaign, but at only forty percent of the asking price for each apartment. He gave his word that no one would ever know what they were paying, so as to keep the "snooty" mystique alive. There was even the possibility that the campaign might rent more apartments if there were still vacancies. The owners were smart enough to realize that a rental of forty percent of the asking price was certainly better than empty apartments earning no income. They would also let it be known in the right circles that the apartments were renting fast, which might also create some demand. It seemed that if there were only a few of anything, people didn't want to miss out.

Andrew took the four-bedroom apartment for himself, since in his mind, he was the most important person in the campaign, with the exception of David himself, and since Andrew was probably financing most of the living arrangements himself. In his mind, he was too old and too successful to live in a hotel room, and he didn't have a place of his own in New York City.

Andrew's assistant called Paul to tell him that they had rented an apartment for him in New York City. In truth, Paul was a little disappointed at first, because he had envisioned himself looking for his own place in the city. It was all going to be part of the great adventure for him. However, when Paul googled The Austin, his eyes almost popped out of his head. He knew that every hotel and apartment looked much better on the internet than in real life, but if this place was half as nice as it looked on his laptop, it was something. The outside of the building was definitely impressive, and the address on the Upper East Side of Manhattan was posh. The pictures of the newly renovated apartments were also something to behold. Paul couldn't contain himself and he counted the days off on his calendar before the apartment was going to be available.

So two weeks later, when Paul pulled up in a cab in front of The Austin in real life and not in his dreams or on the internet, the building did not disappoint him. Paul promised himself that he was going to take full advantage of both living in New York and of his new job. He knew that part of his fundraising job was to entertain potential big donors to the campaign. Depending on who the donor was and the size of the possible donation, the donor might get a personal visit at the person's office, an expensive dinner, an afternoon on someone's yacht or tickets to a premier sporting event. Paul wasn't yet sure which of these scenarios would be his. Andrew had told him that at the beginning, Paul would accompany him to get the hang of it. Andrew might stay the whole time or he might turn it over to Paul to close the deal. Andrew was very smooth in a quiet way, and Paul was looking forward to learning from him. His style was different from Paul's, but it was very effective. At their first meeting in Florida at David's house, Paul felt himself listening to more of what Andrew had to say than what David had to say, even on policy matters.

Right now Paul was up for anything. Paul knew that he was good at turning on the charm, when need be. He was good at finding common ground with clients, and so this was the same thing, only the product he was selling was David and his ideas to make the United States a better and safer place. As he thought about it, Paul could remember himself as a kid selling candy bars to help buy Little League uniforms for his team. Not only was he the kid who sold the most candy bars, but he was also able to sneak a few for himself without anyone realizing it, because his sales had so far outstripped every other kid.

The young entrepreneur Paul realized how good he was at winning people over and getting them to buy things from him. If he could sell that many candy bars for Little League, he should also be able to sell other things and put some of the profit into his own pocket. Paul grew up in a relatively small town in the Midwest at a time when mothers still stayed at home, and for the most part did not work outside the home. He convinced his bemused father to drive him to the local drugstore and his father stayed in the front of the store, but he could still hear Paul's sales pitch. Paul convinced the pharmacist owner to let him sell a few products outside the store by whatever means Paul could think of.

Paul had this all thought out before they even got into his father's car. He would stick to the necessities that people might have forgotten in the store. The pharmacist wanted to know what products the ten-year-old wanted to sell. Paul rattled off toothpaste, toothbrushes, deodorant, shampoo, tissues, Life Savers and M&M's candy. None was heavy or bulky to carry. The pharmacist wanted to know why he picked those candies. Paul said because he knew Life Savers didn't melt and neither did M&M's candy. In fact, he had read that NASA had picked M&M's candy because it didn't melt and it didn't leave crumbs in the space shuttles. Crumbs could float around and possibly cause damage inside the shuttles. For good measure, Paul threw in that after the kids had eaten the candy, their mothers would make them brush their teeth. Hence, the toothpaste and toothbrushes.

Paul was an exceptionally cute ten-year-old with dark curly hair, blue eyes and a winning smile. He had a pretty good idea from the kids who went to the same elementary school as he did, in what neighborhoods the moms were home during the day. Paul canvassed those neighborhoods and found lots of moms who were happy to help a cute little boy with the sale of a product they were going to need anyway. Then Paul had his most brilliant idea. A new condominium had been built about a mile from where they lived. Most of these people worked full time. Paul situated himself at the front door of the building starting about five thirty in the evening. The residents coming home from work were pleasantly surprised to find the little boy with a number of products right outside their building. They were hot and tired in the summer, and not having to make another stop on the way home from work was quite appealing to them.

The condo residents turned out to be his best customers. Some even suggested new products to be added to his items for sale. After the first week, Paul had his father drive him back to the pharmacy. This time his father came all the way to the back of the store with his son. The pharmacist, seeing Paul's father, expected that Paul was coming back to return a lot of unsold products. To the pharmacist's astonishment, Paul took quite a bit of crumpled money out of the pockets of his shorts and laid it on the counter, together with a crumpled piece of loose leaf detailing the sales.

Paul carefully counted out the split of money between himself and the pharmacist. Then he pulled a second piece of loose leaf out of his other pocket with a list of the products that he wanted to sell that coming week. And so it went the rest of the summer. The only thing that Paul kept to himself was that he upped the prices to the people he was selling to. He gave the pharmacist the split of the money he agreed to, but kept all the "overage" for himself.

In the post 9/11 era, and with ISIS bombing airports and train stations all over the world, it wasn't a very hard task to get people to donate to a campaign that stressed wiping out terrorism and keeping America safe from another attack. David also knew that he had to be more knowledgeable about foreign policy and global economics and not just be a one-note candidate against terrorism. Andrew had enough colleagues with the expertise in global economics to help David become more than competent in that arena. As a former governor of

Florida, David had a very good grasp of domestic affairs and programs to more than hold his own.

Paul had asked for and had been provided with a number of books containing policy statements, and he had been reading and familiarizing himself with them. He wanted to be able to hit the ground running when they met with donors. Paul was also a little wary, not of the information, but of the fact that he didn't want to learn one thing and then have David change his mind and possibly say something else. Paul had seen that happen with other candidates.

In Paul's first night at The Austin, he decided to take advantage of the health club. He swiped his card to get in and found it to be bright and well-stocked. There were elliptical machines, Nordic Tracks, treadmills, recumbent bikes, rowing machines and lots of weights and equipment. Paul was just too tired to do anything that required thought about his form, so he turned on a treadmill and got on. He had the remote control and turned on the flat screen TV on the wall. There was a woman at the far end of the room going at it pretty hard on a rowing machine.

He flipped the channels to MSNBC, then to CNN and Fox. Nothing too exciting going on, except the talking heads droning on. He sighed. He supposed that he was going to have to get used to them, and probably pay more attention to what they had to say. Screw it, he thought. I'm off duty. He knew that very shortly being off duty would be a thing of the past.

He turned on the Yankees game. This had not been a good year for his favorite team. They were hovering below their and their fans' standards. With the TV on, he jumped when someone behind him spoke to him.

"Sorry, didn't mean to startle you."

"It's okay. I didn't hear you over the noise of the treadmill and the TV. What did you say?"

"I said that I'm a Dodgers fan and I still don't like the designated hitter."

"I grew up as a Cardinals fan in the National League, but frankly I prefer not to kill off a rally by having the pitcher come to bat. I like having base runners."

"So are you a Yankees fan now?"

"I could become one now that I'm in New York. I just want to see the Bronx Bombers hit some bombs out of the park. You always been a Dodgers fan?"

"Yep, grew up in L.A. As Tommy Lasorda said, 'I bleed Dodger Blue.' My dad was a huge fan, so it's an inherited thing."

"Don't forget that they were once the Brooklyn Dodgers," he teased. "And Don Mattingly, your former manager, was a Yankee great. Donny Baseball."

"I know, I know."

Paul slowed the pace on the treadmill, and jumped off. He wiped his hand on his running shorts and held out his hand. "I'm Paul Bennett. Just moved in today. Proud resident of Apartment 3E."

"Valerie Wilkinson, nice to meet you. I'm in 3A."

TOM

It had turned into a cold, blustery day with the East River sporting white caps and an angry gray sky above. New York was such a different city from Atlanta in so many ways, and Tom was enjoying the differences. It was mesmerizing to look out over the water from his office. Nothing like this in Atlanta. Tom had grown accustomed to "Hotlanta," as Atlanta was often called, not only because of its temperature, but also because of its oppressive humidity. Tom had already gone out and bought himself a lined trench coat and he was going to buy both a winter coat and a ski parka. He felt like a little kid waiting for snow in the winter. The impression he got from his colleagues was that they dreaded the long winter and the sleet and snow. He hadn't really experienced a true Northeast winter, so he was looking forward to it. Another reason he was glad that his apartment was within walking distance to the hospital, so that he could get to the hospital no matter what the weather.

Tom roused himself from his musings, rose from his desk and grabbed his lab coat from the hook on the back of his office door and his stethoscope. He had two patients in particular he wanted to check on before his daughter, Amy, arrived. Tom wanted to be sure the patients were stable before he left the hospital.

"Sue, I'm going to be in the "T" unit to check on a few patients before I leave. I told my daughter to text me when she's here. She'll come up to my office. How much longer are you going to be here?"

"About another forty-five minutes, unless you want me to stay longer," she replied. As far as Tom could tell, Sue was a slightly more than middle-aged woman, who navigated hospital rules and personnel problems with a certain grace, yet firm manner, and made Tom's life immeasurably easier. He knew she had two grown children, and a few quite young grandchildren, but that was about it.

He made a mental note to ask more about her and her family, since she displayed the family pictures quite prominently and proudly. Tom had been wrapped up in his patients, making improvements to the transplant program, working with Karen and her staff on garnering grant money and trying to adjust to a new hospital, its staff and a number of very sick patients.

Sue had been a "gift" from Karen Gallagher to Tom. When one of the older surgeons had retired, Tom had the good fortune to have it coincide with his arrival at Matthews Memorial. Karen had persuaded Sue to take the position with Tom, because Sue had thoughts of retiring. Tom knew that Karen had given Sue more responsibility and more authority, and he suspected more money. Karen was a little like a magician, pulling the rabbits out of the hat when needed to make things happen and to avoid calamity.

Tom was more than happy to give Sue whatever areas of administrative responsibility she was willing to take on, because that freed him up to spend more time on what was truly important to him—his patients. Sue had adapted well to Tom and his rhythms. She kept him advised on administrative matters and had the good sense to inform him of anything he needed to concern himself with, as well as any "storm clouds" on the horizon.

"Thanks, but hopefully, it will be quiet in the "T" unit and I won't be that long. Maybe this is a night when we both can get out of here on time. If I don't see you, have a good weekend, and thanks for all your help. Not sure I would have made it through without you."

Sue's smile at the remark said it all. "There are a few things I do need to talk to you about, but nothing that can't wait until Monday. No barbarians at the gates tonight."

Tom waved as he left the office. He took the elevator down one floor and walked down the long corridor to the double doors and the sign that said "Transplant Wing." Tom swiped his ID card and the doors opened. In contrast to the relative quiet of the corridor, the transplant wing was a beehive of activity and sounds. Sometimes Tom just stopped in his tracks to watch and listen. It was a miracle of modern science, and things had changed so much in the last forty years when transplants were virtually nonexistent. Hell, things now changed at such a rapid pace in so many areas of medicine that it was astonishing.

Tom prided himself at having the "Amendola nose." Tom's father had it, and the family teased him that it was due to the size of his nose. Tom's nose wasn't nearly as large, but he did have the same sensitive sense of smell. He could smell things that others never even knew existed. When he first started working in surgery in general and transplants in particular, Tom always felt that those wings had that awful hospital smell. Tom took a big sniff of the air, and smelled exactly what he wanted to smell. Absolutely nothing.

As he walked to the nurses' station, he saw one nurse typing away furiously on the computer and another walking down the hall with a rolling cart of medication. The sounds in this part of the corridor were the familiar beeps and blips that Tom and every person familiar with medical shows on TV knew. These sounds were like the sounds of home to him. They were comforting to him and they were the sounds of life, as far as he was concerned. Quiet in the "T" unit or alarms were bad. Very bad. They could be the sounds of death that all surgeons fought against with all of their being.

Tom had always felt that he and his team were the army battling sometimes unseen enemies lurking everywhere and waiting to pounce to snatch away his patients. Tom and the team had to be constantly vigilant against the many enemies. The enemies were around 24/7; they never slept. They didn't care if it was Christmas Eve, Thanksgiving or the Fourth of July. They were always there looking for an opportunity to wreak havoc on the patient.

Tom had never quite subscribed to the concept of The Grim Reaper, dressed all in black, looking evil with a sickle in hand. That concept was too benign as far as Tom was concerned. Tom saw death as a horrific-looking monster with gaping jaws and huge teeth waiting to devour anything in its path. Not tonight, Death, if I can do anything about it. Not tonight.

Tom stopped briefly at the nurses' station and the nurse typing furiously looked up at him. "Hello, Dr. Amendola."

"Hi, Jean, how's it going tonight? Is Dr. Wagner here?"

"Yes, I believe he's in with Mr. Rose." Tom thanked her and continued down the hall. Phil Wagner was a fellow, a surgeon who had finished his residency and now was doing more post residency work. For Phil Wagner he was doing his fellowship in cardiac transplant surgery. The fellows were the cream of the crop. They had risen to the top among some very smart and very capable doctors and surgeons. They were like sponges that lapped up knowledge and techniques. The problem was that the fellows virtually lived at the hospital. They put in brutally long hours and they had a very high level of responsibility.

Tom walked into Mr. Rose's room, and saw Phil Wagner looking at the patient with a worried expression on his face. "What's going on, Phil?" There were no hellos or niceties. Just get to the point.

"He's spiked a fever. We have him on antibiotics, but his fever is still climbing. Not dramatically, but still climbing."

Tom's response was "Oh, hell."

Chapter 25

MOHAMMED AND AKRAM

Things were beginning to look up for Akram and Mohammed. The deli owner came through and his friend who owned the trucking company needed more help. The manager wasn't so sure that Mohammed was the right guy, but he only needed the guy to help load and unload the trucks. He wasn't going to speak to the customers, so it didn't matter that his English was only passable.

For his part, Mohammed was glad to be out of the apartment and working. He didn't care if he missed classes at the college. The pay was very good and to his delight, almost all the customers tipped them in cash when they delivered the furniture. For the first few weeks, Mohammed came home sore and tired from all the physical exertion, but recently he noticed more muscles in his arms and was not exhausted at the end of each day. He was also pleasantly surprised with how many of the customers, in addition to the tips, offered them a soda or a bottle of water. It clearly wasn't his dream job, but Mohammed was learning the New York area and the suburbs where they were making the deliveries. The customers were friendly and because Mohammed was boyish looking and shy, they seemed to make an effort to say something nice to him. Mohammed also was willing to move around some already existing furniture, and that won over the customers as well. Mohammed decided that the reputation of New Yorkers as being rude and mean was undeserved.

Life was better. Between the money that the two of them brought in, they went from barely having enough to eat after they paid the rent, to having spending money to buy things and go to the movies or an occasional dinner in a nice restaurant. Mohammed kept the tips for himself and to himself.

The drivers and other deliverymen asked Mohammed out for a beer after work. At first, he was very hesitant about going with them, and drinking liquor in violation of the Koran. He made an excuse the first few times that they asked him to go with them, until he noticed that they had stopped asking him to go along. One night Mohammed heard the drivers saying they were going for a beer, and Mohammed asked if he could go with them. The guys were so surprised that he wanted to go that they bought him a beer. His first, ever. At the first swig, Mohammed thought he would choke. It was yellow and bitter. Then he took a second taste and a third. Maybe not too bad. Somehow Allah would have to understand. Mohammed was in America now and the rules might not apply across the Atlantic. Or some other rationalization that Mohammed would come up with.

On one of the deliveries to Westchester, the truck broke down on a back road in Bedford. The truck was making a rattling noise before it seized and perhaps died for good. They called the dispatcher, who seemed indifferent at best to their plight once he heard that all the deliveries had been completed. He said he'd call the tow truck company. Another forty-five minutes passed and no tow truck appeared, and they called the dispatcher again. When the driver walked around the truck to get better cell service, he was surprised to see the hood of the truck up and Mohammed leaning in.

"You know anything about motors, Mo?" the driver asked in surprise.

"Engines are very orderly pieces of equipment. If you look at it in an orderly fashion, you will soon see the problem."

"Okay, if that's what you think," he replied somewhat skeptically. "Knock yourself out."

Another fifteen minutes passed and there was a lot of banging coming from under the hood. Mohammed yelled to the driver, "Turn the engine on." And with that, the driver heard the engine turn over after a first sputter.

"Well, what do you know! You did it, Mo." Mohammed also noticed that the workers who liked him called him "Mo." He was assimilating into the U.S.

The following Friday Mohammed was surprised to see a larger amount in his paycheck. He looked at the check and then looked again. His initial reaction was to just pocket the money, but he wanted to keep this job and not do anything to jeopardize it. He timidly knocked on the bookkeeper's door. Lou, the bookkeeper, looked up from his computer over half glasses. "Excuse me, Lou, there is too much money in my paycheck this week."

"Oh, yeah, Mohammed, the boss heard how you fixed the truck and saved him a towing fee and repair bill. He wanted to thank you. I should have put a note in with your check. My bad."

"Thank you very much, sir. Will you thank the boss for me, too?"

"You can do it yourself; he's standing right behind you."

"So you're Mohammed. I appreciate that you took some initiative and fixed the truck. That's what I like in my people. Do you know anything about mechanics or was this just a lucky fix?"

Mohammed stammered a little. "I, I do know something about auto mechanics."

"Want to earn some extra cash and do some maintenance for me on the trucks? We can arrange it that we pull you off some of the larger deliveries and you work on the trucks. Let's try it and see how it goes."

"Yes, sir, I would like that, but I need some better tools. It was lucky that we had some tools in the truck with us."

"Okay, we can arrange that. Take a look at the trucks and tell Lou what you need. I don't expect you to do major repairs, but I'm sure there are always things you can do for maintenance that won't cost us a fortune."

"Yes, sir, thank you. And thank you very much for the extra money in my check." The first step up the ladder of success and his second step toward assimilation.

For his part, Akram was not having as much fun. He was still stuck in the deli. He wasn't sure what was grating on him more. That Mohammed was making much more money than he was, that Mohammed was enjoying himself or that he, Akram, was still slicing cold cuts. It was good that they weren't so strapped for money, but Akram always envisioned himself as the leader and the more successful of the two of them, and right now that was not how things were working out.

Chapter 26

VALERIE

Valerie was awash in documents. She needed to familiarize herself with not only all the documents, but also with the associates who were going to be working on the case with her. While she thought Brendan Stewart was a smart guy and a good attorney, he was also very quirky, so she wasn't entirely sure that she wanted to rely on his choice of associates to work on the case.

He had taken a liking to her, and so once in a while, she would have lunch with him. Valerie realized at a few of the partners' meetings that several of the partners didn't like Brendan and thought that the bumbling was all part of an act or a persona. So far Valerie didn't agree that it was an act, because more than once she had seen him spill coffee or soda on himself when there was nothing to be gained by the spill. She knew he kept extra shirts and ties in the closet in his office for those spills. Valerie figured that he was the best client of the dry cleaner which was located around the block from the office. She had seen pickups and deliveries to the office from the dry cleaner on a number on occasions. While Valerie was friendly to Brendan, she didn't want it to seem that she was somehow tied to him.

There was another of the partners who did litigation named Randy Cunningham that Valerie liked better than Brendan, partially because he was not the same kind of physical train wreck waiting to happen that Brendan was. Randy seemed to be a voice of moderation whenever he spoke at partners' meetings. Randy had dropped into her office several times, mostly to bounce some things off her for another opinion on cases, and a few quick visits when he had walked down the hall to get a cup of coffee and to take a break.

The good thing about Randy versus Brendan was that Randy's visits were quick and to the point, whereas Brendan meandered around in the conversation for a while before he ever got around to what he originally came to talk to her about. Valerie had resorted to looking at the clock on her credenza when Brendan first came into her office and then if five minutes had elapsed before Brendan got to the point, telling Brendan that she had to finish an e-mail. A few times Brendan just kept talking until Valerie had actually started typing and then he finally got the hint.

Randy was quite nice looking, and was close to six feet tall and trim. He had dark hair and dark piercing eyes. She had lunch with him a few times with two of the other partners, and it had been a good experience. They talked about business, but they also talked about movies, new restaurants and which were overpriced and which had the best pasta or fish. It was at one of these lunches that Valerie found out that Randy had been divorced about a year ago. When one of the partners had teased Randy about his last date and whether it had been as much of a disaster as the one preceding it, Randy actually blushed. Valerie couldn't tell if that was because she was there, or if it had been that bad.

If Randy hadn't been her partner, Valerie could see herself possibly going out on a date with him. She dismissed that thought very quickly, knowing how messy those relationships could become and how much they were grist for the office rumor mill. It was actually her third thought when Todd came to mind. They talked on the phone, but Todd had not come to New York to see Valerie as often as he'd promised. Valerie had been engrossed in her work and God knows there was a lot of it, but now as she reflected on it, she was disappointed and perhaps a little hurt that Todd had only been to New York once to see her. That long weekend had been fun, but it was more like a tour of the sights in New York City, than anything bolstering their relationship. Even though they were not married, Valerie always thought that at some point they *would* get married. Maybe that was no longer true.

One of the defendants in the case where Valerie represented the plaintiff was refusing to produce documents in response to Valerie's demand for discovery. The defendant was insistent that it was not going to produce the demanded documents because they were not relevant to the issues in the case and they were trade secrets belonging solely to the defendant. Their argument was that to give up this information and these documents would be to give up information that was proprietary to the defendant. The defendant argued that it would suffer irreparable injury if this information was out of their possession in any way. Valerie's position on behalf of her client was that she could not adequately prosecute the claim for her client if she didn't have this information.

The defendant's attorney had made a motion to the court for a protective order so that the defendant did not have to provide the documents. Valerie had made a cross-motion asking the court to deny the protective order and direct the defendant to turn over the documents. This particular judge not only wanted each party to provide affidavits in support of their respective positions, but he also wanted the attorneys to argue the motion in front of him in oral argument.

Valerie had given the task of writing the first draft of the motion to compel, and to reply to the motion for a protective order, to an associate attorney named Davis Mitchell. He was a third-year associate, meaning that he was in his third year after having graduated from law school. Julie Willett had been so eager to work on this case, but the case she was working on and which was supposed to settle, had, in fact, not settled and so she was tied up. The job of writing the brief, a document showing the case law that supported their position, was given to Ann Shoreham, who was a fifth-year associate. Both were capable and articulate. Valerie conferred with them about what she wanted included in the affidavits and the brief. They were each going to submit the first draft to her for her comments and revisions. Valerie was going to do the oral argument before the judge.

In the interim, Valerie started sifting through the massive number of documents in order to be able to take a deposition of one of the other defendants. Depositions are oral examinations in which the opposing attorneys ask questions of a witness or party to the case under oath. The witness' testimony was typed on a computer by a court reporter. Valerie gave the job of organizing the documents according to certain categories to a first-year associate. Valerie jokingly told the first-year associate that by the time he finished organizing the documents the way she wanted, he would be a third-year associate. Judging by the look of panic on his face, Valerie realized that he didn't get the joke. She hoped his organizational skills were keener than his sense of humor.

Chapter 27

AKRAM

Akram found himself relieved and upset at the same time. He was relieved that with Mohammed and him earning money, they could stay in America and not have to return home as failures. They now didn't have to watch every penny earned so carefully. He was upset that Mohammed was now making more money than he was, and that Mohammed was making new friends and seeming to enjoy his life. In truth, Akram was jealous of Mohammed's new friends at work and that Mohammed did not seem to want to include him with the new friends.

Akram was also a little scandalized that Mohammed was going to bars and drinking beer. Although Akram made several remarks about it to Mohammed, after Mohammed brushed him off, Akram kept his opinions to himself. Akram always believed that since he was the smarter of the two of them, that he should also be the more successful. However, it appeared to Akram that success in America seemed in large measure, to be a function of how much money one had. Akram's pride was dealt a further blow when Mohammed came home all excited about his promotion at work from delivery man to mechanic, with a raise attached.

Akram had continued to go faithfully to the mosque, while Mohammed's interest in the mosque waned in direct proportion to how many times he went to the bars with his friends from work. Akram had called the imam exactly as he was told to do, but nothing had materialized as far as a new job through the imam's contacts. Akram made sure the imam saw him every time he attended the mosque. If possible, he tried to say a few words to the imam after the end of every service to further reinforce his presence at the mosque and in the consciousness of the imam.

About two months had elapsed without any job possibilities coming through the imam, when one night the imam had one of his assistants quietly ask Akram to stay after the service, since the imam wanted to talk to him. Akram tried not to get his hopes up about a job, for fear they could well be dashed, or that the imam merely wanted to talk to him about something else. Akram lingered after the service and then the imam motioned for Akram to come with him to a room in the back of the mosque.

"So my friend, how are things going with your new life in America?" was the opening line of the imam.

"To be truthful, they are not going as well as I would like. I am still working in the deli, because I have not been able to find a better job. I am looking for other possibilities."

The imam nodded his head slowly. "Sometimes Allah's plans are different from ours and his timetable is not set by us. I have noticed that you have been a faithful follower and I am sure that Allah has noticed the same. The job I had originally hoped would open up for you did not, but as I said, Allah works in his own way and in his own time. I think I have the possibility of a better job for you."

Akram's face lit up. "That would be wonderful. What kind of job?"

"I have a contact who needs someone to work in his office. It is a company that does money transmitting. They send money to people in other countries and they receive the money sent here. It is a good job, and I am told, pays well. However, it is a job which requires discretion and confidentiality. It seems to me that you are a prudent young man, and would fit well in this company. Are you interested in this type of job?"

"Oh, yes, I am very interested." Anything to get away from cold cuts and Slurpees, thought Akram.

"Good. Here is the contact information. The company is located in Queens. Call the owner tomorrow and I think he will want to meet you in person. Let me know how the interview goes. Here is his phone number."

The following day Akram called the owner of the money transmitting business and two days after that, met him in person. The business was housed in a nondescript building in a strip shopping center. There was a hair and nail salon, a self-service yogurt store and the money transmitter office. The strip shopping center seemed fairly busy and as Akram entered the office, he was face to face with several huge signs saying the business was under twenty-four-hour surveillance. Even if the signs were not posted screaming about the surveillance, it was very obvious that there were cameras everywhere.

Akram told a young man behind what may have been bulletproof glass that he was here to see "Wally," the owner. After only about two minutes, a short, heavyset man with a bushy mustache and a "comb-over," came out to retrieve Akram. He did not give Akram his name, but Akram was pretty sure this man was not "Wally." They walked down a poorly lit corridor and then made a sharp turn. The second corridor was markedly different and better. The short, heavyset man stepped aside and motioned Akram to go ahead of him into the office. He then closed the door behind him, and left Akram in the office with a man.

Wally was sitting behind a desk in a moderately sized office with a large computer monitor on his desk, in a well-lit and well-organized office that smelled faintly of smoke. This office was in sharp contrast to the outer office and the space in the front of the office where customers came in to either send money or pick up the money sent to them. Those areas were cluttered and dingy looking, whereas the offices in the back were clean, organized and freshly painted. Akram thought this was a somewhat backward marketing technique, where the space presented to the customers was unappealing, but the back offices were quite pleasant.

Whatever his real name was, it was not "Wally." Wally was about five-foot eight, with dark hair and a neatly trimmed beard, which was flecked with gray in his sideburns. Wally was definitely of Middle-Eastern descent. Akram guessed that Wally was somewhere in his fifties, but it was difficult to tell whether it was early or late fifties.

Wally stood up from his desk and held out his hand to Akram. "Nice to meet you. Please sit down."

After a few minutes of the interview, Akram could detect a faint accent, but he couldn't exactly place it, so he couldn't be sure where Wally was from. Even though Akram's English was good, he noticed how much better Wally's English was than his own. Wally was not a native English speaker, but he was close.

Wally asked Akram a number of questions about his family and his life back in Saudi Arabia, about how long he had been in America, and what he had been doing and with whom he was in contact since he had been here. Wally seemed more interested in Akram's personal history than he did about any sort of business experience or business goals Akram might have. Akram had been nervous that Wally would look down on him since his only work experience in America had been in the deli. Wally glossed over that quickly and then asked Akram about his computer skills. Akram didn't tell Wally that he was enrolled in college. He would much rather have a full-time job and make money, than jeopardize his getting the job by saying he needed hours off to attend school. Akram decided he would deal with the Immigration Service about his student visa when the time arose in the future. Right now he wanted this job.

Wally asked Akram if he would be willing to perform a few tasks on the computer to demonstrate his skills. Akram gladly agreed to do that. He felt that he could show off his computer skills to Wally and make an even better impression.

Wally then circled back in his questions to Akram about his personal life. He wanted to know if Akram belonged to any organizations, and again asked about the people he socialized with. It was a short list, since Akram put in a lot of hours in the deli and hadn't really had much of an opportunity to meet people in a social setting. Akram casually threw in a few questions about whether Akram had ever been arrested or convicted of a crime.

When the interview was over, Wally walked Akram down the hall and set him up in an empty office. He turned on the computer and gave Akram a list of the things he wanted him to do on the computer.

"When you've finished what's on the list, come back to my office, Akram."

In less than fifteen minutes, Akram was back in Wally's office. Wally motioned him to sit down and looked back at his own computer and checked Akram's work.

"You're quite good on the computer and you're quick. I like that. I'm offering you a job here."

Although Akram was thrilled and would have taken almost any salary Wally offered, he held back and asked politely about the salary. When Wally told him about the actual salary, Akram felt his heartbeat rise substantially. He took a second to catch his breath, which Wally misinterpreted to mean that Akram wasn't pleased with the offer. Wally then hastily threw in that if Akram's work was good he would get a raise at three months and again at six months.

Akram beamed and had to contain himself not to jump out of the chair with delight.

"Can you start next Monday?"

As much as Akram wanted to start right away and start making good money, he knew that his boss in the deli had been good to him. "Wally, I would very much like to start work next Monday, but I know it is the custom in the United States to give your employer two weeks' notice. My boss has been good to me and I feel that I must do the right thing and give him the proper notice. I will start work two weeks and one day from today, if that is okay with you."

Wally smiled at two things. One was that Akram's English was still a little stilted and formal. The second was that based on their conversation he could see that the kid wanted to do the right thing. "Sure, kid. I like it that you want to do the right thing and that you show some gratitude."

Wally also thought to himself that if this kid was going to follow the rules in the U.S., even though he hadn't been here that long, how much more would he follow the rules of Islam against the infidels?

Chapter 28

AMY

Amy walked the length of the train platform and up an incline and found herself looking at the main concourse in Grand Central Terminal. It had been a few years since she had been there, so she stepped aside as the crowd surged forward into the terminal so she could take in the sights.

Her favorite had always been the information booth in the center of the terminal with the clock on top. She wondered where each person standing in the line at the information booth was heading, and she liked to make up stories about the lives of each person. She also loved the domed ceiling with the constellations painted on it.

This was going to be a great weekend, and she was looking forward to spending three days alone with her father in New York City. As she thought back, she couldn't ever remember spending any time alone with him. His free time had always been limited, and when he was away from the hospital, he took all three kids out together, or her parents and the three kids went places together as a family. Being the youngest, Amy felt that a lot of time she was just tagging along. It was her mother who made the effort to take each kid out alone. Even though her mother had been dead for three years, Amy still missed her so much. No one could ever take her place.

They had a lot planned for the weekend. Tonight they were going out for dinner so that each of them could unwind a bit and not have to worry about being on a timetable or missing the start of an event. Tomorrow they were going to a Broadway show and Sunday they were going to see the Rangers play hockey at Madison Square Garden.

Amy rolled her suitcase behind her as she exited Grand Central, and managed to hail a cab going uptown. She was going to meet her father at the hospital and then they'd go back to his apartment. As was par for the course, her father seemed more excited about showing her around the hospital than showing her his new apartment. Amy sighed to herself as she thought that some things never changed. Her father was always wrapped up in his patients. Amy could think of many nights and weekends when her father was supposed to be off duty and another doctor was covering, but yet he went back to the hospital if something was going wrong with a patient. As a kid, Amy could never understand it, because it seemed to her that his patients were more important to him than his family.

Her perception of her father changed, however, after an experience that took place when Amy was fifteen. Of course, as a teenager, she thought everything her parents did was wrong or stupid. Especially her father, who seemed to disappear from events because he was needed at the hospital. Amy was a very good basketball player, and as a sophomore she was promoted from the Junior Varsity to the Varsity. Her team was playing in the county finals and Amy had been given more and more playing time as they continued to win the games that put them in the finals. Amy wanted both her parents, and in fact everyone she had ever known, to come watch her play.

Amy told her father when the finals would be with two weeks advance notice. He told her that since the game was on a Saturday night, he would not be doing surgery that day. He had another doctor covering for him, as well as the residents on staff at the hospital. Amy knew that she would not be a starter in the game, but that she would still be getting significant playing time. Shortly after the game started, one of the seniors came down with a rebound, but also landed very awkwardly and sprained her ankle. The ankle swelled up fast and it was apparent that she was out of the game for good. Amy expected that another girl who was a junior would go into the game to replace the injured player. Instead the coach turned to Amy and said simply, "You're in."

Amy was thrilled to be put in so early in the game. She scored her first basket and then settled in to the rhythm of the game. When the first quarter came to an end, and Amy walked over to the sidelines to sit down, she looked up to where her parents were sitting, except that only her mother was sitting there. The disappointment on her face was clear. Once again, her father had picked his patients over her. And he had promised her that he would be there. Her mother had tried to explain at the end of the game, that it had been an emergency. Amy's teenage reaction had been, "Whatever." That was the outward reaction as if nothing mattered, but inside she was seething.

The following morning when she came downstairs to the kitchen, her father was sitting at the kitchen table with a large mug of coffee in front on him. Her mother was leaning against the kitchen cabinet, with a very somber expression on her face. Her brother, Steve, who was never up early, was sitting at the table with her father, and her brother's eyes were red from crying. One of his closest friends, Chris Hughes, had been in a very bad car crash. His parents had begged the nurses in the Emergency Room to find her father, who went to the Emergency Room to help the parents, despite the fact that it was in the middle of the playoff game. He stayed with Chris' parents for most of the night, even though and perhaps especially because, things were not looking good and Chris might not make it.

This was the first time that Amy finally got it about her father. Mr. and Mrs. Hughes wanted her father to come to the Emergency Room and help them, even though emergency medicine was not his field. People relied on her father; people depended on him not only for his expertise, but for his compassion and caring. It put things in perspective for Amy in a way that she had never seen or had the maturity to understand before about her father. Amy went from being resentful about her father's patients and his obvious commitment to them, to being proud of her father. If something ever happened to her, she wanted her father, or someone with as much of a feeling for his patients, to take care of her.

Amy arrived at the hospital and presented herself at the front reception desk. Her name was on the list of approved guests, she was issued her electronic pass and was ushered to a back elevator where Tom's assistant, Sue, greeted her and led her to Tom's office.

Sue opened the door to Tom's office and led the way in. "Can I get you some water or a cup of coffee while you're waiting? Your father wanted you to text him when you arrived. Right now he's in the transplant unit. I think he wanted to check on a few patients before he left the hospital for the evening. I'm sure you're used to this," Sue finished almost apologetically.

Much to her own surprise, Amy did not give a sarcastic response. "I know he has a lot of responsibility on his shoulders. I don't think I would want all of that on me, but somehow he seems to flourish with that."

Sue responded by saying, "Let's hope no one we love ever needs a transplant, but if they do, I want your father to be the surgeon."

Chapter 29

TOM

Tom opened the door to the restaurant. Since the bar was in the front, there were wall-to-wall people near the entrance. The first time he'd been to the restaurant, he would have turned around and walked out, but Karen Gallagher had assured him in advance that no matter how noisy and crowded it was near the bar, the two back rooms were quiet and the food was very good.

The hostess made her way through the throng of thirsty patrons to the second of the two back rooms with Tom and Amy in tow. Tom thought to himself that this was a schizophrenic restaurant, because the back rooms were a completely different place from the front. Even the name of the restaurant, Duo, reinforced Tom's belief. The bar was manned by young men and women appearing to be in their late twenties or thirties, while the restaurant had older waiters dressed in white Oxford cloth shirts, black pants and red ties.

Amy and Tom were seated at a table for four, which was a luxury in New York restaurants, where the tables were squeezed together as tightly as possible. The waiter appeared almost instantly after they were seated to take their drink order. As the waiter moved away from the table, a woman and two men were being seated at their table by the hostess. Valerie recognized Tom in the second before he recognized her. She smiled at him and then he realized who she was. She stopped for a second at the table, and Tom rose from his seat to shake her hand. Tom introduced Amy to Valerie and explained that they were neighbors in the apartment building, and Valerie introduced the two men as her clients. It was just noisy enough in the restaurant that Tom couldn't catch their names. The men proceeded to their table and Valerie lingered for a moment.

"Funny, how I never see you at the apartment, and then meet you here. Sort of like in *Casablanca*, 'Of all the gin joints in all the towns in all the world," she said.

Tom laughed. "Probably because we work too much and don't spend enough time at the apartment enjoying the amenities." Tom turned to explain to Amy that they lived on the same floor and still never saw each other.

Valerie said, "I know it sounds like a pick up line, and it's not meant that way, but do you come here often? This is my first time."

"I've been here a few times. It was recommended to me by one of the doctors at the hospital. I really like the food and it's close. I don't know about lawyers, but I know more than a few doctors who like to imbibe once they are not on call. They have a pretty good wine list here, too."

"Good to know." Valerie seemed as if she wanted to linger a little longer and talk, but then she said, "I better get back to babysitting my two clients. Nice to meet you, Amy. See you soon, I hope, Tom." With that she turned and headed toward her table.

After a glass of Merlot and an appetizer of calamari which he shared with Amy, Tom felt himself relax. It had been a tough week in the hospital, and he was glad it was over. Tom had made a point of telling the senior resident and the fellow who were going to be on duty, that if at all possible, he didn't want to be called back to the hospital this weekend.

When the fellow, Travis Becker, couldn't mask his surprise, Tom said, "Look, I'm going to be honest with you, and this is not for public consumption. This is the first time my daughter is coming to visit me in New York from Yale, and I really don't want to spoil it and have to leave her alone. We have theater tickets and Ranger tickets, and this is special for her. Dr. Compton is on call and covering for me, and you know he's a great guy. I'll leave it to your discretion, but I hope between the two of you, you can handle anything that comes up."

Travis nodded and smiled, after having been taken in to Tom's confidence. "Dr. Amendola, I understand what you're telling me, and I have confidence that when you return on Monday, the hospital will still be here and all of your patients will be up and tap dancing." Tom liked this young man, who did seem to have a sense of humor amidst all the serious medicine going on.

Tom returned from his recollection of the conversation earlier in the day and said to Amy, "So tell me what's going on in New Haven?"

Tom waved to Valerie as they left the restaurant. Since they'd stopped at the apartment earlier to drop off Amy's suitcase and let her freshen up before dinner, when they finished eating, they decided to go for a walk. It was a beautiful night in New York, with the moon full and just a slight breeze. As they returned to the apartment, the doorman let them in the front door, and they walked toward the elevator. Valerie was waiting for the elevator as they approached it.

Valerie heard the footsteps behind her and turned around. "Okay, so who's stalking who? Twice in one night!"

They rode up together in the elevator and Tom asked Valerie how she liked the restaurant.

Chapter 30

TOM AND AMY

Saturday morning rolled around and Amy, who was not used to going to bed as early as she had the preceding night, woke early. She went into the kitchen to make coffee, and the smell of the French vanilla coffee brewing woke Tom. He walked into the kitchen in a tee shirt and sweat pants.

As he came into the kitchen, Tom said to Amy, "It's hard to get my body to sleep late on the weekends, when I'm up before dawn the rest of the week."

"Hi, Dad, want to go work out before we eat breakfast? You said there's a nice health club in the building, right?"

Tom's body winced in his mind. He had been putting in a lot of hours at the hospital and had yet to fulfill the promise he made to himself when he moved to New York that he would get in a regular tennis game at least two days a week. Right now his body wanted to sit, drink coffee and read the newspaper. He probably had too much to eat and drink last night, and he was paying the price this morning.

The other promise Tom made to himself was that this weekend was going to be all about Amy and whatever she wanted to do. "Sure, love to get some exercise," Tom lied. "Just let me put on sneakers."

As they arrived in the health club, there was one man really going at it on the rowing machine. He nodded as they walked in. Amy jumped on the elliptical machine and Tom got on the treadmill.

After a few minutes, the man got on the treadmill next to Tom. Paul could see that the young woman had her ear buds in with her iPod, but Tom was watching the news. Since Paul was now working on the campaign, he forced himself to talk to everyone. He had a captive audience with Tom, and the man was watching the news, a perfect opening.

"Hi, I'm Paul Bennett. I live in 3E."

"Tom Amendola. I live in 3B. Nice to meet you."

"This is a great health club. They have so much equipment and no is ever here. I usually have this place all to myself. It's nice to have a little company."

Tom nodded. "That's my daughter over there. She's visiting for the weekend and it was her idea to work out early this morning. Honestly, I would have preferred to read the newspaper."

"You look like you're in pretty good shape, so you must use the equipment." The other thing Paul learned was to compliment everyone. Everyone was a potential donor and a potential vote.

Tom laughed. "Not in the shape I'd like to be. It's easy to be complacent and lazy about exercise. You look like you work out regularly. You were really moving on that rowing machine when we came in."

"Thanks, I sit at a desk a lot of the day and I'm out for business at night. If I didn't work out, I'd have gained fifteen pounds." Now was the time to mention what he did for a living and drop the candidate's name. "I'm on the staff of David Collins' presidential campaign. I'm the associate director of the campaign."

"So this early, almost two years before the election, he already has a campaign staff?"

"You'd be surprised how much has to get done early to make sure the campaign is in full swing when the primaries start. It's a huge undertaking in lots of areas. Do you know about David Collins and what a great guy he is?"

Before Tom could answer—and it was going to be a nondescript answer, since Tom knew the name and that David Collins had been a governor of Florida, but not much else—his peripheral vision caught someone walking over to one of the other machines. It was Valerie.

She smiled and said, "We meet again. We never see each other and then we see each other three times in twelve hours. Good morning, Paul," she nodded in Paul's direction.

"You guys know each other?" Tom asked.

"Yeah, Valerie and I are gym rats. We work out a lot and at odd hours, so we see each other."

Tom was a little relieved that Valerie and Paul knew each other, because if it had been Atlanta, Tom wouldn't have thought twice about someone striking up a conversation with him, but in New York, Tom saw that people kept to themselves. Even in the hospital, unless the person worked on your service, there wasn't much conversation as you walked the hospital corridors.

The weekend flew by. On Saturday night, they saw *Fiddler on the Roof*, which Tom had seen on Broadway when he was in high school. He had loved it then, and loved it even more so now as an adult. He was now able to understand the depth of love between a husband and wife, despite what life could throw at you. Amy loved it as much as he hoped she would.

Then on Sunday afternoon, they headed to Madison Square Garden to watch the New York Rangers take on the Broad St. Bullies, a/k/a the Philadelphia Flyers, and duke it out on the ice. This was anything but a love fest, as *Fiddler on the Roof* had been. These players skated with an intensity you could feel from the stands. They body checked each other into the boards and it was obvious that these teams disliked each other. Amy seemed to enjoy the game as much as she enjoyed the play.

In light of how much Amy loved basketball, Tom promised that the next time she came to New York, he would get tickets to either the Knicks or the Nets, or perhaps to one of the local college teams like St. John's, Seton Hall or Iona.

The weekend came to a much quicker end than either Tom or Amy wanted. It was clear to both of them how much fun they'd had and how much they truly enjoyed being together. Tom insisted on taking Amy back to Grand Central to get her train. The hug each of them gave the other was genuine, and when Amy said she wanted to spend another weekend with her father, Tom felt she really meant it. She promised to call him when she was back in her apartment.

"Next time you come down, I will make sure that I don't have a case on Monday morning so that you can stay Sunday night and go home on Monday. Must be nice not to have any classes on Monday morning. Wait until you get out into the real world."

Chapter 31

WALLY

Wally got a call in his office in the middle of the afternoon from the imam. He told Wally to be sure to make sure his cell phone was on with the news alerts, and also to be sure to turn on the TV if he had one in his office for news in the next few hours. If the initial part of the plan went well, then the imam would contact Wally about setting in motion the second part of the plan. Wally knew what his part of the plan entailed, but he was also virtually certain that he was only a small part of the second plan.

He wasn't sure how many parts of the plan the imam controlled, and he would never have asked, since compartmentalization seemed to be a key component. You couldn't give up information to the authorities you didn't possess. The problem was that the more you broke up the parts of the project, the more people you needed to involve, and who was reliable and discreet then needed to be taken into consideration.

This project had been a long time in coming to fruition. It would be wonderful if all parts of the project came together as planned. Wally picked up the phone in his office and was going to dial Akram. He thought better of it and put the phone down. He took his cell phone out of his pocket and placed it on his desk. He picked up the remote and turned the TV on. He drummed his fingers on the desk and waited. And waited. He found himself reciting long forgotten prayers in Arabic asking Allah for strength and guidance. Surely Allah would bless this work against the infidels.

In all the time that Wally had worked in his office, he had never thought the office was the least bit quiet. Today he could hear the second hand move on the clock on the wall. He felt a bead of perspiration run down his cheek from his temple. This is not the time to be nervous. This was the time for a steady hand, a bold heart and a firm resolve.

Finally, after what seemed to be an eternity, Channel 2 broke into the scheduled programming with a news bulletin. Wally listened to the first few sentences from the news anchor. Then he switched stations to Channels 4 and 7. They were reporting the same thing about dirty bombs. Almost simultaneously, his cell phone lit up with alerts. Wally exhaled a very deep sigh. Now he had to execute his part of the plan.

Wally buzzed Akram on the intercom. Just as he did, Akram's phone had gone crazy with news alerts and he barely had time to glance at them before Wally's voice came over the intercom and startled him.

"Akram, I need you to come to my office immediately!"

"Wally, I just got texts on my phone that dirty bombs have gone off in New York City."

"I know that and I just told you that I need you to come to my office immediately!" Only this time the tone was even more emphatic.

Akram jumped up from his chair and headed for Wally's office. In the few seconds that it took to get to Wally's office, several thoughts raced in his mind. One was that he had never heard that tone of voice from Wally, who was usually soft spoken. Akram thought that Wally wanted him to do something important to safeguard further the money flowing in and out of the office to all parts of the world.

Akram knocked on the door and entered Wally's office as one motion. Wally was typing furiously on his computer.

"Shut the door," he barked at Akram. "The imam told you when he helped you get this job with me, that there would come a time when he would need your help and that you would repay him. Well, that time is now. Are you ready to keep your promise to the imam?"

While Wally was in no mood for long or flowery speeches, he felt he needed to emphasize the promise Akram had made and make sure the young man was really truly ready to do his part.

"Yes, I remember. I gave him my word." Akram was not yet connecting the dots, because he saw the money transmitting business as a for-profit company, which had little, if anything, to do with the imam and the mosque, except that the imam gave him the lead on the job. Akram wasn't sure if he could ever remember actually seeing Wally at the mosque.

"Well, now is the time for you to keep your word to the imam and for us to strike a serious blow against the Satan America."

Akram was so surprised by the words that he took a step back in the office.

Wally continued as if he had not noticed Akram's surprise or his step backward. "The dirty bombs that were set off today are the work of our brothers. While New York City is reeling from this, and concentrating on the dirty bombs, we are going to wreak havoc in other ways. We are now going to cause ruin in the banking business. We all have our particular role to play in this. Let me explain what I need you to do now. Are you ready and committed to Allah?"

Akram nodded his head, but wasn't sure if any words had come out of his mouth.

"Good, then listen to me and this is what I want you to do." After he finished and Akram was about to go back to his office, Wally said, "*Allahu Akbar*."

Akram repeated "*Allahu Akbar*," but he was so numb and his hands were trembling so much as he returned to his office, that he was not sure his fingers were going to be able to type on the computer.

If Akram had been born in America, or if he knew American idioms better, he would have understood the saying, "There is no such thing as a free lunch."

Chapter 32

TOM

Tom checked in with Sue a few more times at regular intervals. After the second call to the office, she told him she had been called to the Emergency Room to help log in patients. She gave him her cell phone number. She told him that a large decontamination center had been set up, and that there had been a steady stream of patients coming to the Emergency Room, but that the pace had picked up considerably as time wore on.

"Sue, look, I'm not going to call you while you're busy, but do you think that about every two hours you can call me and let me know what the hell is going on? I feel really helpless just sitting in my apartment, yet I have some fever and I'm still kind of weak, so I don't think I can make it in. Plus, the police are really stressing not to go outside until they have assessed the air quality."

"Don't worry, Dr. A., I already let Karen Gallagher know that you had been out sick yesterday as well. She understood completely. She's got a lot more on her mind right now. But I promise to call you. I'm really scared, but I'm happy to have something to do."

"Sue, I think that's the definition of courage. You do your job and help people, even if you are afraid. I have every confidence in you."

He heard what he thought was a little chuckle on the other end of the phone. "Okay, talk to you later."

Tom went back to lie on the bed and was hoping for something more substantial in the way of updates from the mayor. Were they just playing it close to the vest or did they really have no more pertinent information? Tom's guess was that the mayor, NYPD and Homeland Security knew a lot more, but they were figuring out how to disseminate it to the general public. Meanwhile, the talking heads on television continued to drone on. So far no one had taken responsibility for the attack.

Chapter 33

PAUL

Paul felt like the proverbial hen on a hot griddle. He had checked his phone for what seemed like a million times, and the TV was blaring in the background. There had been the initial burst of information right after the dirty bombs went off, but then it seemed as if everything had stalled. Everyone was repeating the same information over and over. He had cleaned off the cut on his cheek and he had a decent sized bruise. He still was getting busy signals on his cell phone, so this had turned into several hours of torture for someone who was addicted to his cell. He was pacing up and down in the apartment and it didn't appear that much was going on in the street from what he could see from the apartment windows. It was already dark outside, so there really wasn't much to see in the street. He made himself a roast beef sandwich, more from a need to do something than from being hungry.

He toyed with the idea of going to work out in the health club, but when he thought about it, it didn't seem like a very good idea, especially since he didn't know if the doorman was still at the front door and if there was a possibility that intruders could get in to the building. Then he remembered the conversation he'd had with Valerie earlier that the doorman would let them know if he was going to leave.

Grabbing his keys and his phone, he looked through the peephole, saw no one in the hall and opened the door to go to Valerie's apartment. When the doorbell rang in Valerie's apartment, both Valerie and Brendan jumped. Valerie looked through the peephole, saw it was Paul and opened the door.

"Hi, come on in." As Paul walked in, Brendan was sitting on the couch in the living room. Valerie introduced the two men. Paul literally did a double take when Brendan got up from the couch to shake his hand. Never an imposing figure even in his suit, now Brendan looked like something from the Salvation Army. He had on a pair of Todd's sweatpants which were way too long for him and so drooped over his socks. His dress shirt was dirty in the front, and the sleeves were rolled up. Because it was Brendan, Valerie was used to the fact that he often looked like an unmade bed, and that was when he was wearing all of his own clothes. Now in this patchwork of clothes, he really was something hard to describe. Valerie quickly explained the clothing situation to Paul.

Paul got to the point without further pleasantries. He wanted to know if Valerie was getting any cell service, and if so, if she had any new information. He then wanted to know if she'd heard from the doorman as to whether he was still manning the front door or if the night man had come on duty. Valerie said she had tried to call the concierge downstairs, but no one was answering.

"That's what I was afraid of. These guys will bolt in a second. I don't really blame them that they want to go home. I guess the question is, are they safer staying here than out on the streets? I'm thinking of taking a spin downstairs to see what's going on. Want to come with me?"

Brendan was taken aback that Paul was suggesting that they go downstairs together. However, something must have clicked on in Brendan's Y chromosome, and much to Valerie's surprise, Brendan not only agreed to go with Paul, but he also jumped up off the couch.

"Let's go; we'll be back in a few minutes and let you know what we find out," Paul said.

Valerie agreed. "Okay, but I am obligated to say 'Be careful'."

As Paul and Brendan left Valerie's apartment, Paul made a detour back to his apartment. Paul turned to Brendan and said, "Wait a sec, I think we ought to have some protection with us, just in case." Brendan nodded and waited for Paul outside his apartment. Paul returned with a baseball bat in hand. Brendan looked a little wide eyed when he saw what Paul had retrieved from the apartment.

They got on the elevator and when the elevator door opened to the lobby, the lights were on in the lobby, but dimmed. The lobby was deserted, which was strange in and of itself, since there was normally activity in the lobby and often it was clustered around the concierge's desk. But the concierge's desk was dark and the desk was completely bare.

Paul headed toward the front door with Brendan in tow. "Hey, Bud, how's it going here?" Paul asked. Paul had no idea what the doorman's name was, despite the fact that he went in and out of the building a minimum of twice a day, and on some days more than that. It was more a commentary about Paul's arrogance than about anything else. If you weren't someone who could further his career or do something to add some substantial dollars into the campaign war chest, Paul took no notice of you.

Joel was still on duty on the front door, even though his shift had ended. He looked like a frightened kid, although he was in reality older than he looked. Joel's response was, "Not much going on in here or outside."

Joel saw the baseball bat in Paul's hand and gave him the faintest of nods.

"You're not seeing a lot of people out on the street?"

"Nope. Right after the dirty bombs went off, it was kind of a madhouse out there as people were running to try to get inside. It's kind of scary looking out there."

"How so?"

"Well, it's odd that it's so quiet outside. Even in a snowstorm, there are people and cabs moving around. Not like that now. There have been some police cars going by telling everyone to stay inside, but that's it."

"Anyone trying to get in who doesn't belong here?"

"That's what I was afraid of earlier. That's why the manager told me to stay inside the building and not stand outside. He thought it would be easier to keep people out if there was at least a locked door between us."

"Where's the manager now?"

Joel shrugged an "I don't know."

"Well, was he here in the lobby to tell you to stay inside?"

"Nope. He called me on the phone and told me what to do, but I haven't heard anything from anyone in a long time."

Paul nodded. "You planning on sticking around tonight?"

"I'm not sure what to do. I spoke to my wife and she said she's home with our son and they're okay. I don't know whether I should try to get home to them. I'm afraid to go outside and breathe that crap in the air."

"Might be smarter to stay here. Besides the radiation which could make you really sick, you could get mugged or killed if you met up with a bunch of guys. You have anything to eat?"

"No."

"What do you normally do when you're on duty?"

"I get food from the kitchen for the restaurant."

"That's on the other side of the building. Brendan and I will stay here at the door while you go find something to eat. Grab something and bring it back here. You think any residents are going to want to get back in now?"

"With all the renovations, there are almost no residents. I think they were going to start advertising for new tenants soon."

In a few minutes, Joel returned looking more unhappy than when they first started talking to him. "The restaurant is locked up and everyone's gone. How come they all left and I didn't see them leave?"

"I guess they were on the other side of the building. Do you know if they live close to here?"

"The chef owns a small building not too far from here, and some of the restaurant staff lives there. Maybe he let the others go there. I live in Queens," he moaned.

In a rare moment of humanity from Paul, he volunteered, "Listen, I'll go upstairs and bring you down something to eat. Do you want Brendan to stay here with you for a while?"

Brendan, who had remained mute throughout the interchange between Paul and Joel, seemed a little bit startled that Paul was volunteering his services. Brendan somehow sensed that Paul was a tough guy, and being with him gave Brendan a sense of comfort. That's why he had agreed to come on this foray to the lobby in the first place. Now Paul wanted to leave Brendan behind at probably the most vulnerable place in the building with a doorman who looked to be about one hundred and fifty pounds soaking wet.

Paul saw the pained expression on Brendan's face. "What?"

Brendan stammered, "Ah, well, I really don't know if I'm the right person to stay. I, ah, don't have a weapon and I don't know any martial arts."

"Oh, shit, Brendan, grow a pair. Then I'll stay here with Joel. Do you think you're okay to ride in the elevator by yourself or is it too scary? Go bring back some food for the guy. You can handle that, can't you?"

Chapter 34

TOM

Never in his life had Tom been so grateful for a landline. He was able to call Amy and tell her he was okay. She had been frantically trying to call him on the cell as had her two siblings and a bunch of his friends, who then tried Amy. Not much more information had been forthcoming from NYPD and Homeland Security, except that they were working diligently to do what was necessary to try to contain the radioactive material in the air. It seemed that there were an enormous number of people being treated for radiation in the New York City hospitals and that ambulances and fire trucks were transporting people to the other boroughs. No one seemed to have a realistic estimate yet of how many people were being treated.

NYPD was preventing anyone from driving into New York City and no railroads or subways were running into the city. With the roads closed, the ambulances were having a much easier time transporting patients to the hospitals. NYPD had also effectively stopped all civilian traffic from moving within the city. New York City was shut down and now that darkness had descended on the city, it was more than eerie-looking outside.

Tom asked Amy not only to call back the friends and family who had called her asking for him, but he also asked her to call his assistant at the hospital, Sue, and Betty Crowley, the head nurse on the transplant unit, and have them call him back on the landline. It had become so automatic to give everyone your cell phone number. But now with the cell towers flooded with calls and everyone mostly getting busy signals, Tom realized his mistake about telling people which phone of his to call. He was hoping that Amy might have better luck getting through from outside the city.

Tom also asked Amy if they were getting any more or different news about New York City, since they were out of the immediate area. Amy confirmed that the news was sketchy at best about the dirty bombs, but that they were getting the information that New York City was essentially closed down tight. No matter who you were or where you wanted to go, you weren't going to be let into New York City any time soon.

Tom could hear the fear in Amy's voice and he did the best he could to reassure her that he had been sick when the bombs went off and he been in his apartment the whole time. He didn't want to tell Amy, but he was trying to figure out a way to get to the hospital tomorrow, if his fever was entirely gone. Tom didn't want Amy to worry, so he wasn't even going to mention it. He knew he couldn't take a twenty-minute walk to the hospital and be exposed to the radiation, but he didn't think he could get the hospital to send anyone for him, nor did he think he could persuade the police to pick him up. There had to be a way, so he just had to keep thinking of possibilities.

Tom was startled by his doorbell ringing. As he looked through the peephole and saw who it was, he was relieved. Valerie came through the open door with an odd looking man in tow. Valerie introduced Brendan to Tom and gave him the now familiar explanation about Brendan's makeshift wardrobe. Brendan explained that he and Paul had been to the lobby and the whole story about the lobby being deserted except for the doorman. Brendan was clutching a plastic bag, which he explained contained food for Joel and said that he was on his way back to the lobby.

Valerie also told Tom that Paul was still down in the lobby with Joel, but that no one was certain how long Joel was going to stay. "Perhaps, we should start thinking of a contingency plan," she said. "We seem not to have very much information from the authorities, and we don't know how long this state of emergency is going to last. I think the three of us are the only ones on this floor, and maybe Joel will be able to tell us what floors the other tenants are on. Joel told Brendan and Paul that he heard by phone from the manager of the building early on, but nothing at all from him in the past few hours. We may well be on our own."

Brendan said that when they first went down to the lobby, Paul had suggested that they ought to check out the layout of the building. "It's a pretty good idea. We only know about the front door, but we ought to know how many other points of ingress and egress there are in the building."

"Spoken like a true lawyer, Brendan. Let's leave ingress and egress aside for a few minutes and just say we need to know how many doors there are and how secure they are," Valerie countered.

"It would certainly be helpful to know how many of us there are who are actually in the building now, and not just how many total tenants there are. We don't know how many in the building were exposed to radiation and what levels. We could have people become very sick in the building. We don't know if we call EMS if they will come get them and take people to a hospital or if you are supposed to get to a hospital on your own. I've never treated anyone exposed to radiation and I don't have the proper equipment or medicine here in the apartment."

"I need to go back downstairs and bring this food to Joel. He may be the key to everything because he probably knows more about the building itself and the tenants than anyone else. We need to try to keep him here in the building."

Valerie jumped in. "I'll go downstairs with you. I think I probably know him the best of all of us. Let me try to find out what's really on his mind. He's probably worried sick about his wife and son and wants to be with them, yet I think he also knows it's not safe to be outside alone."

Tom said, "I don't think he has much choice about going anywhere right now. The trains and subways have been shut down according to the major networks on TV. That will certainly help us to persuade him to stay. How can he possibly get to his family?"

"Once we come back upstairs, I think the four of us should talk about what to do next. Maybe we will have more info tomorrow morning from NYPD and Homeland Security which will lead us in a direction. Right now everyone's tired and on edge and the lack of information is infuriating to me."

"You're right. Will the three of you come back to my apartment so we can talk?"

"Okay, Tom, I think we should be back in a few minutes and we'll come here. I'm really scared about this, and I'd feel better if we brainstorm."

Brendan had chosen to remain silent throughout much of the interchanges down in the lobby, and now in Tom's apartment. Finally, he spoke up. "Look, I don't live here and I'm only here because of Valerie's kindness in taking me in. Before we went down to the lobby, Paul went back to his apartment and got a baseball bat to bring with us. Do either of you have any weapons?"

"Weapons?" Tom and Valerie said in unison.

Brendan continued as if he hadn't even heard their skepticism. "Right now we're less than twelve hours into this crisis. We don't know if the situation is going to be resolved quickly or not. If not, we may well find out that things could get very ugly and we need to be able to defend ourselves. Surely this thought has crossed your mind?"

Chapter 35

THE AUSTIN

Valerie and Brendan returned to the lobby with the food for Joel. The quiet that had descended on the lobby was eerie. In the distance they heard some voices and both Valerie and Brendan stopped just outside the elevator door. Valerie realized that it was Paul's voice they were hearing. Paul and Joel had moved away from the front door and were standing about half way between the elevator and the front door.

Brendan handed the bag to Joel who eagerly took it. Paul said to the other three, "Let's all go over to sit on those couches while you eat something. I was telling Joel we should check out the building and see where everything is. I've never been past the front lobby on this side of the building. On the other side of the building, I've never been past where the restaurant is located. We have to be sure things are closed up tight and there are no open doors or windows. We really have to know what we're dealing with. As soon as you're finished eating, we should go take a look around."

"We told Tom Amendola we'd go back up to his apartment when we're done down here and talk about what to do," Valerie said. "I think we have to start getting a plan together if this situation isn't resolved soon. Tom is a surgeon, and that's a good thing for us to have a doctor around."

"So how many tenants are there who are actually in the building now?" Paul directed his question to Joel.

"I'm not really sure. I only started working here recently. The renovation work is still being completed on most of the building. The few tenants who live here all seem to work and come back in well after rush hour."

This answer caused Paul to turn on Joel. "You gotta do better than that, buddy. Think about who you saw come in." By now Paul's tone of voice had turned to anger.

Valerie realized that the more Paul pressed Joel, the more Joel was going to freeze up, so she stepped in with a much friendlier tone. "Listen, Joel, how about you write down the names of the people you remember coming in and their apartment numbers, and after a time, maybe that will jog your memory for other tenants whose names are not coming to you right now."

Paul was about to start up again on Joel, when Valerie gave him a withering look which shut him up tem-porarily. She continued on. "Paul, why don't you and Joel take a look around the building. See if everything is locked up and meet us upstairs in Dr. Amendola's apartment when you're finished. Joel, you okay with that? You're the one who knows the building better than any of us and you can show Paul the way."

"What should I do about the front door?" Paul jumped in this time, and took his cue from Valerie with a less demanding tone. "You told me no one has come in the front door for hours. I doubt any of the tenants are going to try to come home now when NYPD has said it wants everyone off the streets and to shelter in place. If people were near home, they tried to get here, but I think now that ship has sailed. C'mon, buddy, let's go take a look around."

Joel nodded and then in an uncharacteristic display of annoyance, turned to Paul, and said, "My name is Joel."

"Okay, okay. Got it. Now let's take a spin around the building."

Chapter 36

THE AUSTIN

After a few minutes, the doorbell to Tom's apartment rang and he opened it and let Paul and Joel in. Brendan was leaning against a wall in the living room with a can of soda in hand. Valerie was seated in the wing chair and Tom motioned Paul and Joel toward a seat on the couch.

"So what did you find out?" Valerie said, looking directly at him and hoping to bring Joel into the conversation.

"There are loading docks in the back of the building which are locked. They seem pretty secure. The restaurant is toward the back of the building and the kitchen is at the very back part of the building. That doesn't look too great, because there's a door and few windows. The door's okay, but the windows could be broken into without that much effort."

"How would somebody access the back of the building?" Brendan asked.

"There's an alley which isn't all that apparent, but you can see it and some enterprising person who's desperate might want to take a look to see where it goes. You'd be out of sight from the street," Paul said with a heavy sigh.

Tom said, "Do you think that we can secure the door and the windows in the restaurant better? Were you in the restaurant looking toward the back of the building?"

"No, we took a quick look from the alley. And I mean quick. We didn't want to stay outside for more than a few seconds. Joel said he doesn't have keys to the restaurant and he has no idea where they are," Paul said.

Joel volunteered that he had nothing to do with the restaurant for his job, so he was pretty much in the dark about how the restaurant was run. Then he added "The restaurant has one of those fancy grates covering the door when the restaurant is closed."

Before the conversation could continue any further, the TV, which had been providing background noise, suddenly lit up with a news bulletin. Tom grabbed the remote and increased the volume. Channel 4 broke in with a message from the mayor. He was behind a podium and had on a dark green fleece jacket with his name and the logo of NYC on his left breast pocket. The police commissioner was standing to his right and the chief of FDNY was to his left. All three men looked tired and haggard.

Usually any press conference by the mayor engendered a gaggle of reporters and cameramen. Tonight it appeared that the three of them may very well have been in a room by themselves just facing a camera. The mayor didn't have to ask for quiet in the room, and there was no background noise or camera flashes.

"Good evening. I want to keep everyone informed as to what is going on and what we've been doing over these past few hours. First of all, New Yorkers were smart and heeded our instructions to get inside if you were outside, or to shelter in place. We have shut all incoming roads into the city as well as stopped mass transit into the city. Kennedy and LaGuardia airports have halted all incoming flights. We allowed the departing flights to leave. Now both airports have ceased all operations.

"When the bombs went off, we used the technique called 'load and go' with Metro-North, the Long Island Railroad, and the subways to get as many people out of town in as quick a manner as we could. Shutting down roads into the city allowed us to have access to essentially empty roads for emergency vehicles to travel without impediment. There were some major traffic jams on the FDR and the West Side Highway as people exited the city. That has subsided now as people understood that it was safer to stay inside and stay where you are.

"We have sampled the air in numerous places in the city, and in the three vicinities where the dirty bombs went off the air has been contaminated. In areas of the city away from the hit zones, the air is contaminated, but the radiation levels are not off the charts. In the hit zones, which is an area of a mile radius, the radiation levels are high. Fortunately, there was almost no wind today and tonight, so the wind is not moving the contamination significantly.

"We are employing a new and previously top secret technique known as 'scrubbing.' It's a sophisticated technique which contains chemicals that basically neutralize the contamination by eating into its essential components. The scrubbing is being sprayed from the air and from the ground. Right now we are concentrating on the hit zones, but we will spread out to encompass other areas in the city. You will probably see or hear helicopters and small planes overhead spraying, and you will see trucks spraying this mist-like substance.

"Since this scrubbing technique is extremely new and, in fact, cutting-edge technology, we are not exactly sure how long it will take before it gets the radiation down to safe levels. The Department of Homeland Security is also getting more of these scrubbing chemicals from the labs where it has been manufactured and shipping it to us as fast as possible.

"We are still getting reports from the hospitals as to the numbers of people who were exposed to the radiation and are currently being treated and decontaminated. Right now we don't have an accurate count, so I really don't want to speculate on the number and be wrong. Every hospital in New York City has an Emergency Disaster Plan, and they have all been activated. They have drills and practice for all types of disasters, so I am confident that they are handling this crisis better than anywhere else in the world.

"There is no need for panic. We are less than twelve hours into this crisis and we are already working very hard to solve the problem. I have been in touch with the governor and the president who have both offered and are sending troops and resources to us in the city.

"Right now, stay where you are. Check on your neighbors and offer them a hand if they need it. Share what you have with those around you. We're New Yorkers and we're tough, but we're also compassionate and caring.

"I will be back in touch with you tomorrow at the latest. If I have something important to tell you before then, I will come back on the air.

"Until then, be tough, be smart and be aware. God bless the United States of America and the City of New York. Good night and Godspeed."

Chapter 37

THE AUSTIN

It took a few seconds after the mayor finished speaking before anyone in the room said anything. Finally, Tom broke the ice and verbalized what everyone had been thinking. They were happy with some real news about the crisis from the mayor, but there were more questions raised by his address than had been answered.

"I guess it was good that the mayor addressed the city. At least they have a plan of attack and they have some new technology to try to neutralize the contamination."

Paul snorted in derision. "That was the biggest load of bullshit I have heard in a long time. He didn't give any details on this 'scrubbing' crap. For all we know, they're making this whole thing up to pacify the unwashed masses."

Brendan injected himself into the conversation with some force to his argument. "He's telling the truth and here's why. The whole world is watching New York. Our friends and our enemies. He can't just make up shit as he goes along. He's going to be held accountable for every word he says. The president and the governor are not going to let him get up in front of a camera, and probably billions of people around the world who are also watching, and say things that are completely untrue. Every word he said will be analyzed and re-analyzed.

"The president and Homeland Security are helping in every way possible, because the greatest city in the

world has been attacked and crippled by some crazy
fanatics. I'm willing to bet that every word he said was
written by someone in Washington. That's why it took
so long for him to show up on TV. Every word he said
was scrutinized by the powers that be. How this is handled will be the model for the country and the world. If
we can neutralize the dirty bomb, then we have taken a
huge weapon and a huge threat out of the hands of the
terrorists."

The other four people in the room were impressed
by not only by Brendan's words, but also by the
forcefulness of his delivery. The thought raced through
Valerie's mind that they were seeing a flash of the trial
attorney that was Brendan. He apparently could rise
to the occasion.

Valerie surprised herself how calm she had been all
night. She felt she was drawing strength from being
with the others, but she also felt that she was able to
call on a part of herself that allowed her to analyze situations for her clients in court and make rapid decisions
under stressful conditions. "I think Brendan is right.
The mayor is not making this stuff up, and he's getting
a ton of help from behind the scenes.

"The red flag in my mind is when he was talking
about the technology being 'cutting-edge.' I don't know
if that's code for experimental. We don't know if this
technology has ever been tried or if it works. That's the
wild card in my mind. Notice that the mayor said they
don't know how long it will be before the scrubbing
works. I suppose the caveat between the lines of what
he said may also be *if* this scrubbing really does work."

"Okay, so where does this leave us?" Tom asked.
"We may be better off than a lot of other people because we're here in our own luxury apartments, and
we're warm and safe and dry. It doesn't seem that we

have been exposed to the radiation and if we stay inside, hopefully we'll be alright."

"God, what the hell is the matter with you? Don't you get it? While we might be 'warm and safe and dry' as you so quaintly put it, we could be trapped here for who the hell knows how long. And the fact that we're in a luxury apartment probably makes us a target if this radiation goes on for any period of time. People are going to get desperate and they're going to be scrounging for food, water and clothes, if it gets much colder.

"If you were stuck in an office building, how much food do you think is going to be there? If you're stuck in the lobby of some building because they told you to get off the streets, how long do you think you're going to stay there with no food or water before you get desperate enough to venture out and try to score food and water? We have to act now to protect ourselves before some marauding bands are going to take whatever we have. This has all the trappings of turning into a jungle. I hate to say it, but the fabric of civilization as we know it could be shredded." Paul finished what he had to say, and for a minute slumped down into a chair.

"You're right. So what do we do now?" Tom directed the question mostly to Paul.

"We have to secure the building as best we can, so that it will be hard for anyone to get in. Maybe if it's too hard to get in, they'll get discouraged and go loot somewhere else."

Valerie turned to Joel, who had been sitting in silence. "Joel, can you get us in to the restaurant? We should take whatever food is in there. They must have a supply of staples and canned goods. We have refrigerators in our apartments for the perishables. "

"I don't have a key to the restaurant, but I do know there are tools in the loading dock. We can use them to break in to the restaurant."

"Good thinking, Joel. What else can you think of?"

"Maybe there is stuff we can use later on."

"Good, Joel, keep thinking. Maybe you, Paul and Tom can go down to the loading dock and see what you can find to get into the restaurant. Do you think there is some sort of rolling cart Brendan and I can use to move the food up here? I think we should get on this now and not wait until tomorrow morning, just in case someone decides to beat us to the punch. Paul is right that the longer this goes, the more dangerous it will become."

Chapter 38

THE AUSTIN

The night turned out to be a great deal longer than anyone had expected. The job of getting into the restaurant was much more difficult than it looked at first blush. There was a metal grate which was pulled down to close the restaurant. It looked to be decorative at first, but the decoration camouflaged the true nature of the grate. The metal grate also had a padlock on it to hold it in place. All five of them were surprised that in a luxury apartment the restaurant was closed with a metal grate and a padlock, especially since the restaurant was located within the apartment building itself.

"Who the hell did they think was going to break into a restaurant in the building, when there was a doorman, a concierge and numerous staff members bustling around?" Brendan asked. "Did they think the tenants would break in if someone was in dire need of a grilled cheese sandwich?"

At first, Valerie was inclined to agree with Brendan, but then as she thought about it, it dawned on her that they were probably protecting the extensive wine cellar. During the few times she had eaten in the restaurant, she thought the food was good, but not excellent. However, she remembered that they had touted the restaurant's vast and expensive wine list.

Valerie explained this to the group, and said that they even hosted a wine tasting evening every other month. None of the three of them who were tenants had ever been to the wine tasting, but now Valerie could visualize the signs she had seen in the past for the previous wine tastings.

Joel was able to get them into the loading dock and the engineering room. The engineering room proved to be the more helpful because there were all kinds of tools and equipment. They couldn't find any metal cutters which looked large enough to cut the padlock. Then Paul let out a triumphal whoop. He found the forklift and thought they could use it to ram the metal grate. The triumph was short-lived since they couldn't find the keys for the forklift. "Goddamn it, the keys have to be here somewhere. No one takes the keys to a forklift home with them at night," Paul complained.

The five of them searched the area where the forklift was parked with disappointing results. "Who's the foreman of the engineering department?" Tom asked Joel. "Does he have an office?"

Joel pointed around the corner and said it was the first door on the left. Tom went to find the foreman's office and came back shortly thereafter with a disappointed look on his face. "The office is, of course, locked. The door has no windows, and doesn't look as if it would be that easy to get into it. This is the most paranoid group I have ever seen. Everything is locked and then what's inside that is locked again. It's probably easier to break into Fort Knox than it is to get into anything here. I think we're wasting time trying to find the keys to the forklift."

Joel handed all four of them hammers and wrenches. "Let's see if we can either break the grate by hammering it or by pulling it open with the wrenches." Paul and Tom each probably had a good fifty plus pounds on Joel, who was thin and wiry. He made his living opening doors and carrying packages for elderly tenants, not doing heavy manual labor.

No one commented that Joel handed hammers and wrenches to Valerie and Brendan as well. It seemed that tonight everyone was going to have to help as best they could. As they walked through the halls to get to the restaurant, each of them was lost in their own thoughts. Of all of them, Paul was probably the strongest and fittest. He was a big man and he worked out regularly.

When they arrived at the metal grate in front of the restaurant, Joel said, "I think we should try bending the grate with the wrenches. We don't need to take down the whole grate, we just need a hole big enough for us to get in. There must be some motor to get the grate up and down, so we need to get in to the front of the restaurant and maybe we can find the controls."

Joel looked at them. " Are you going to say you did this to the grate? Because if my boss finds out I did this, I'm going to get fired. I need this job."

Tom jumped in before Paul did, because he knew that if Paul spoke, he was going to say something abrasive and obnoxious. Tom had already seen Paul stiffen after Joel's remark.

"It's alright, Joel. We'll take the blame. Right now it's more important that we preserve the food from the restaurant. We don't want it to spoil or for someone else to take it. We don't know how long we're going to be stuck here, and the food will be very important. We'll pay for the damage and the food." Tom was hoping that this crisis would end early enough that the damage to the grate and taking the food wouldn't actually be an issue with the management of the building.

"Let's get to work. Any ideas where to start?" Paul looked expectantly at the group.

Tom said, "Look, this is just a guess on my part, but I think we should start at the point where the grate meets the edge. That might be a weak point where the grate attaches."

"It's as good an idea as any. You guys go to the left edge and try prying the grate away from the hinges and I'll start on this side and we'll see which way makes it give first. Valerie, why don't you and Brendan go back to the loading dock and see if you can find a rolling cart of some kind. We got sidetracked and forgot about that. Also, bring back anything that looks like rods or poles or anything that we might be able to use as a weapon. "

Tom followed up. "You two stay together. Don't get separated and don't go into different rooms. If you see or hear anything, start screaming and we'll come. Come back in not more than fifteen minutes, no matter how much you've done."

Valerie nodded assent. "Come on, Brendan. Let's go."

Paul said over his shoulder. "Each of you should take a hammer with you. Stay alert."

Chapter 39

AKRAM

There was a flood of emotions and thoughts pouring through Akram's head. He wanted to be loyal to Wally and to the imam, who had both treated him well. Wally had been a good boss to him. He was someone intelligent to talk to, and once in a while they went to the diner together for lunch. Now that Akram thought about it, the conversations at lunch mostly centered on sports. They never discussed politics or current events. Akram wasn't that interested in American football or basketball, but Wally clearly was. In order to have something to talk about with Wally, Akram started reading the sports pages and watching ESPN on TV. Mohammed's brothers were trying out for semi-pro soccer teams, so Akram had a much better idea of that sport.

Mohammed was busy with his work and his new friends, and Akram felt they had grown apart and had nothing much in common anymore. Akram had not become as Americanized as Mohammed, but he had grown to like the U.S. Not everything about America was worthwhile, but there were many things very intriguing about New York. Akram was very taken with the fact that almost everywhere you went in New York City, there was water nearby. That was a huge departure for him from Saudi Arabia and the desert. Akram went to Jones Beach, the Statue of Liberty and rode the Staten Island Ferry. He took a trip on The Circle Line.

On the day that Akram went on The Circle Line, it started out as an overcast day, which probably kept a lot of people off the boat. As they neared the Statue of

Liberty, many of the people who had stayed inside for most of the trip came out on deck. As luck would have it, or as Akram would have phrased it, Allah smiled on him that day. A young woman with dark hair and a killer smile stood next to him at the rail. She broke the ice by saying what an impressive sight the Statue of Liberty was. Akram realized that she was talking to him, sort of. He had done some reading about the Statue of Liberty before he had gone out there, and so now he had some interesting facts to tell her, which Akram thought made him seem smart. That was the ice breaker, and the conversation continued.

After a few minutes the conversation had progressed to other things about Manhattan. Both of them were engaged in the conversation, and as The Circle Line headed away from the Statue of Liberty, Akram said he was going to get a cup of coffee and asked if he could get one for her. Her name was Holly, and Akram thought it was the most beautiful name he had ever heard. It rolled off his tongue. Holly said she would like to come inside with him to have the coffee.

Partially because he was shy and partially because he didn't know how to act around American women, the times that they met after that encounter were in public places and during the day. Holly liked it that Akram wasn't coming on strong and that the things he suggested they do together were non-threatening. They went to the movies, they went to museums and they went to the Bronx Zoo.

Now Akram was in a panic, because Wally had called America "The Great Satan," and had told him that their "brothers" had set off the dirty bombs. There were a number of things that Wally had told Akram to do as part of this great plan. Now Akram wasn't so sure he wanted to do these things, because he had grown somewhat fond of America, and he had grown very fond of Holly. If he did what Wally was telling him to do, Akram realized that if caught, he probably would end up in jail. What Wally was asking him to do would also mean the end of the money transmitting business, Akram's job and his lifestyle, which was becoming comfortable. It would also mean the end of his relationship, or whatever he should call it, with Holly.

The first thing that Wally told him to do was freeze all the money in the accounts at the money transmitter business. That meant that any funds deposited with the company to be sent overseas were not going to their intended destination. All of that money was to be taken and placed in a master account that Akram never knew existed.

The second step was the mirror image of the first. Any money that had come into the money transmitting business from overseas to be given to someone in the United States was also to be removed from the individual accounts and placed in the master account.

Akram wasn't exactly sure what Wally was going to do with the money in the master account, but he was fairly certain he could take an educated guess. Wally was going to take all the money in the master account and do something illegal with it, since this money didn't belong to Wally. Wally had long ago taken his fees for his services on these accounts. This meant that all the money being diverted into the master account definitely was being stolen from the customers.

That was the first phase of what Wally told him to do. It was going to take some time to move all the money into the master account. Akram wasn't sure what Wally was going to tell him to do with the master account and where all this money was going.

Wally had yet another phase of transactions he would want Akram to perform, that Wally had not yet shared with Akram.

Chapter 40

THE AUSTIN

In the first five minutes after Valerie and Brendan went to find the cart from the loading dock, Paul stepped back from the metal grate with sweat pouring down his face. His shirt was soaked with sweat and he was gasping for air. He had spent those five minutes bashing the metal grate with a hammer, and he had virtually nothing to show for it. At this moment, both of his elbows hurt from repeatedly hitting the metal grate with the hammer. "Son of a bitch. This thing was meant to survive a tank assault. You guys able to open the grate?"

Tom and Joel had been working at the other end of the grate with the wrenches. They had been able to bend back a few of the metal rings attaching the grate to the track, but it too had been slow going for them. "Some progress, but not much. Come take a look."

Paul came over to survey the situation. "At this rate, it's going to take us hours to get through. The other problem I hadn't thought about until now is if we bend the grate off the track, we aren't going to be able to use the motor to raise it. We've got to find something to give us more power to break through this goddamn thing."

If this had been a Greek tragedy, and things had not been going well, it would have been time for the *deus ex machina*, literally "the god in the machine." The god would swoop in and rescue those who needed rescuing to end the play.

The next best thing happened. They did indeed hear a machine and as the three of them turned toward the sound of the machine, Valerie came around the corner driving the forklift. Brendan was standing on the first step of the forklift and holding on for dear life.

"What the hell? How did you find the key?" Tom asked. "We all searched for it."

Valerie let out a whoop of joy. "The key was hiding in plain sight. I guess they never expected anyone other than employees of the building to use the forklift, so they didn't lock the key away. It was on the floor right under the driver's seat. It had moved pretty far back under the seat!"

Valerie slowed the forklift to a crawl. "Guess you guys need me. You certainly didn't make very much progress. You need a smart woman to bail you out." The sarcasm in her voice was evident.

Ever the alpha male and a chauvinist, Paul said, "Get down. I'm going to ram this thing into this goddamn grate and it's going to be toast."

"The hell you are. I'm driving this thing and I'm going to take this bad boy down. Get out of the way!"

"Jesus, Valerie, you can't do this."

"Why, 'cause it's a man's job? Have you ever even driven a forklift, like you're some kind of forklift expert?"

Tom was not a chauvinist, but he was skeptical of Valerie's plan. "Hold on a sec, Valerie. Before either of you ram this grate, we should think this through. There are a bunch of things that can go wrong, no matter who's driving. You're going to have to hit this with some force. You could get thrown off the forklift; it wasn't meant to be used as a battering ram.

"Then, suppose that the metal splinters and impales you. We have no ability here to stop massive bleeding or remove metal from someone's body in the lobby of a building. Those are activities best done in a fully equipped ER."

The smirk on Valerie's face was replaced with a frown. "Suppose I don't ram it with any speed but just keep putting pressure on the grate until it snaps? There probably is some weak point. Didn't you guys make any progress in breaking the grate?"

"Well, we got some of the rings off the track on the side over there."

"Then that's where we should concentrate our efforts. I'm not totally unprepared either."

With that, Valerie pulled out a hardhat and a pair of safety goggles that had been on the seat next to her. She proceeded to put them on and looked appropriately ridiculous, like a kid playing dress up.

That sight broke the tension as everyone started to laugh. Finally, Joel who had been standing quietly and who had been intimidated throughout the interchange, spoke up. "Stay here for a minute, I have another idea." He returned shortly thereafter with one of the curtains which he had ripped off one of the windows.

"This is big enough that you can wrap it around yourself several times, and maybe stop any metal from hitting you."

"Good idea. Give it to me."

Valerie stood up and wrapped herself in the curtain. It went around her three times. "Okay, ready to go. Let's do this."

"C'mon, Valerie, we all get it that you're a liberated woman, but this is..."

Before Paul could finish, Valerie cut him off. "If you dare say, that you should do it because you're a big strong man, I swear I will ram YOU with this forklift. Now get the hell out of my way."

With that, Valerie adjusted her goggles and pushed the hard hat down further on her head. She backed up the forklift and angled it over to the right side of the grate. She backed it up again to straighten out the fork-lift so that it was now at a ninety-degree angle to the grate.

"You guys should back up and get away from the grate."

At this point all four men realized that they were dealing with a very determined, if not half-crazy wom-an. She didn't have to tell them twice to move back. They all wanted to move to safety, yet they also wanted to see if this insane idea was going to work and if the insane woman was actually going to do this. They def-initely wanted to see the stubborn grate go down in de-feat.

Valerie waited a few seconds to let them move away and take cover. Then she gave the forklift the gas. Despite all the conversation about the perils of hit-ting the grate too fast with the forklift, Valerie gunned it as best she could. She felt the forklift hit the grate with some force and she felt a jolt in her body. It all happened in what seemed like slow motion. Then with a sharp crack, the hated metal grate gave way with a tremendous crash and the grate looked like twisted rub-ble.

Valerie let out a very loud "Yes!" and she heard the cheers behind her.

Chapter 41

THE AUSTIN

"I hope this wasn't overkill. If this thing blows over today, and we just plowed a forklift into the front of a restaurant, we're going to have some 'splaining to do,' like Lucy Ricardo."

"Don't be stupid, Tom. These are dirty bombs that went off. It's not like this is a snowstorm which is going to be over in twenty-four hours as it moves up the coast. The effects of radiation are going to linger. Even with this new scrubbing thing that they're trying, there's no guarantee it's going to work or if it does, how fast it's going to work. We're going to have to fend for ourselves."

As they surveyed the damage, they also saw that the forklift had gouged a hole in the sheetrock in the front wall of the restaurant. Joel was the first to pick his way through the rubble. "Boy, Ms. Wilkinson, you really are something. I never saw anyone drive a forklift like that! Someone hand me a hammer. I think I can break a big enough hole for me to get through and open the door, so Ms. Wilkinson doesn't have to ram the door. Although it would be fun to see you do it."

As Joel proceeded to hit the sheetrock with a hammer to make a larger hole, the other four picked their way through the mangled grate. It took some strength to move the larger pieces of the grate and some pieces were very mangled. Those mangled pieces they wrestled with the wrenches to try to make them smaller to move them out of the way.

Valerie jumped down off the forklift as a rush of adrenaline surged through her. She had felt some flashes of adrenaline in the past when she won a case in court and bested a nasty opponent, but nothing like this. The closest she had come to this much adrenaline was the first and only time she had gone zip lining. Right now she was almost a little breathless. Brendan looked like a deer in the headlights. "My God, Valerie, you're wonderful. Who knew you could even drive a forklift, no less drive it like Mario Andretti. Wait until I tell them in the office what you did."

Right now the office, court and clients seemed very far away. Valerie had a sobering thought. If she, a civilized woman, attorney and officer of the court, could drive a forklift through a metal grate with hardly a thought, what could happen in the outside world when and if people became desperate? "Yeah, yeah, no big deal. C'mon, Brendan, stop standing there like an idiot and help us move this crap out of the way."

It took some time with a lot of grunting and growling, but they moved what was left of the grate out of the way of the front door to the restaurant. Joel had managed to open up a large enough hole in the wall for him to wriggle through into the restaurant. He was pushing to open the door from the inside as they were pulling debris away from the door on the other side.

Joel turned on the lights in the restaurant to get rid of that other worldly look of half dark. The inside of the restaurant was in sharp contrast to the space outside the front door littered with debris. The tables were set with china, cutlery, water glasses and china. If you looked into the restaurant with your back to the front door, everything seemed normal as if the restaurant was about to open. Apparently, this look of normalcy struck all of them as they paused for a moment.

No one said anything as they marched toward the kitchen at the back of the restaurant. All of them would have been turned away for dinner if they had appeared in the restaurant the way they looked at this moment. They were covered in dust, not only on their clothes, but in their hair as well.

Paul's shirt and hair were still soaked in sweat. Tom had a rip in the sleeve of his fleece jacket and a piece of the material was hanging. Valerie's face was smudged with dirt and it was apparent where the goggles had been covering her eyes, because the rest of her face had a coating of dust. Brendan still had on his white dress shirt from earlier in the day. It was dirty from his sojourn in the streets of New York to get to the apartment. Now there was a big black smear across his chest on the shirt. Joel had long ago taken off his tie. His black pants were covered in white dust from crawling through the hole in the sheetrock. The front pocket of his white shirt was ripped.

As they arrived in the kitchen, it was in sharp contrast to the front of the restaurant. It was apparent that the kitchen staff had left in quite a hurry and without cleaning up. There was a stack of dirty pots and pans in the large sink. The counters were littered with serving spoons, forks and small pools of various colored liquids, most probably the remains of sauces and gravies.

As everyone checked out the mess in the kitchen, Joel volunteered that there had been a large private party in the restaurant at lunchtime, which had closed it to the normal lunchtime crowd. Apparently, they had cleaned up the front of the restaurant to make it look fresh and presentable, and decided to clean up the kitchen afterwards. Then they ran out of time.

"Did the restaurant staff let management know they were leaving when the dirty bombs went off?"

Joel shrugged. "I dunno. They left through the back of the building, because I didn't know they had gone either. The restaurant staff are a very close knit group. They stick to themselves and they don't mingle with any of the other staff. I don't even know a lot of their names."

"Okay, doesn't really matter now," Tom replied. "Let's get organized and figure out how to get the food out of here. Did you guys get a cart from the loading dock?" he asked looking from Valerie to Brendan.

"Well, we kind of got sidetracked when we found the forklift. Did we even see a rolling cart, Brendan?"

"I honestly don't know, Valerie. It got kind of hectic back there. I'll go back to the loading dock and find one."

"Let us know if there's more than one. If you can bring two with you, do it."

Joel said, "I'll go with you and see what else we should bring back from the loading dock and the engineering room."

"Let's see what's here. We should probably organize the food by perishables and non-perishables. Where should we pile the food?"

Paul smirked and said, "I'll make it easy." With that, he swept his arm across two counters and everything on the counters ended up on the floor with a series of crashes and clangs.

"For God's sake, Paul, did you think that was going to make it better? Now we have a pile of broken glass all over the floor that we have to walk through. Nobody here has on work boots." Valerie shook her head in disgust.

Chapter 42

THE MAYOR

Ryan Bernard, the mayor of New York City, the New York City Director of the FBI, the chief of Emergency Management Services and several deputies for the three people, sat at a conference table in a secure location. A few of the deputies who couldn't fit at the table stood in the background or leaned against the walls of the conference room.

They were waiting for the Director of Homeland Security, Jordan Reid, to appear on the large flat screen TV. When the screen flickered on, the people in the conference room were surprised to see not only Director Reid, but also the president.

The mayor was taken aback by seeing the president on the screen without the mayor having been informed in advance. "Director, oh, ah, Mr. President," the mayor stumbled. "We weren't expecting anyone important. Sorry, that came out wrong, Mr. President. We're very happy to have you."

"No need for any apologies, Ryan. I know you guys are stretched to the limit. We're all on the same team. So what updates do we have now?"

"Well, Mr. President, the EPA people and my people in Emergency Management Services are telling me it's too soon to tell if this scrubbing is actually working. They're not sure if we have to do a second spraying in the most severely affected areas. From what I've been told, this scrubbing was in its final stages of testing in the lab, but of course, it hasn't actually been tried in a real emergency. New York is the guinea pig.

"The readings on the radiation are not coming down fast, but they say that doesn't necessarily mean that they won't. Of course, it doesn't necessarily mean that they will either. We're dealing with so many unknowns that we can't plan accurately.

"If we try to be optimistic that the scrubbing will work, my people are also saying that we need more of this product both for the very badly affected areas and for the areas in the city away from where the dirty bombs went off. Can you supply us with more?" The mayor stopped his soliloquy for a moment and let out a huge sigh.

The president deferred to Jordan Reid on this. Jordan said, "We have to check if we sent the whole supply to you in New York. They might have sent it all or they might have kept some in case some other city was hit. I'll let you know tomorrow."

"Look, Jordan, I don't need an answer tomorrow on this. I need an answer tonight. Right now, within the hour." The frustration in the mayor's voice was very evident.

Jordan was not about to be boxed into a corner on this. "I said I'll check and I will."

"Jesus, Jordan, you're not the one sitting in a city contaminated with radiation with millions of people depending on you. You're a couple of hundred miles away probably sitting in a goddamn bunker."

The president broke in and said, "Ryan, Jordan will be back to you in two hours." As he said this, the president was glaring at Jordan. "Jordan will be back to both of us in two hours. Right, Jordan?"

Through clenched teeth, Jordan said, "Yes, Mr. President."

"Okay, Ryan, what's next?"

"I've asked the governor to call up the National Guard. Since we're only a few hours from the bombings, it's going to take time for them to mobilize. Right now I'm going to have them assemble just outside the city's limits. The police and fire department are going to need help—big time. They'll be working round the clock for now, but they can't keep that up. That's when I'll have the National Guard move in. We think we're going to need help from the army as well. How many troops can you give us?"

"Tell us how many you need and we'll start mobilizing them. The army is very good at doing big things on a moment's notice."

"I think we're also going to need trucks and tanks. This could get ugly and we probably are going to need a show of force. I hope we won't need to use that force.

"Now comes the two interrelated and thorniest problems. I have a couple of million people literally, who are sheltering in place. They are not going to want to stay that way for very long. Some of them are in their offices, some are in stores and lobbies of buildings. You get the idea. We don't have a good idea of where people are at this moment.

"We're trying to decide now if we should try some food drops first or try evacuating people first. Both pose a very serious problem of logistics and exposing people to radiation. We don't have nearly enough hazmat suits for the entire population. Right now we don't even have enough for the police, fire department and National Guard. How many hazmat suits can you send us?

"While it's critical for the big picture that the scrubbing works, it's even more critical in the short term that we know it's at least producing some results so we know what to do with the population in the immediate short term. The last thing we want is for people to panic and go out in the streets right now. They're going to panic if they think we're not doing something to help them or they think they're going to starve to death. This is more than a rock and a hard place. If we don't do something quickly, we're going to be crushed by that rock. You guys gotta help us now!"

The president was listening to every word. "Ryan, I'm going downstairs now into the Situation Room with Jordan. We have so many smart people and so many resources, and the group that is waiting in the Situation Room knows specifically what's available more than I do off the top of my head. In two hours I will get back to you from the Situation Room with as many answers as we have at that moment. We'll then be in a better position to tell you what we can do for you and when."

"Thanks, Mr. President, we'll all be waiting for your call."

The flat screen went dark and the people on both ends of the call exhaled as both sides felt an incredible burden on their shoulders.

Chapter 43

THE AUSTIN

The adrenaline was still pumping through Valerie. Her ride on the forklift was such a departure from anything she had ever done in her life and anything that she ever would have expected to do, but somehow it felt great. She wasn't sure if her face was actually grinning, but internally she knew she was doing cartwheels. She forced herself to focus on what they needed to do in the restaurant.

There were a number of big refrigerators, and two small freezers, so they thought they had struck pay dirt. As they proceeded to explore the kitchen further, that was a false assumption. Paul headed for the refrigerators first. In the first, there were eight gallons of milk, three large tins of coffee and two fancy boxes with packets of tea, jars of mustard and huge industrial tubs of mayonnaise. There were at least fifteen dozen eggs. There were three apple pies unopened in boxes, one blueberry pie with three slices missing, one cherry pie with one slice missing and half of a coconut custard pie. There was a large bag of cookies which looked to contain chocolate chip, oatmeal, chocolate, chocolate macadamia and sugar cookies.

In the second refrigerator, there was lettuce of every variety imaginable and marked neatly on the outside of plastic bags. There was iceberg, Bibb, romaine, spring mix, endive and radicchio, to name a few. To compliment all of this lettuce of every ilk, there were jars too numerous to count of salad dressings, again in industrial sized containers. Paul read them out loud. "Italian,

French, Balsamic, Vinaigrette, Caesar, Creamy Caesar, Russian, Thousand Islands, Raspberry Walnut, Citrus, Lime Vinaigrette, Yogurt and Smoky Russian Bacon. Who the hell knew there were this many kinds of salad dressing?" Paul said to no one in particular. There were also a few bags of celery and two of baby carrots.

He moved on quickly to the third refrigerator, hoping for better results. This third refrigerator was apparently the one for meat. There was a small platter of roast beef and a small platter of salami which looked to have been rewrapped, sitting in the back of one of the shelves. Paul was looking for steak, burgers, chicken, veal and pork. He knew they were going to need some substantial food and not just salad dressing and desserts. "Shit. Goddamn, Shit!" he yelled loud enough to get Valerie and Tom's attention.

By now Tom and Valerie had gone through the cupboards and cabinets. They had put what they had found on the counters now vacated by Paul having swept everything onto the floor a few minutes earlier. Valerie and Tom had rounded up five loaves of bread, some small dinner rolls, a number of cans of College Inn chicken broth, tomato soup and consommé, twenty cans of salmon, a huge stock pile of cans of tuna, a few packages of ground beef, three large turkey breasts from one freezer and two good sized turkeys from the other freezer.

"What did you find, Paul?"

"Shit, not all that much. I would have thought a restaurant would have had much more in it."

Valerie responded, "My guess is that the restaurant was going to be closed tomorrow after the party that Joel mentioned. They probably get deliveries every day, so that's one thing. The other is that the restaurant staff slipped out the back, with everything they could carry with them."

"Valerie's right. No one saw them leave. Joel didn't even know they had gone. If you look around at what's left, they probably carried off what was easiest to take. The stuff that's left is what's heaviest, bulky and not so easy to carry. They either took a chance that this was going to be a long siege, or they were hoping that they could blame the theft on someone else. Maybe some of the staff they thought were still gonna be here."

Paul and Valerie nodded at Tom's statements.

Tom waited a minute and then continued. "We found what appears to be a huge freezer downstairs, but it was has some sort of combination lock on it. We can't see into the freezer, but if it has a combination lock, presumably there's valuable stuff in there. Maybe expensive cuts of meat would be my guess, but it could also be useless things to us like caviar.

"We don't think that Mario Andretti here can get the forklift through this restaurant and downstairs to get to the freezer. I think we should try to find out if the combination is written down somewhere. They were sloppy about the key to the forklift, so maybe we get lucky and find the combination somewhere.

"Did anyone see anything like an office for the chef or maître d'? That's a good place to start."

They spread out in the kitchen and pantry areas looking for something that resembled a code. After a few minutes, they were discouraged. "We don't know what the hell we're looking for. Do we actually think that the code to this freezer, which might contain all kinds of expensive food, is going to be written on a slip of paper that screams at us 'freezer code?' The guys in the loading dock might be stupid, but I doubt the chef is that stupid. This lock might need two codes from two different people to get in. I think we're wasting our time," Paul concluded.

"Wasting our time about what?" Brendan and Joel had returned with a rolling cart. "Not too easy to get it into the restaurant after Valerie's escapade with the forklift. How'd you do with getting the food?"

"Okay, I guess." Paul gestured in the direction of the counter. "There's some stuff in the refrigerators, but nowhere near as much food as we hoped. Let's just hope that this doesn't go on for too long. We're going to have to be careful, and maybe ration what we have. Let's get everything out of here and onto the cart. Separate the perishables onto one shelf. We should get ourselves out of here pronto as well."

"Where's Joel, Brendan?"

"He's coming with another cart. He was gathering hardware, blankets in case the power goes off and all kinds of other things, some of which I can't identify."

"Alright, let's get going."

Chapter 44

AKRAM

Wally was sweating. He wasn't sure if it was from stress or exhilaration. He buzzed Akram on the intercom. "Akram, have you finished with the accounts?"

"No, not yet. There are hundreds of accounts. Some of the accounts have very little money in the account and some have a lot. There is no way to tell what's in an account until I access each one."

"How many more accounts do you have to do?"

"I can't tell. The list you gave me is alphabetical. It would have been better if they had been listed numerically, so I could tell how many more accounts I still had to access. Some of these customers have several accounts."

"Well, what letter are you up to?" Wally asked with clear annoyance in his voice.

"I'm up to 'N,' but I would guess that there will be a lot of accounts starting with the letters 'R, S and T,' but probably not a lot of accounts with names starting with 'X, Y and Z.' Whose bright idea was to do this alphabetically?"

"Never mind that now. It is as it is. Just keep working. Let me know the minute you are done."

Akram had calmed downed somewhat from when he first left Wally's office. He certainly wasn't going to tell Wally, but it took him more than a few minutes to start accessing the accounts when he first returned to his office. His hands were shaking so badly that he couldn't type.

At first, Akram thought he should just go back to his office, pick up his jacket and walk out the back door. He considered doing that as he watched the news of the dirty bombs on his phone. He truly didn't know what to do. There was no one for him to call for any sort of help or another opinion about what to do.

He tried taking deep breaths to slow his heart rate, and that did help a little. As his heart rate went down from hysterical to very upset, he was able to think a little more clearly. He finally decided that it was too risky to just get up and leave. Wally would certainly know if he just bolted out the door. Akram wasn't sure what Wally would do to find him and maybe even have someone kill him, if Wally somehow thought that Akram had betrayed him. More importantly, Akram thought Wally would be even more upset if he thought that Akram had betrayed the grand plan of the brotherhood. Akram wasn't sure who this brotherhood really was, how many people were affiliated with it and how much power and reach they had.

Akram decided it was better for him to play along as if he believed in the cause, whatever the cause was. Right now, Akram hated what the brotherhood had just done. Akram believed in Islam, but in his reading and study of the Koran, Akram did not see anything in Islam that told its believers to perpetrate random violence and death in the name of Allah.

Akram had never been forced before today to act on his beliefs or contradict others who held radical beliefs. He simply couldn't justify killing people randomly because they were Americans. In his time living in the United States, he mostly saw hardworking people trying to make a living and provide for their families. Sure, there were excesses, and sure there were problems, but Akram didn't think that the average person he saw on a day to day basis, had any control over the policies of the United States. They were cogs in the wheel.

He decided that he would do what Wally was so insistent that he do with the accounts, if only to buy himself time. Time to think and time to formulate a plan to get out. Akram had a hunch that Wally was not going to stick around for long after his piece of the grand plan had been carried out, but that was not a certainty, only a guess.

If Wally disappeared with all the money that was going into the master account, then Akram felt that he would try to disappear immediately thereafter. Hopefully, by then, Akram felt that no one would be able to identify him and do him harm from the brotherhood. Then another thought crossed his mind and he almost gagged.

Certainly, the authorities would find out that Akram worked for Wally. With Wally most probably in the wind, Akram realized, to use another American idiom, that he would be left "holding the bag." Even though Wally said he only knew a part of the plan, Akram was certain that Wally knew a lot more than he had let on to Akram, and that he had a well-thought-out plan to save himself, which probably didn't include Akram.

The thoughts were flying so fast through Akram's head. Then another thought flashed through his mind. Suppose Wally wanted Akram to flee with him? Where would they go? Could he get home to Saudi Arabia? Did he want Wally to know where he was? His home in Saudi Arabia would probably be the first place the American government would look for him. That was so obvious it was laughable. He also didn't want to bring danger to his family's home. More importantly, he didn't want to bring shame and disgrace to his family. No, he had been raised better than that. Akram cursed the fates that had now turned his life upside down.

His life had taken a definite turn for the better in the last several months. This was due in large part to the fact that he had taken this job with Wally. He was not living hand to mouth, and he was not in danger of having to return to his family as a very large failure.

Then something else stabbed at his heart. He thought of Holly. Could he ever tell her what had happened? Worse still, could he ever tell her his part in all this, albeit unwittingly? He probably would never be able to see Holly again to explain things to her.

Chapter 45

VALERIE AND BRENDAN

It didn't take that long to put the food from the restaurant on the rolling cart, but they realized that it was going to take two or more trips. They couldn't pile up the food too well on the cart because they had to get the cart over the debris that was littering the lobby in front of the restaurant. They had already moved the largest pieces out of the way, but there were still enough pieces of metal and sheetrock to make rolling the cart over them impossible.

Plan B was to wheel the cart as close as they could get it to the door to the restaurant, carry the food to the cart from the restaurant, and then move the cart as best they could through the mess and the "debris field." This took a lot more effort and time then they had expected. Then Valerie and Brendan rolled the cart through the lobby to the elevators, while the others repeated the process of moving the food out of the restaurant so it could be loaded onto the cart.

When they reached the third floor, they unloaded the cart onto the floor of the living room of Valerie's apartment, and then Brendan made an about-face and quickly took the cart back to the elevator. Neither Brendan nor Valerie said anything in the trip up in the elevator, and the only thing that Valerie said was as they reached her apartment was, "Let's just put this on the floor in my apartment for now and we'll try to organize when we have everything up here." Brendan nodded in agreement.

As the door to her apartment closed behind Brendan, Valerie thought that this was the only time in her professional life that two attorneys had been together and no words had been exchanged except for one sentence. She caught sight of herself in the mirror and almost gasped at what she looked like. Her hair was covered in dust and was matted down. The goggles still hung from her neck. Her face was even more filthy than her hair. She grabbed a paper towel in the kitchen and ran it under the faucet. As she rubbed the wet paper towel over her face, the amount of dirt that came off was remarkable. Plus, it felt good to feel the cool water on her face. She hadn't realized how much she had been sweating.

As she looked over the mess that was now on her living room rug, she picked her way through the items as best she could and started picking up cans of soup and chicken broth and tried to organize them in groups and put them on her kitchen counters.

In a few minutes there was a knock on the door. Valerie grabbed and pulled it open with one hand and continued to pick up cans in the other. Tom and Brendan rolled the cart in as far as they could until they were blocked by the food on the floor. "Valerie, you have to be more careful before you open the door like that, without even looking. You made an assumption that it was us. We didn't say anything, and it could have been anyone just looking to get in."

"You're right. I wasn't thinking, Tom. I was concentrating on trying to organize this stuff before you guys came back with the next load. Is this it?"

"No, but I think that one more load on the cart will probably do it and we can carry up the rest. Joel has the second cart loaded with all kinds of supplies from the loading dock and engineering that we might need.

We'll have to split up the food into the refrigerators and then figure out what to do with the things he has."

"Like what?"

"There are tools, blankets, and some metal rods that he thinks we might want to use as weapons, and a whole lot of other things." Tom started shaking his head in disbelief as he said the word "weapons."

"I hope that we're overreacting about this. Every time I say that, Paul jumps down my throat. I really don't know. What do you think?" Tom posed the question to both Brendan and Valerie.

"We've been at this for a lot longer than I thought it was going to take. I was just focused on what we were doing without thinking of the bigger picture for a while."

"You've been very quiet, Brendan. What do you think?"

Brendan looked down at his feet and then shuffled from one foot to the other before he spoke. "How well do you know Paul? "

"He's a neighbor, that's all. All of us are fairly new to this building, and in New York, I gather you're lucky if you do more than nod at your neighbors in the elevator. Why do you ask?"

Brendan didn't answer right away.

"C'mon, Brendan, you're thinking something or you wouldn't have asked the question. You might as well tell Tom and me now."

"There's something about him that I don't like. There's a thread of something vicious or maybe even violent about him. I can't quite put my finger on it. I don't know what would happen if you crossed him. He's probably not very much of a team player. If push comes to shove as they say, I wouldn't expect much from him, if it didn't suit his needs."

He turned to Valerie. "You weren't watching his face, after you refused to let him drive the forklift."

"What about his face? I thought he was a chauvinist, and didn't like it that he wasn't going to drive the damn thing. There's probably a ton of guys who wouldn't have liked that either and that I didn't give in to their overdeveloped male egos. I'm not sure that makes them violent."

Brendan shrugged. "Think what you want. I just think that we need to keep an eye on him. It's more of a vibe than anything else. That instinct, vibe or whatever you want to call it, has saved me more than a few times on trial."

"All of us are under stress with this dirty bomb, and all that we did tonight with the restaurant was more than any of us thought it was going to be. We're all tired, dirty and stressed. I don't think Valerie was dismissing or disrespecting what your thoughts are. We will pay attention, but I don't know that tonight was necessarily a good indication of the future."

Now it was Brendan's turn to shake his head in disgust. "Don't kid yourself. The stress may only get worse. Much worse for all of us."

Chapter 46

THE MAYOR AND THE PRESIDENT

The flat screen TV came on from the Situation Room in the White House. Even though he was the mayor of one of the largest cities in the world and New York City touted itself as the "Greatest City in the World," Ryan Bernard felt insignificant realizing that he was speaking to some of the most powerful people in the world in the Situation Room. Like all Americans, he had seen the Situation Room portrayed in the movies and on television many times. He had seen the still pictures of the Situation Room when the Navy Seals had killed Osama bin Laden and the president and his Cabinet members watched anxiously in real time.

Now, however, all eyes in the Situation Room were focused on him. "Mr. President, I truly appreciate that you have gotten back to me in two hours as you said you would. We can only do so much here without your help." Ryan stopped talking and waited for the president.

"Well, Ryan, we have some good news for you. There is still some more of the scrubbing agent that remained at the labs. We are happy to give you every bit of it that we have. The people at the Defense Department are very eager to hear what readings you're getting on the radiation levels. I don't expect you to have the exact numbers now, but tell us to whom they can speak directly. They want to hear about the levels as your people took the readings each hour. Let the scientists continue speak to each other, since I'm sure each side is going to have a great number of technical questions for the other that we won't understand.

"Our people at DOD were somewhat discouraged that the readings hadn't gone down to what are considered safe levels after the first spraying. They are in favor of giving New York a second or 'booster shot' as they call it. That's the good news.

"The bad news is they don't have too much of this product left. They say it's not enough to spray the entire city again. They are huddling now to discuss where they think you should spray again to get the greatest results."

The president hesitated and the mayor picked right up on the hesitation. "There's more bad news, right, Mr. President? Go ahead, lay it on us."

"Yeah, unfortunately, there is. They think it's going to take a few weeks to produce more of the scrubbing agent. There's some organic component to it that has to grow in the lab. They don't know if they can speed up the process all that much. I'm really simplifying this, and as I said before, the scientists are already working on this. I've told them how much of a priority this is and that I want the labs working around the clock.

"I spoke to the head of the lab myself, and this is only in the last two hours since you and I have spoken. The head of the lab tells me that they are going to try to speed up the process for the organic component. Here's the wild card. The lab really doesn't know if they will get the same results and the same efficacy, if the process is sped up. It might alter the end result of the product in ways they are not too sure of."

"I understand. We have a lot of unknowns here which is making this situation a whole lot worse. As they say, we are shooting at a moving target." The mayor's tone sounded deflated.

"Look, Ryan, as we know, this scrubbing agent was in its final testing stages. We gave you the best we have. DOD is the first to admit that. They were obviously hoping that they'd never have to use this product at all, but if they did, that it wouldn't be for a long time in the future. That would have given them more time for testing and improvement."

"I get it, Mr. President. We're all trying to do the best we can during this shit storm. Oh, excuse me, Mr. President, I didn't mean to say 'shit' to you."

"Ryan, that's not the first time I've ever heard the word. You are living in the eye of the shit storm, and we're trying to help you get out of it. Not an enviable place to be." That remark brought a chuckle from all the people in the Situation Room and in the mayor's conference room.

"Mr. President, thanks. I'd like to move on to the other things we need. I asked you how many hazmat suits you can give us."

"I'm going to let Jordan address this. Jordan, go, you're on."

Jordan Reid, had obviously had a "come to Jesus" moment in the last two hours. Apparently, behind the scenes, the president had excoriated Jordan, the director of Homeland Security, for being difficult, if not downright uncooperative with the mayor in the conversation the three of them had.

Jordan answered, "Right now, we can give you about nine hundred hazmat suits. We will fly them out right now into Kennedy or LaGuardia or wherever you want. We are going to have them loaded onto a plane tonight. They will be in New York in a couple of hours.

"I've also directed my team to locate as many hazmat suits as we can from other federal agencies. We're also going to beat the bushes from other states to round up even more. We should have a handle on that tomorrow morning, and we'll get them to you as fast as we find them. We're getting people out of bed right now to find out what each agency has in its possession. But nine hundred hazmat suits should get you started when you add that to what you already have in your possession."

They had yet to get to the hardest issue.

Chapter 47

AKRAM

Akram purposely was slowing down the work of moving all the customers' money into the master account to try to give himself time to think about what he was doing at this moment. More importantly, Akram was thinking about what he was going to do tomorrow, the day after that and the days to come. Akram did not want to end up in prison, or worse, in Guantanamo. He was clearly aiding and abetting a terrorist activity and he was afraid to consider the consequences of what this was going to mean for him.

The only person he could think to reach out to was Mohammed, so he called him on his phone. Fortunately, he the call went through. "Mohammed, it's me. I have only a few minutes and I have to speak very quietly."

"Akram, where are you? I've been very worried about you, but I couldn't get through on my cell. Are you in Manhattan or in Queens?"

"I'm at work in Queens. Shut up and listen. I'm in big trouble. Wally is somehow working with the terrorists. He's part of their plan. He's taking the next step in helping the terrorists financially through his money transmitting business. I don't have time to go into it on the phone. I need to get out of here NOW. I can't go home. Do you have any friends who live in Queens whose house or apartment I can go to for now?"

"Yes, I have a couple of friends who live in Queens. Do you want me to text them and see if it's okay?"

"No, I need you to tell them I was stranded at work and I need to go there. Don't give them a choice so that they could possibly say no. Give me their addresses. Which friend lives closer to here?"

"It's my friend Ralph. He's a good guy. I'll tell him you're coming. You need to make up some good story to tell him about why you're going there and not home. But how are you going to get there? I don't think the buses or subways are running. They want everybody to stay inside."

"Are you home, Mohammed?"

"No, I went to pick up two of our men and the truck who got stuck on the road. I got the truck running and we were headed back to the company when the bombs went off. All the roads into New York City were closed down. We're stuck in Westchester."

Mohammed paused. "Okay, I'll tell Ralph that I'm stuck in Westchester and you forgot your keys to the apartment. But how are you going to get there?"

"I'll walk if I have to. Just text or call him so he's knows I'm coming. I'll explain things to you when I get there. Thanks."

Akram hoped that maybe there was still time to save himself from a total disaster and possibly prison, if he got out now. He got up to go to the bathroom and to give himself another few minutes to think and the prac-ticality of the fact that it looked as if he had a lengthy walk ahead of him. He doubted that any stores were going to be open for him to go to the bathroom or buy a cup of coffee. He was very worried about going out in the radiation, but he was more terrified of staying with Wally and the brotherhood.

There were pots of coffee brewing in the office. By now, the coffee was probably going to be so bitter and old that he could chew it rather than drink it. As he left the bathroom, he stopped by the coffee pots and poured himself a large cup. He went back to his office with the coffee. A few minutes later, Wally bolted into Akram's office. "Are you finished yet?" he asked without preamble.

"Almost. There are a lot of accounts. Many more than I originally thought." Akram took a large gulp of his coffee. He did it right in front of Wally. The coffee provided the prop that he thought it would. The steam was coming up from the coffee cup. Someone trying to leave the office would not be drinking a fresh cup of coffee.

Wally turned on his heel and as he was walking out of the office, he threw out the comment over his shoulder to Akram. "Hurry up. I have more things I need you to do. Let me know when you're done. We can't waste time." Since Wally had already left the office, there was no need for Akram to give Wally an answer.

He waited about thirty seconds and stood just inside his office to listen for any sounds in the hallway. It appeared that Wally had gone back to his office. Akram went back to his desk and grabbed three power bars he had in his desk. He walked back across the room and shoved them in the pocket of his coat which was hanging on a coat rack. From his days working at the deli, Akram had developed a sweet tooth. He had tried many of the foods in the deli. Although he was hesitant to taste them at first, Akram had taken a real liking to Twinkies. However, he noticed that people snickered when he said he liked Twinkies, and so if he ate them, he did so at home. Right now, Akram wished he had Twinkies rather than power bars with him.

He also picked up a paperweight from his desk and put that in his other coat pocket. Akram wasn't sure if he would actually use the paperweight against Wally if it came to that, but it was all he could think of that would fit in his pocket if he had to defend himself.

One more thought popped into his head. Akram was desperate to get out of the office, but this was the one truly rational thought with some foresight to it. He raced back to his desk and yanked open the top drawer. He rummaged through the top drawer and found what he wanted. He grabbed the USB flash drive and inserted it into the computer. He began downloading the program onto the flash drive. It was quick, but at this moment nothing could be fast enough for Akram. After what seemed like an eternity, the download was complete. Akram pulled the flash drive out of the computer, put it in his pocket and then casually walked to the door of his office and took a fast glance.

Since he didn't see anyone in the hallway, in one fell swoop, he grabbed his jacket and baseball cap off the coat rack and headed in the direction of the back door. He didn't bother to put them on and waste any time. Akram was praying that he would have the less than one minute he needed to get out the back door and then a few more seconds to cut through the parking lot. If he had that much time, he could probably fade away without Wally finding him or knowing how long Akram had been gone before Wally realized it.

The cold air in the parking lot hit him in the lungs and took his breath away. Akram continued walking to the back parking lot, where many of the employees of the stores parked. Abutting that parking lot was another parking lot separated by a curb, and thankfully not a chain link fence. As Akram made his way through the second parking lot, he moved behind a van and stopped for a minute to put on his coat and baseball cap. Both parking lots seemed fairly empty. No doubt people were spooked by the dirty bombs and had gone home.

Although he had purposefully not been running to attract any attention to himself, he was walking fast. He thought his heart was going to come out of his chest, it was beating so hard. He took a minute to zip up his jacket, and pull the baseball cap down hard on his head. He also pulled his scarf over his nose and mouth and tried to catch his breath. It wasn't only that he had been walking fast that was making his heart pound; it was pure unadulterated fear. It felt as if a vise was constricting his chest.

Akram realized how afraid he was of Wally. This was a side of him that Akram had never seen before. Wally had always seemed to be sort of laid back. That was until today, when a whole new Wally appeared. Akram was also afraid of the whole situation, that people were willing to wreck such damage on the people of the City of New York. Their reasons did not seem clear to Akram, nor could he think of any valid reasons to inflict this on innocent people. He was also afraid of the part he had played in this. He was afraid of the retribution to come.

He poked his head tentatively around the side of the van to look toward the back of the building where the company was. Part of Akram expected Wally to come running after him with a gun or a machete, but the parking lot was still and there was no movement coming from the direction of the building he has just exited.

Then it hit Akram that there was no movement or sound anywhere around him. It was eerily still.

Chapter 48

THE AUSTIN

All five of them sat down on Valerie's couches as Joel and Paul brought the last items of food into her apartment. They were exhausted physically and emotionally. No one cared that they were filthy and that they were tracking dirt into what a few hours earlier had been a beautifully clean and well-appointed apartment. No one cared that they were messing up the couches. What had seemed initially to be almost a lark or adventure to get the food out of the restaurant, had turned into an extremely trying task.

After a few moments of watching everyone catch their physical and mental breaths, Valerie spoke up. She had been in the apartment longer than Joel and Paul, trying to do some organizing, and so she gave them her ideas. "I can't fit all the perishables into my refrigerator. Why don't I take one of the turkeys and Tom and Paul you each take one and put them in your refrigerator? While I was waiting for you guys to finish downstairs, I tried organizing some of the canned goods. As you can see, I didn't finish, but they are mostly stacked by content, so we have an idea of what we have." There was still a fair amount on the living room floor.

"Anything new on TV from the mayor?" Paul asked.

"I don't know. Let's turn it on and see," Valerie answered.

It seemed to dawn on all of them at almost the same time that they all had lives and jobs that they were very involved in before this day. Tom said he needed to excuse himself and go back to his apartment for a few minutes and call his family and the hospital. That seemed to spark the same thing in all of them.

Tom unlocked the door to his apartment and it shocked him how calm and organized everything was compared to Valerie's apartment, which looked like a tornado had blown through it, with so many things just parked at random on the living room floor.

Tom called Amy first from his landline. Once again, he said a silent prayer of thanks that he had a landline from which to call. This was the first time he noticed that the light on the voice mail was blinking. He had no idea how many messages were on the voice mail and right now he didn't care. Amy answered before the first ring had been completed. "Dad, are you okay?" The worry in her voice was so obvious that it was painful to hear.

"Where have you been? I know the cell phones are all just getting those weird busy signals. I've been calling you on the landline and there was no answer. Where are you now? Everyone has been calling you and you didn't answer. We're all frantic. You didn't go out in this, did you? They keep saying that no one should be going out in New York City. Why haven't you been answering or calling back with all the messages we've been leaving?"

Tom finally cut her off because he felt the rant was just going to continue. "Okay, Amy, take a breath. Calm down. I'm fine. I haven't gone out at all since..." He was going to say "since the bombs went off," but changed his mind to try to soften things. He said instead, "Since everything happened."

"I've been in the apartment building, but not in the apartment itself. There are a few of us who live on the same floor in the apartment. We got together to try to figure out how to handle the situation here. We decided that it would be better if we all worked together."

Tom paused for a few seconds to consider how much more to tell her. "We think we need to be prepared in case this quarantine goes on for some time. There's a restaurant in the building." Again, Tom hesitated about what to tell her.

Tom decided that if this crisis ended well, he would then tell Amy the whole story about breaking into the closed restaurant. With a forklift! At that point when the crisis was behind them, it probably would even be a funny story. Right now she was getting the edited and sanitized version. "We took the food that wasn't being used in the restaurant so that it wouldn't go bad and that we would have food in case we have to stay inside the apartment for a while." Tom couldn't think how he could water it down any more.

Amy was upset enough that she wasn't totally picking up on the nuances of what her father was saying. What Tom had said to her was ambiguous enough that it could possibly be interpreted several ways. During any normal time, no one would ever have been able to imagine Tom breaking into a restaurant as an active participant. It was so out of character for him, and Tom was betting that Amy wouldn't even be thinking in the direction of a break in. Tom was fairly certain that he had never used the words "break in" in his description of what had transpired.

"What are you going to do, Dad?"

"For now, we're all doing what the mayor has told us to do. We're staying inside. It's not the worst place to be stuck in my apartment. You saw it; it's hardly like being in jail. Since you're removed from the city, what are you hearing on TV? We're not hearing very much here. The mayor says he will come back on TV tomorrow morning to update us."

"I think we're getting all the same info on the networks. Social media is lit up with all kinds of conspiracy theories as to who is behind this. All kinds of speculation as to what this new product is that's supposed to be cleaning up the radiation in the air. The talking heads are all over the media, but that's mostly what it is, talk.

"There are also people saying that New York City is doomed. That the city will be under a boatload of radiation forever. That it will never come back.

"They say that the authorities don't even have a realistic idea of how many people are still in New York City or even where all the people are. Every time somebody gets on TV talking about New York, it just gets worse and worse." As she was saying that last sentence, her voice cracked and she started to cry.

"Amy, don't cry. I don't think these people know what the hell they're talking about. It's just too soon. You know that the talking heads have to fill up time on TV. They keep talking endlessly. That's what they do."

Even as he tried to put up a brave front for Amy, Tom felt sick in the pit of his stomach. In truth, he didn't know what he was talking about. He was trying to make both of them feel better. She was repeating what the talking heads were saying on TV and in social media, but in fact, they might be right. New York City might well be doomed and in it millions of people, including him.

"Look, honey, right now I'm in the apartment and I'm safe. That's what we have to stay with. Anything else we say is pure speculation. Let's stay with the facts we know, even if there aren't very many of them. The good news is my landline is working and we're having a conversation, and we can continue to have conversations, so you will know how I'm doing until this gets resolved. I gather that there are lots of people who only have a cell phone and they can't talk to their families to let them know that they're okay. We're much luckier. Listen to the hard news. You might have info that you can tell me that I won't know being in the city.

"I'm going to call your sister and brother, but if for some reason I don't get through, you call them and let them know I'm okay. I told you I was sick, so I wasn't in the hospital yesterday or today. I need to call and find out how things are going in the hospital, which must be a madhouse. I also need to know how things are going with my patients. It's getting late. Try to calm down and get some sleep. I'll talk to you in the morning. I love you, honey."

"Love you, too, Dad. Please be careful. We don't want you to do anything heroic. I need you. I lost Mom. I can't think of losing you, too."

"Amy, I promise you. I will not do anything stupid. I must admit that I was tempted to try to go into the hospital when I first heard what happened, but I didn't. I'm right here. I intend to be around to walk you down the aisle and to see my first grandchild. That's a promise. You okay now?"

A very small and meek "yes" came back to him.

"It's gonna be okay. I'll talk to you in the morning. Bye for now."

As he hung up, Tom felt like a knife had just gone through his heart. For most of his adult life, Tom had been very focused on his patients and put them first. They needed him and their lives hung in the balance. Laurie had always been there when the kids needed something, but when Amy said, "I lost Mom. I can't

think of losing you," it shook him up much more than
he would ever have imagined.

Chapter 49

VALERIE AND PAUL

Back in Valerie's apartment, she had given out bottles of water and soda to her three "guests." Paul was the first one to gain back some semblance of energy. It might have been the caffeine in the diet soda, but in any case, he got up off the couch and asked if he could use her phone. Valerie showed him the phone in her bedroom and walked out of the room to give him some privacy.

Valerie expected that Paul was going to call his wife and that made her feel a little guilty because she hadn't thought to call Todd. He had been strangely absent from her life since she had been in New York. He hadn't kept his promise to come to New York once a month as they agreed when Valerie took the job, and there was a strain between them when he had come to visit. As soon as Paul got off the landline, she would call him. He might have left messages on her cell phone, but she couldn't access them. Now Valerie felt even more guilty that Todd was probably frantic. He didn't know where she was and if she had been in the path of the dirty bombs, or if she was still alive .

Paul was getting back to himself, and so what was important to him was business. Here was the opportunity of a lifetime to catapult David Collins into the limelight as a great leader in a crisis and a great philanthropist, without appearing to try to politicize a horrific catastrophe. Paul was in the eye of the storm and he could provide David with valuable information he might not otherwise have access to. Paul scrolled down his contacts in his cell phone and found David's number. Even though he knew that the cell wasn't working, it was so automatic that he hit the button on his phone to make the call. He called himself an idiot, picked up the phone on Valerie's nightstand and dialed the number, even though it was well after eleven p.m.

This was David's personal cell phone and the phone rang a number of times and then went to voicemail. Of course, Paul thought. The phone number which was showing up on David's phone was not Paul's; it was Valerie's. David would have no idea who Valerie Wilkinson was. Paul left a message and explained where he was and that he had no cell phone service and that he was calling from Valerie's phone.

Paul then dialed his wife, Debby. The irony of the situation did not escape him. David was more important to him than Debby. Debby started crying when she heard his voice. Now Paul felt really guilty for not thinking of calling her hours ago.

"Don't cry, Debby. I'm okay. The cell phones are all just making this fast busy sound, so none of them is working. I had to find someone who had a landline, and believe me, they are few and far between. I've been trying to call you."

Debby had a million questions for him, and he had some answers, but not as many as she would have liked. He tried to be patient with her, but as they spoke, it became increasingly clear to him that although he felt he was okay, anyone hearing of this disaster would be both incredulous and fearful about all that happened in New York. In one way, this could end up being a disaster far worse than 9/11. The two planes that purposely crashed into the twin towers had killed almost three thousand people. These dirty bombs had the potential to kill far more than three thousand. Millions of people had been in New York when the bombs went off. The numbers of people killed by radiation today or in the days and weeks to come, could be many times higher than three thousand.

Paul realized that Debby was a source of valuable information for him. He didn't know what the rest of the country was hearing and it might well be very different from what he knew. If he could put together info from what Debby knew and what he knew, this could give David Collins the edge he needed to become the next president of the United States. If it was because of the help Paul had given David during a time of unprecedented national crisis, well then Paul had just punched his own ticket to a major job in the administration, maybe even as chief of staff.

After a few more minutes on the phone, Paul found out that the information being disseminated around the country was sketchy, and there was nothing new. Most of what was out in the media was rumor and conjecture. Maybe this presented another great opportunity for Paul. Since there wasn't much information out there, the real time information he had might prove to be invaluable.

"Listen, I will tell Valerie—this is her landline— that you might call back if you find out anything. If not, I will call you again tomorrow. This phone is in Valerie's apartment, and my apartment is down the hall. There are a few more people who want to use this phone to call their families, so I gotta go. Leave a message on her voicemail if there is anything. I'll tell her to check her voicemail and let me know. Otherwise, I'll call you tomorrow. Love ya. Bye for now."

A few seconds after Paul hung up the phone and before he could even walk out of the bedroom, the phone rang and it was David Collins. David sounded truly worried about Paul. "My God, Paul, where the hell are you? We know you're in New York. Are you okay?"

Paul tried to sound calm and in control, but as he answered David's questions, he thought he sounded less sure of himself and the situation. This was not how he wanted to appear to David, but the gravity of the situation was sinking in. Paul tried to shake off how he felt and said, "David, there's so much going on and we don't know much. I'm safe in the apartment building, and I can tell you what I can see and hear. I'm not that far from the newest Ground Zero. This is a great opportunity for you. We have to figure out how to capitalize on this for you."

"How is this a great opportunity for me? This is a disaster of epic proportions. We don't know how many people are dead and if New York City will be a ghost town."

Paul wanted to scream on the other end of the phone. This guy couldn't be that dense. "I think that you and I and Andrew need to talk about some strategies. Maybe you should spearhead a relief operation. Collect donations. Buy tons of food to send to New York. Make a huge donation of your own money for food or medicine. You'd really be doing some good for a lot of people who are going to need it. You will be perceived as the greatest philanthropist of our time, not to mention that this is the kind of leader people want. They would want this type of leader to be the president."

"Yeah, I get it. Of course. I'd be doing good things for the country and it wouldn't hurt that I was seen doing good things."

Paul could almost see the light bulb come on over David's head. Paul knew that Andrew would get it in a second. Maybe he should have called Andrew first, but he didn't want to give up the brownie points with David. Paul knew that he could probably just leave this idea with David and let Andrew run with the ball, but he didn't want to be cut out of the loop. After all, it was his idea.

"The three of us should talk tomorrow morning. We don't want anyone else to beat us to the punch. Right now I'm in a neighbor's apartment using her phone. I don't know when and if my cell will be working, so I might be using this phone with this number again. My name won't come up on your phone. Let me call you tomorrow morning and you can conference in Andrew. Call him tonight and tell him what I said."

"Okay, good work. I want you to be careful. I want you to be safe." Paul was touched by the tone in David's voice. Paul had grown used to a much more rough and tumble environment, where emotions were kept under wraps. David surprised him.

"Thanks, David. Talk to you tomorrow. Bye."

Chapter 50

WALLY

Wally ran out of patience waiting for Akram to finish putting all the money in the master account. The guy was usually so quick, thorough and willing to please. Maybe that was the problem. Akram was probably trying to be too thorough. Right now Wally couldn't care less if they missed a few stray accounts. He was sure by now that Akram had probably gotten the vast majority of the accounts moved.

He buzzed Akram on the intercom. When there was no response, Wally was angry. This was not the time for coffee or bathroom breaks. There was important work to be done. Wally slammed the phone down and charged out of his office to find Akram. The door to Akram's office was open, but he was not in the office. Wally turned on his heel and walked down the hall to the bathroom. He banged on the door with his palm. "Akram, you in there?"

The voice that answered him was two octaves lower than Akram's and clearly was surprised that Wally was banging on the bathroom door. Definitely not Akram. So where was he? Wally walked up and down the hallway, looking into each office and getting more and more agitated that he couldn't find Akram. The few offices whose lights were on were empty. There were two small empty offices which were dark. Wally stormed back to Akram's office. The lights and computer were on. Wally walked behind the desk to look at the open computer screen. Akram had the computer program open and it appeared he was in the customers' accounts. That was where he was supposed to be, and it looked as if he had been working on accounts starting with the letter "T."

Wally hurried out of the office and asked the one other employee who had been in the bathroom when Wally knocked on the door, if he had seen Akram or had seen him leave the office. He said no. Could he have gone out to get something to eat? This seemed an unlikely scenario in Wally's mind, especially since he had been pushing Akram so hard to get the money into the master account, to say nothing of the fact that there was radiation in the air. Wally walked back into his own office and sat down at his desk. He checked the master account and saw that there was a large sum of money in the account. Wally didn't know if this was all the money or not.

He tried calling Akram on his cell phone, but the cells were not working and he only heard the fast busy signal. Something was wrong, but Wally couldn't put his finger on it. Akram was a nearly perfect employee. He did everything Wally asked him to do, and he did it quickly. He was a quick study. It didn't seem that Akram had become very Americanized in his lifestyle. The imam said that Akram was a faithful follower and was at the mosque every week. That was usually the first indication that things were changing in a Muslim's life—when he started missing weekly prayers at the mosque.

Something was wrong, but Wally couldn't identify what was nagging at him. He walked back into Akram's office and looked around again. All of a sudden it hit him. When Akram was in the office, his cell phone sat conspicuously on the right-hand side of his desk, with the blue light of the phone blinking contentedly. The cell phone was gone. Then there were the real telltale signs. Akram's coat and baseball cap were gone from the coat rack from the corner of the office. Akram has been spooked for some reason. He had bolted out of the office and was gone. Wally had no idea how long he had been gone. He tried to remember exactly what time it was that he had last been in Akram's office and spoken to him. Wally had no idea because he had been so focused on what he himself was doing.

This could turn into a real problem. Apparently, Akram was not the faithful follower that Wally and the imam thought him to be. Wally had to decide what to do and what was most important to the mission right now. Akram would have to be taken care of. He knew too much and was a very bad loose end. Wally knew where Akram lived. He would need to have someone go there and solve the problem. At this moment, Wally had other more pressing things to take care of.

Chapter 51

VALERIE AND TOM

Tom needed a few moments to compose himself after the call with Amy. The best way to do this was to focus on his patients. He called Sue on her cell from his landline, but the calls still were not going through. He tried calling his office phone, but all it did was ring and go to his voice mail. He tried Sue's number that went to the phone on her desk. That went to voice mail also. He assumed that Sue was still down in the Emergency Room. He didn't want to call Betty Crowley in the Transplant Unit right now because he knew they were shorthanded in the unit and she probably didn't have much information from the ER. The ER and the transplant units were as far apart in the hospital as was possible, in an attempt to keep the immunocompromised patients away from people presenting with unknown diseases and germs in the ER.

He walked back to Valerie's apartment and knocked on the door. "Hey, Valerie, it's Tom."

Valerie looked through the peephole this time and then let him in. "Paul is on the phone in my bedroom, so while we're waiting for him, let's move some of the stuff into your apartment so you can put it into your refrigerator, and then we can finish up and bring the remainder to put in Paul's refrigerator."

After a few minutes, Paul came back into the living room and Brendan then went to call his wife.

Paul said, "I'll move the rest of the stuff into my fridge while Brendan is on the phone with his wife." After the food and the remainder of the things on the rolling cart were moved to Paul's apartment, they ultimately ended up back in Tom's apartment.

Paul said, "I'm beat. I don't think there's much else we can do tonight. I worked it out with Joel that he'll stay in my apartment, since you already have Brendan staying with you. Let's get together tomorrow morning and see if things have changed and then we can decide if there's anything we can do." With that, Paul closed the door and left.

"Well, so far he's playing nice. Maybe Brendan was wrong about him. I guess we'll have to wait and see. I'm not much of a drinker, especially since I don't drink before surgery, but tonight I could really use a drink. Want a beer, Scotch, or wine?"

"Yeah, what are you going to have?"

"I'm thinking of a single malt Scotch. But have what you want."

"How about a Merlot or Cabernet Sauvignon?"

Tom brought out two glasses and the bottle of Merlot. "Give it a minute to breathe while I get the Scotch."

"This has been quite a night. I'm exhausted and exhilarated at the same time. I keep thinking of what we're going to tell John 'the stuffed shirt' concierge and management. I suppose that I'll have to pay for the restaurant damage. I also can't imagine what my partners are going to do when they hear I used a forklift on a metal grate. You know Brendan can't wait to tell them."

"Look, we're all in this together. We'll all chip in. I just hope that we have to deal with that sooner rather than later. None of us has had a real chance to reflect on this whole problem. I'm not sure how I'm going to feel about this in the morning, if we don't have some good news. I tried to be the brave father when I was on the phone with Amy just now. Who knows?"

"How about we do what I tell my clients *not* to do? For tonight, we do the 'ostrich' imitation and stick our heads in the sand. Let's talk about something else. Tell me about your work. I got a very condensed version when we first met. I think transplants must be so interesting and so rewarding."

Surprisingly, the conversation moved from Tom's work to his kids and Laurie's death in not too long a time. Valerie was a good listener, which was born out of being an even better questioner from her job. Valerie was not just being polite. Tom was a kind person and that came through in a short time.

Valerie lived in a world of litigation where everybody was tough. She wasn't used to kindness, compassion and collegiality. She lived in a male-dominated world where most of the hot shot litigators were men, whose egos could fill Madison Square Garden.

Despite her resolutions when she had first arrived to take advantage of being in New York and all it had to offer, she had been bogged down in work. She hadn't been to a Broadway show or a museum, or a professional baseball or football game. When Tom then turned the conversation around to her, she felt a little embarrassed that her life was so one sided. She had war stories, but she wanted more than that. It was a refreshing change that Tom wanted to hear not only about her work, but about her.

He was also a very good listener, a quality she prized. Even though his work was literally a matter of life and death for many people, he had a sardonic sense of humor. He was able to laugh at the mistakes he had made in his life and he had some great stories about non-life threatening mistakes the residents working for him had made.

The bottle of Merlot was almost empty when Tom went into the kitchen for another bottle of wine. He returned with an ice bucket, more Scotch and the wine. "No, don't open another bottle. I practically polished this one off myself. I haven't had this much wine in a very long time. I can't be hung over tomorrow."

"I'm not doing a bad job by myself with this Scotch either. How about a cup of coffee or decaf instead? We can both switch over."

Valerie nodded and she followed him into the kitchen. "We have all kinds of food from the restaurant, but I would really like a piece of one of those pies. I put two of them in your refrigerator." Tom was a few inches taller than she and he was definitely older. She could figure that out by the age of his children, how long he had been in practice and by the gray at his temples. When she did the math, she took a good guess that Tom was probably somewhere between fifteen and twenty years older than she. Right now it didn't seem to matter. As she stood next to him in the kitchen, he even smelled good.

Valerie stopped for a second. This was so weird, she thought to herself. They were sitting in Tom's apartment drinking, exchanging stories and now having coffee as if this were the end of a date. She had hardly even had a conversation with him before today. It seemed that the outside world didn't exist. They had done such a good job of employing Valerie's "ostrich" imitation that they had forgotten the disaster around them. Maybe for a time tonight that was not such a bad thing.

Chapter 52

THE GOVERNOR

The State of New York is also known as the Empire State. Its governor, the Honorable Nicholas Gallante, loved the moniker. New York was huge, sprawling and almost frenetic. It was an Empire, his Empire. He was in the first year of his second term as governor and he was immensely popular. He had won the election last year by a landslide. The reason for his popularity was that he had somehow managed to balance the resources of the state between Upstate and Downstate, long sworn enemies like the Hatfields and the McCoys.

He had brought jobs by luring light manufacturing and pharmaceutical companies to Upstate New York. If he was revitalizing Upstate and that economy was doing much better, it was easier to shake loose dollars from the legislature for projects such as the MTA, subways, Metro-North and the Long Island Railroad. The building of the new Tappan Zee Bridge over the Hudson River between Rockland and Westchester Counties had not only created a huge number of jobs in the construction industry, but it had also calmed the ire of commuters who fumed over being perpetually caught in traffic over a too small and antiquated bridge built in the early 1950s.

Despite the fact that Nick Gallante was the consummate politician, he was also a decent human being and the plight of the people caught in the disaster in New York City, gave him a knot in his stomach. The governor was none too pleased with His Honor, the mayor, for speaking to the director of homeland security and anyone else in Washington with a title without him. What truly pissed him off was that His Honor, the mayor, had spoken to the president of the United States without him. The president, for God's sake! He, Nick Gallante, was the chief executive officer and the governor of the Empire State and he should be speaking to the commander in chief. That definitely irked him.

Governor Gallante decided to call the president himself and then he would call His Honor, the Mayor, with help from the state. Now was not the time to straighten out His Honor, the Mayor, but that time would come. They would have a "Come to Jesus" talk, as soon as this crisis was more in hand. His Honor, the Mayor, badly needed resources from the state right now, and certainly in the future. His Honor, the Governor, was more than prepared to offer those resources and help because lives depended on it, but also because there was no better way to make the electorate love you than to offer generous help in a time of natural or manmade disaster.

The voters of the state needed to see him on TV, and they needed to see him often. Right now, His Honor, the Mayor, was trapped in a contaminated city, but His Honor, the Governor, was able to move about the state freely. However, he had already decided that he should stay at the Capitol in Albany and look "Governish," his own made up word. This was the gubernatorial equivalent of looking presidential, as he liked to say. When it was possible for people in New York City to go outside and move about, then His Honor, the Governor, and His Honor, the Mayor, would hold some joint press conferences in person.

Governor Gallante of the Empire State had a productive and positive phone conference with the director of FEMA and the president himself. His Honor, the

Governor, told everyone on the conference call that he had declared a state of emergency and called up the National Guard. He told them he was ready, willing and able to send them in as soon as he had coordinated with the mayor as to the safety of the National Guard with the radiation levels and the prized hazmat suits.

"Mr. President, I know that the mayor is over-whelmed with all that he has to deal with, and who can blame him. Nothing has ever happened like this, thank God, so there's no play book, but I will talk to him to make sure he and I are on the same page and we have spoken before we speak to you again. I know you have huge national security issues to deal with as well. We are very grateful for all your help, Mr. President. Thank you."

The call was brief, but effective as far as His Honor, the Governor, was concerned. He spoke to the president personally and confirmed who had the New York State resources at his disposal and that he was every bit the team player, but nonetheless the leader of the Empire State.

Chapter 53

VALERIE

With Tom looking on in the hallway from his apartment to make sure she got back safely to her apartment, Valerie opened the front door to her apartment and gave a quick wave to Tom before she went inside. She made sure to double lock the door. She had totally forgotten about Brendan since he was on the phone with his wife when she left her apartment to go to Tom's. The door to the second bedroom was closed and the light was out. It had been a trying day for Brendan as well, so he must be sleeping. It was probably just as well, since she didn't feel like getting into any explanation of why she had been at Tom's apartment so long.

Her apartment looked the worse for the wear after all the supplies had originally been dropped off here. It looked far different from when she left the apartment to go to work this morning. As she walked into her bedroom, the guilt hit her. She hadn't called Todd and he must be frantic by now. She rushed to the phone and called him. He picked up on the first ring. "My God, Val, are you okay? I've been worried sick. I didn't know if you were even alive." The anguish was clear in his voice.

Now Valerie had a double dose of guilt. Things had certainly been less than perfect between them since she came to New York, but she never meant to put him through hell, which is probably where he had been in the last few hours. This was all while she was enjoying a very nice evening with Tom.

They stayed on the phone for almost a half hour as she explained all that had gone on since the bombs went off, but leaving out the last part of the evening. She had the cover story that no cell phones were working and she said the land line service was spotty. Valerie said that this was the first time she had been able to get through. Todd didn't know anything more on the other side of the country than she did in New York. Valerie promised to call him tomorrow as soon as she could get through, or if he could get through first.

"I need you to take care of yourself, Val. I love you. You should probably come back to L.A. as soon as this is over. All we have here is earthquakes," he joked. It was the first light comment all day. They both laughed.

"Love you, too, babe. Call you tomorrow."

As soon as she hung up, her eyes filled with tears. She wasn't quite sure what she was crying about. Todd, the loss of their relationship, the bombs, the uncertain future of her life and God knows what else. Any one of those seemed like enough to cry about. She sat on the edge of the bed for quite a while as she thought about the day and she tried to figure it out. Maybe that was the problem. She was trying to think through what was an emotional situation. It was all too new to try to sort it out now.

Valerie caught a glimpse of herself in the mirror and then looked down at her jeans and her shoes. She couldn't go to bed this filthy. She walked into the bathroom and ran the water to warm up it up in the shower. She stripped down and threw everything in the hamper. The dirt and dust had seeped through her clothes, and even her underwear was filthy.

As the warm water poured over her, the tears poured down her cheeks. Valerie had gotten to where

she was by being tough.   There was no "tough" now.
Only raw emotions.

Chapter 54

THE MAYOR

The mayor, his aides, the deputy mayor, the police and fire commissioners were huddled around the conference table in New York City's version of the Situation Room. The mayor was adamant that they had to come to some sort of agreement between and among the most powerful people in the city, about what they wanted to tell the governor and what they wanted the National Guard to do.

Right now since the scrubbing wasn't having the immediate results they wanted, they had to deal with two extremely difficult, if not mutually exclusive choices. The first choice was to have the police and fire departments, with help from the National Guard, move people marooned in offices buildings, restaurants and schools, into large places like Madison Square Garden, armories and basketball arenas in local colleges. From there, people could be checked out for radiation poisoning, fed, housed for a short time and ultimately evacuated from the city. The mayor lamented once again that neither Yankee Stadium nor Citifield, where the Mets played, had built a stadium with a retractable roof. Each was an open air stadium. Right now the temperature outside was far too cold to relocate people to either place, since nights in New York in the fall were always cold and often close to freezing.

The logistical problem was that they couldn't merely load people into trucks and buses and relocate them. The radiation levels were too high to have people go out in the streets unprotected. That meant that they had to put hazmat suits on people before they could be moved. A daunting task at best for who knew exactly how many people.

The second choice was to have the police and fire departments, aided by the National Guard, bring food to people stranded in office buildings and stores, etc., to tide them over and buy time until the radiation came down to acceptable levels. They wouldn't have the logistical nightmare of moving thousands of people through a contaminated atmosphere, but the big questions were, how many times would they have to bring food to people and could they do it fast enough?

The fire commissioner was adamant in his position. "All I can envision is another Superdome fiasco as they had in 2006 from Hurricane Katrina. Remember what a horror show that was with people stranded there with no working toilets and the place looking like a pigsty? We all felt that no human being should be subjected to conditions like that, especially since it was engineered by the city of New Orleans. If that wasn't the worst publicity for New Orleans and FEMA, I can't think of anything which surpassed that. The New York and national media will somehow get their people in hazmat suits into those places, and we will look as bad as New Orleans. They will call it the breakdown of civilization as we know it.

"Mr. Mayor, you know I am not one for playing politics where lives are at stake, but if this plan goes south, and it most probably will, you can kiss your political career and your ass goodbye. You will be the most vilified man in New York, if not the entire United States. Sorry for being blunt with you, but this is too important a decision for us not to speak our minds and give you the best advice we can. This is the time for us to help the citizens of New York City as well as watch your back."

The fire commissioner had barely finished speaking when the police commissioner dove in.

"You are a hundred percent wrong, Joe." This, of course, angered the fire commissioner to no end and he came back with a sarcastic remark, which in turn, made the police commissioner turn red in the face.

"Cut it out, both of you. This isn't some stupid turf war. I don't want to hear it." The mayor squelched both of them and then motioned with his hand for the police commissioner to continue. "Let's hear your idea."

"We can pull this off with the NYPD, FDNY and the National Guard. We can start in four quadrants of the city simultaneously. We will evacuate people building by building and street by street in an orderly fashion. Once we bring them to a place like Madison Square Garden or a hospital for them to be checked out, if they're okay, then we evacuate them out of the city. They won't be languishing for days like people were at the Superdome. Anyone who has radiation poisoning will be given treatment. Anyone not sick, gets evacuated. We do it and move on to other people."

The mayor said, "Let's be realistic. How long do you think it's going to take to evacuate two million people? We have the folks who live in Manhattan, plus who knows how many were stuck here when the bombs went off? It could take weeks. How the hell are we going to deal with that? We don't know for sure how many people we have to evacuate, but it's probably between a million and a half to two million people."

Now the deputy mayor, who had been quiet the whole time, jumped in and addressed the mayor directly. "Look, Ryan, I think Phil is right," referring to the police commissioner.

"Everyone who's stuck in the city wants to see you do something, for God's sake. Many people are in their apartments and they have some food and they're relatively safe. They can last for at least a few days, if not longer. We evacuate the people stuck in office buildings, schools, etc. Those are the most vulnerable. We don't know if they have any food. That's going to be a huge problem because there's going to be mass panic, and people are not going to stay inside if they're starving. They'll risk going out and looting. We'll have more people exposed to potentially lethal radiation.

"Every person we evacuate is one less person we have to deal with again. We mark them off the list. The governor has said he'll help with the evacuations. We move them to Dutchess, Orange and Putnam counties for now and if we have to go further upstate, we'll do that. If we have to house people in the Capitol with the governor, so be it. He says he wants to help us in any way he can. FEMA can provide those temporary trailers for housing.

"We evacuate people in hazmat suits and then we reuse those hazmat suits to bring more people to safety. Maybe by then, that scrubbing will have worked and we won't have to put everyone in a hazmat suit. We just put them in a closed vehicle."

The mayor nodded and put his hand up to stop the police and fire commissioners from again both trying to talk over each other, or yelling at each other would be more accurate. "I'm also afraid that if we start doing food drops that we will definitely draw people out in the streets and into the contamination. We also won't know where people are coming from or what building they were in. We could easily have rioting in the streets.

"If it comes to it, we ultimately might have to do food drops, but that's a recurring thing, which isn't helping us reduce the number of people in the city. Plus, it's really going to drain our manpower.

"I want to know the exact number of hazmat suits the feds have actually sent us and how many more are on their way."

The mayor looked at the police commissioner again. "I want you to figure out those quadrants you were talking about and give me some real idea of how we break up the city. Get back to me in an hour.

"Joe, I want you and the FDNY on board with this. No push back of any kind. Got it?"

"Got it, you have my word. You're the boss."

"Okay, now I need the communications people to tell me the most efficient way of reaching people who are stuck here. I understand the cell carriers are working on the cell phone traffic, but if the cell phones aren't back on, how do people let us know where they are, so we can rescue them?

"I want to go on TV by 7 a.m. tomorrow to tell the city what we're doing. The plan doesn't have to be refined to the last detail, but I want to give them something concrete. I'm going to call the governor to tell him what we're doing and get him working on the evacuation plan and where people will be going. We meet back here in an hour for an update."

Chapter 55

WALLY

Wally was good on the computer, but not as good as Akram. The younger you were, it seemed the better you were on the computer. Wally was upset that Akram had fled the office, and that was a problem right now as well as for the future.

There would be repercussions that Akram had knowledge of the operations of the money transmitting business. More importantly, Akram obviously knew why Wally was asking to move the customers' money into the master account. Akram would have to be a total idiot not to know that by performing those actions, Wally was stealing the customers' money. The fees for the money transmitting business were taken up front, so the remaining money most certainly belonged to the customers.

Wally would have to answer questions from those brothers to whom he reported. They would be very dissatisfied with Wally. The question was, could he deflect some of that dissatisfaction to the imam. After all, Akram came to Wally directly as the result of the referral from the imam. The imam had done the initial screening of Akram or he would never have made it to Wally's office in the first place for Wally to meet him.

The imam was very well connected within the brotherhood. Would that be enough to protect him or would he be able to blame Wally as well? Those were questions that would be answered in the future. Wally supposed that at least that would give him time to reflect on the problem and perhaps be able to come up with some good explanations, or perhaps excuses.

Today's immediate problem had to do with the next step in the plan. The explosion of the dirty bombs was only the first phase, although it was monumental to have pulled it off against a city like New York, where they thought they had the best anti-terrorism units in the world. The second step for Wally, and he presumed for anyone else in the brotherhood in the money transmitting business, was to hack into the correspondent banks. They wanted to transfer as much money from their customers' accounts in the banks as they could within a very limited period of time. This was no simple feat, since banks had been so much more security conscious in recent years, and the fire walls had become ever more sophisticated.

In one casual conversation Wally had with one of his correspondent banks, the banker mentioned that as a security precaution, they had hired a company to try to breach the bank's fire walls and get into the bank accounts. Several weeks later, Wally made up a question so that he could have another phone conversation with the same banker. In the course of the conversation, Wally brought the conversation around to the company hired by the bank to try to breach the fire wall. The banker was proud to tell Wally that there was only one point on which the bank had failed the test.

Since the banker was so proud of their having passed the test, Wally was able to casually ask about the one point of failure. This banker was an older guy with a big mouth. He was living in the past when banks were brick fortresses with big steel vaults and that was more than enough security. Wally asked him about the other areas where the bank had apparently done quite well in the security test, but that gave Wally much more insight into the probed areas.

Today, Wally was supposed to hack into the banks with which he was doing business. Wally really was not sure if this was a feasible goal of the brotherhood. He had been given some instructions about how to proceed, but there were so many variables and a good deal of finesse needed, which Wally didn't think he possessed. Wally had been counting on Akram to perform this hacking.

At least Akram had performed the task of getting a sizeable amount of money into the master account which Wally would cash in, but Wally was not happy that he might have to tell his superior that he had failed in the hacking. Wally had no idea if the other money transmitters had succeeded in their hacking endeavors. Part of him hoped they would fail too, so that he wouldn't look bad. He just didn't want to be the only one who failed.

Then they would be on to the third phase of the plan, but phase three was waiting for the second phase to be completed since the second phase needed power.

Chapter 56

VALERIE

The digital clock said 7:10, but the sky looked gray outside the window. Valerie wasn't sure if it was just a dreary day or if this had something to do with the dirty bombs. The thought of the latter made her so anxious. She had been exhausted when she finally went to bed, but she had only slept well for a few hours. Then she had tossed and turned for what seemed like a very long time. The last time she remembered looking at the clock was 5:33 a.m. to be precise, so she must have fallen asleep for about an hour and a half. Her dreams had been filled with weird images and people chasing her. She couldn't remember what else, and maybe that was a good thing.

She wanted to turn on the TV and find out what was happening, but she was truly afraid to do so. She hesitated with the remote in her hand. She finally succumbed to curiosity over fear and clicked the remote. There was a banner which said the mayor was going to be broadcasting at 7:30 a.m.

Since there were still about twenty minutes until the broadcast, she got up, threw on a pair of sweatpants and a sweater and headed for the kitchen. *Do the normal things. Make coffee, have something to eat. Try to keep the anxiety at bay,* she thought to herself. Then she laughed a harsh laugh out loud as she walked down the hallway to the kitchen. "What the hell is normal any more? We might be living in a post-apocalyptic world where nothing is ever going to the same. Shit, we might all be dead in a month. Maybe we'll all be dead in a week." As she uttered those words, although quietly, her whole body turned cold.

She started making coffee almost by rote, trying to ignore the cans all over her kitchen counters. Then the flood of events from yesterday raced through her mind and she remembered that Brendan was asleep in her second bedroom. The only thought which warmed her was her few hours of respite with Tom. For a second, she questioned if the time together and the conversation really had transpired. That time together had been a gift. She needed some time to reflect on it and she wondered what Tom thought about last night. She tried to keep the good thoughts flowing, because the fear and anxiety were overwhelming her at the moment.

As much to keep herself busy and try to push away the fear, Valerie decided to heat the oven and cook the turkey. Maybe if she kept busy, she wouldn't have to think of the implications of being in New York City the morning after dirty bombs had gone off. It was now only a few minutes until the mayor was going to speak on TV. At least the coffee smelled good, and represented some semblance of normalcy. However small.

Even though she knew Brendan was in the apartment, when he said hello, he startled her. "Sorry to have scared you. I've been awake for a while, but I didn't want to get up and wake you. Once I smelled that great coffee, I knew you were up. How did you sleep?"

Valerie shrugged. "Not very well. The coffee's almost made. Grab two mugs from that cabinet behind you. The mayor is supposed to speak at 7:30. I'll go turn on the TV in the living room. If we have any appetite left after he speaks, we can eat breakfast."

It was almost 7:40 when the mayor came on TV. He had on a different shirt and tie from the ones he had been wearing last night, and looked as if he had shaved and combed his hair. Despite that, the bags under his eyes were evident and he looked very pale.

"Good morning, to my fellow New Yorkers and citizens of the United States. We have been working very hard all night and I have so much to tell you. During the night, I have had several conversations with the president and the governor, who have offered, and are making good on their offers of assistance. I have also spoken to the Department of Homeland Security, the FBI, the EPA, FEMA and the Department of Defense.

"I am going to be as honest with you as I can. There is much that we do know and there is much we do not yet know. First, let me tell you what we do know and what we are doing. The Department of Defense and the EPA think we can bring down the levels of radiation by doing a second scrubbing. The Department of Defense is sending us as much of the scrubbing material as it still has and we are going to start the second scrubbing today.

"Second, we are going to start a sweep of the city and get the people who are in the most vulnerable places out of the city first. That means people in office buildings, schools and stores where they are stuck without food, a real place to sleep or in places where there is inadequate heat. We will be sending in the National Guard with NYPD and FDNY. Now here's a little bit of the tricky stuff. Since the radiation levels are still high for the moment, the first responders will be in hazmat suits and will be bringing hazmat suits with them to take people out with them.

"Everyone who comes out with the first responders will be taken to central locations, checked out for radiation and then taken out of the city. If the person isn't sick, then that person will be evacuated and either taken home if home is outside the city, or taken to some temporary housing set up by FEMA out of the city, if home is in the city. If the person is sick, treatment will be administered. "

The mayor tried to inject a little levity. "Remember that you are not going on vacation. Don't take every piece of clothing you own. Don't bring your scuba equipment or bowling ball. Each person can take a small carryon bag, like you can put in the overhead bin of an airplane. Bring your medications and any important papers you need.

"Now we need your help on a few things. First, if you are in a place like an office building or school, for example, we need you to e-mail us or call us if there's a landline, to give us your exact address, what kind of building you're in, what the conditions are and how many people are there. We are going to set up four quadrants in the city and that's how we'll work the grid. If nothing works and you can't communicate with us any other way, hang whatever you can outside the building, something like a white shirt. The cell phone carriers tell us they are working feverishly to get the cell phones up and working again, which will make things a lot easier. We are posting the numbers and e-mail addresses on the bottom of the screen and they will stay up on the screen even after I go off the air.

"The second thing we need your help on is that it is IMPERATIVE that you stay inside. DO NOT go outside yet for any reason. You will become sick from radiation poisoning. STAY INSIDE until you hear from me that it is safe to go outside or the first responders come to get you.

"The third thing is that if you are home or in some-one else's apartment, you need to work together and share what you have. Check to see how your neighbors are doing. Check on anyone living alone or anyone with young kids. Check on the elderly or anyone with a handicap. Be smart about the food you have. Don't eat everything you have in the house in one day. You might have to make the food last for a few days, be-cause the delivery man is not coming to the door with pizza or Chinese food tonight and the supermarket won't be open tomorrow.

"Be a good human being and remember that we are all in this together.

"I will speak to you again tonight.

"God bless you all, the City of New York and the United States of America."

The broadcast ended. The mayor, who appeared calm on screen, had sweated through his shirt.

He had also managed to get through the broadcast without saying that they had no idea if the second scrubbing was going to work any better than the first application, which hadn't done much. He had also managed to get through the broadcast without using the word "evacuation."

Valerie and Brendon, who were used to parsing language for their jobs, did pick up that the mayor did-n't say that the first scrubbing had been effective and they picked up about rationing food, even though the mayor didn't use that word either. The "forklift caper" was looking better and better.

Chapter 57

TOM

With all the exertion yesterday coming as it did right after he had been sick and nauseous the two days before, Tom slept well until early morning when the exhaustion abated, but the seriousness of the situation crept into his consciousness and he awakened with a start. He flipped on the TV to see the banner that the mayor was going to address the city later that morning. The only good thought which popped into his mind was the few hours he spent with Valerie last night.

Tom was used to reading people's facial expressions and body language, but that was with his patients. By the time the patients got to him, they were so sick and in need of a transplant, that sometimes their emotions were masked by the fact that they were in such bad shape. They just didn't have the strength to emote very much. He realized that he wasn't great about reading those emotions in a social setting. As he reflected on their time together last night, he was fairly certain that he had correctly read Valerie and that she was in no rush to end the time they spent together. She seemed interested and for the first time in a long time, Tom thought he might be interested as well.

Socially, Tom felt he had been out of circulation since Laurie's death. The relationship with Paula back in Atlanta was superficial. Despite the fact that Tom didn't want to admit it at the time when he took the job in New York, he really didn't take Paula into account in making that decision. He also knew that Paula was so firmly entrenched in Atlanta that she would never adapt to life in New York City. Now after having lived here for several months, he could think of about ten things right off the top of his head about New York City that would make Paula cringe, if not revolt outright. New York was growing on Tom, and he realized he liked his job, and despite all the congestion and problems, he liked the city.

It was easier to have a companion for the dinners and events, he attended. It prevented all of his female friends from perpetually trying to fix him up with their single friends, and Paula provided that cover. Until after Laurie's death, Tom had never realized what an attraction two little letters had on women. The fact that he had M.D. after his name, apparently made him an eminently eligible "catch." Tom didn't want to be a "catch," and after Laurie's death the last thing on his mind was getting back into a relationship anytime soon. But something was different about Valerie. To his own surprise, he realized he would like to spend more time with her and get to know her better. She was different from Laurie, and a breath of fresh air from Paula and her ever-present perfume.

He got up and took his second hot shower in less than twelve hours, which made him feel a little better, and the coffee was ready by the time he was out of the shower. It was too early to call anyone even on the eastern seaboard, no less anyone in the west. He tried Sue's cell phone, his office phone and her office phone with no success. Just ringing and then the voice mail came on. He tried the Transplant Unit with the hopes that he would get Betty Crowley, the head nurse on the unit. Still no answer. That made him extremely uncomfortable, but it seemed a lot of the personnel had been moved to the ER, and that's probably where they still were. If the Transplant Unit was operating on a skeleton crew, which was most likely the case, they didn't have enough people to answer phones.

The staff in the hospital was in the same predicament as other people in the city, which was that they weren't supposed to go outside and so they were stuck in the hospital. He couldn't find out if the hospital was overrun with casualties of the bombs, but his strong suspicion was that they probably were. He sat down in the chair to try to think this through. Every part of him wanted to be in the hospital taking care of incoming patients, and he considered chancing it to try to get to the hospital.

If he could get through to the hospital, maybe they would send an ambulance to get him so that he could be picked up right in front of the apartment and brought to the ambulance bays, which were just a few feet from the ER. That would give him minimal exposure to the radiation. However, since he was not getting through to anyone, it seemed crazy to think he could walk to the hospital without becoming another casualty himself.

If the mayor said in his address to the city this morning that this scrubbing technique was working and the radiation levels were coming down, maybe then he could get to the hospital. His phone call with Amy also rattled around in his brain, where he promised her he wouldn't do anything dangerous and that he would be around to walk her down the aisle at her wedding.

The address by the mayor was not what Tom and virtually everyone else in the city wanted to hear. When the broadcast went off the air, Tom sat there for a few minutes with a sick feeling enveloping him. He needed some human contact. He needed to share this bad news with the others who were in the same predicament and see their reactions. Even though it was still early, Tom took a chance that Valerie and Brendan were awake and up, and so he walked down the hall and knocked on Valerie's door. To his relief, they were both up and sitting in the kitchen.

As Valerie ushered Tom into the kitchen, and he said his hellos, Valerie offered Tom a cup of coffee and a seat at the table. "Did you hear the mayor this morning? What did you think?"

They kicked around their thoughts and although they may have focused on different parts of the talk, all three of them had the same reaction. Despite the best spin the mayor had tried to put on things, there were too many unknowns and the message between the lines was ominous.

"We should probably find out what Paul and Joel are doing this morning."

Tom did an abrupt about-face from what they were discussing. "Why does it smell so good in here?" Tom had dismissed the thought that it smelled like Thanksgiving in the kitchen, but the wonderful smell persisted in his nostrils.

"I started cooking the turkey. I think you should cook the turkey you have. It was clear the mayor was telling us we should be careful with the food we have, if not start rationing it."

"To be honest, Valerie, I have no idea whatsoever of how to cook a turkey. Do you want to do it for us?" Tom was careful to say "us" and not "me." Tom looked sheepish at best.

"It's going to take a while for this turkey to cook. Go pre-heat your oven and then I'll come in and help you. It's really not all that tough," she said with a laugh. "While the oven is heating up, you should come back here. I think we should talk about what to do. It really gives me the creeps to say this, but we might be in this for the long haul."

Chapter 58

THE MAYOR AND THE GOVERNOR

His Honor, the Governor, and His Honor, the Mayor, had numerous conversations about the state of the city. The governor had called up the National Guard as requested by the mayor, and the National Guard members were appropriately attired in hazmat suits. They had to learn how to suit up properly and they had to wait as the hazmat suits trickled in from all parts of the country. The feds had flown in a large number of hazmat suits from Washington during the first night after the bombings as they said they would, but after that the hazmat suits came in sporadically from other parts of the country. The total need for the hazmat suits far exceeded the number required by the National Guard themselves. Therefore, the city did not have anywhere near what it needed to evacuate people stranded in the city.

To make matters worse, the scrubbing didn't make as large a difference as everyone hoped in bringing down the radiation levels. The levels had come down, but not yet to levels which made it safe to go outside. The product still remaining at DOD had been sent to New York, but there was not enough left to re-spray the entire city a second time.

There had been several waves of people swamping the emergency rooms in the city. The first wave was shortly after the dirty bombs went off. There had been thousands of people who had not heeded the warnings to get inside and stay inside, or had not been fortunate enough to get inside quickly. Three days after the dirty bombs went off, there were many people who thought that the radiation was gone, since they couldn't "see" it and the city wasn't moving quickly enough to rescue them. They took matters into their own hands and went outside. This produced the second wave of very ill people coming to the emergency rooms for treatment. Social media and network TV did their best to try to dissuade more people from going outside.

The engineers at DOD were working around the clock to try to produce more of the product, but no one was sure if the resulting accelerated product would be the same as the original product. There was a good deal of dissent about producing more of the product in its current state, since the original scrubbing wasn't working all that well. Some of the engineers argued that they should continue producing more scrubbing and douse the city with as much scrubbing as possible, while other argued for a change in the composition of the scrubbing. The engineers were going to try both alternatives, but they were in uncharted waters. All of this would take time, a commodity the city did not have.

The mayor insisted that they start the evacuations as planned, although at a much slower rate than he wanted due to the physical constraints. In the first quadrant, the National Guard was able to evacuate two blocks consisting of mainly small office buildings, but by the third block they ran into trouble. When people saw the National Guard trucks evacuating people from office buildings, others ran into the street to try to get into the trucks despite the fact that they were not in hazmat suits and were exposed to the radiation. The National Guard had to contain a riot in the street and fired shots in the air to get people to go back inside. Some people had to be physically restrained as they literally tried to climb over other people to get to the hazmat suits.

A similar thing happened in the second quadrant after only two buildings were evacuated. One of the major problems was to go into a building and get the people stuck inside suited up. Some of the suits were too small and some were so large that that person couldn't walk because he was tripping over the suit. It took time to get the people dressed in the suits and then into the trucks.

Simultaneously, in the third quadrant, the National Guard went into St. Thomas Aquinas High School. Fortunately, most of the kids had already gone home when the bombs went off, but there were still kids left at the school for after school clubs and sports. The teachers had been able to keep the kids fairly calm and they rationed the food left in the cafeteria refrigerators. When the National Guard arrived in the school, the kids helped each other get into the hazmat suits and the evacuation went smoothly. They didn't have enough hazmat suits to get all the kids in the suits at one time. The Guardsmen promised they would return for those left behind. In less than an hour, the Guardsmen returned for those who didn't make the first trip. The remaining kids and the teachers were waiting expectantly, but there was no panic. There was a spirit of camaraderie as they helped each other.

In some places, the presence of the National Guard trucks, in and of themselves, was causing an uproar. Many refused to believe that the Guard would, in fact, come back to rescue them and so there was chaos as people insisted that they had to be in the first truck to leave. Many just wanted to get in the truck, even without a hazmat suit. They had to be forcibly removed from the truck and quickly brought back into the building and out of the radiation. These problems slowed down the evacuation, in some places, to a crawl. The radiation testers were still showing high levels of radiation, and as the winds blew, they changed the readings. It just wasn't safe to be outside in the radiation unprotected without a hazmat suit.

The phone conversations between His Honor, the Governor, and His Honor, the Mayor, deteriorated as well. "What the hell is going on? I'm hearing from the commander of the Guard that there were riots and a free for all! I thought you had this figured out to have an ORDERLY evacuation. And I stress the word "ORDERLY." His Honor, the Governor, was screaming.

His Honor, the Mayor, was exhausted, stressed and beside himself. His first thought was to blow the governor out of the water, but he held himself in check. He knew he needed to try to keep his anger under control, not out of any sense of misguided virtue, but also because he needed the state's resources and he didn't want to start a fight on yet another front with the governor.

"Look, Nick, we just started this process and everyone is edgy from all that's happened here. Everyone wants to be the first one on the truck to get out. You know what people are like when they want to be the first to do something. Think of what it's like when people want to get off a plane or leave a stadium. Now magnify that about a thousand times because they think they might die. We're trying to get to the people who are stranded in offices and schools first. They're the ones who have no resources, maybe very little food or perhaps no food at all. They're in the worst shape and we're trying to get to them as fast as possible. They took shelter as quickly as possible when the bombs went off and these weren't places anyone should have to stay without any resources.

"Did the commander tell you about St. Thomas Aquinas High School on West 25th Street? About how well that evacuation went? That's the other end of the spectrum. There are going to be plenty of stories like that. I went to a Catholic high school just like Aquinas, and the values instilled in those kids by that school were never more evident than today. Imagine the incredible relief of those parents when they heard their kids had been evacuated and also how well their kids had behaved.

"I really think we have to start telling those stories, instead of talking about the people who are acting like animals. I've spoken to the commander of the Guard as well, and I told him I don't want any of his men firing shots into the air. Some kid in the Guard panicked and fired his weapon. I told the commander I don't want this to happen again. It just feeds the terror and we certainly don't need that."

The governor was just as quick to respond. "Look, Ryan, I told the commander he has my approval to tell his troops to do what they need to do to maintain law and order and to protect themselves. Whatever it takes. The whole world is watching what's going on in the city. It can't seem like it's bedlam and that the inmates are running the asylum. We have to be in charge and it has to show to everyone."

"Oh crap, Nick, you are not running this show. You're two and half hours away sitting in your office, and the world outside your office has not turned into a shit show as it has with mine. Don't tell me how to run this city. You're not here! Now let's deal with the plans to evacuate people out of the city."

Chapter 59

AKRAM

Akram's cell phone pinged. Mohammed texted the address for his friend, Ralph. Akram entered the address in his GPS and could see that the house was close to four miles away. In the few blocks that Akram had already walked, he saw that stores were closed and the iron grates pulled down and locked. He had encountered a few people running in the streets and Akram felt himself tense up as anyone came toward him. He had clutched the paperweight in his pocket tighter each time anyone came near him, but so far anyone he saw ignored him and looked as if they were intent on getting to their destination.

He had not seen any buses running, and had seen a few cabs when he first left the office, but the off duty signs were on. As Akram turned a corner, he saw a police car with the speakers on telling people to get off the streets as quickly as possible or shelter in place and not venture out. Akram froze against the side of the building and then backed around the corner from the block from which he had just come. He didn't think the police had seen him, and he didn't want to find out what the police were going to do to people still outside.

Akram had been pondering his choices as he walked, and neither choice seemed good. He didn't want to stay in the office with Wally, because he didn't believe in the cause of the brotherhood, since it's goal was to kill innocent people. Akram was terrified that he was a loose end to Wally and most probably expendable, since he now knew too much about Wally's stealing the clients' funds and that Wally was definitely involved with the brotherhood. Akram balanced that against walking to Ralph's house exposed to the radiation. He was praying the radiation had not reached high levels in Queens yet, and that he could get inside quickly.

Akram pulled his scarf tighter around his face and pulled his baseball cap down harder on his head. He looked at his phone and realized that he had to make a left turn into Ralph's street. It was getting appreciably colder as darkness settled on the city like a blanket, but Akram was sweating from the exertion of half walking and half running, to say nothing of his fear.

He checked the address on the door of a house in a very middle-class neighborhood, and went up the stairs. He pulled his cap off, smoothed down his hair as best he could, and undid his scarf so that it was not covering his face. Then he rang the doorbell.

The porch light flicked on and a large man answered the door. Akram hoped that he smiled at this man and introduced himself. Ralph gave Akram a genuine smile in return. "Akram, come in. Mo called to ask if you could come here, but that was a long time ago, so we assumed you went somewhere else."

Akram explained that he had to walk from the office and how long it had taken. Ralph introduced Akram to his wife, Gail. They wanted to hear if he knew anything more about the dirty bombs and what he had seen on the streets.

"We were just about to have dinner, so please come in and have something to eat with us." Ralph and Gail were so welcoming to him of their home and their dinner, that Akram got choked up. They were so typical of the Americans that Akram had met during his stay in the United States. Good hardworking people. What had they possibly done that the brotherhood hated them so much that they wanted to kill them indiscriminately?

They sat in the den and talked for some time after dinner, with Ralph and Gail asking questions about Akram's family, growing up in Saudi Arabia and his new life in America. Despite his best efforts, Akram yawned out loud. Gail asked if he would like to take a shower and go to bed early. Akram eagerly agreed. He was emotionally spent from the upheaval of the day, the fear and the long walk.

Gail showed him the bathroom and laid out clean towels for him, and Ralph gave him a pair of his pajama bottoms, which they all laughed were going to be way too big on Akram.

A little after four a.m., Akram awoke with bad cramps and a wave of nausea. He barely made it to the bathroom and vomited several times. It took him a few minutes to get up off the bathroom floor where he was sitting after vomiting. He walked back unsteadily to the bedroom. It was still dark outside, which only made Akram feel worse. He crawled back into bed and then started to shiver. About a half hour later another wave of nausea washed over him. There was nothing left in his stomach, but he still retched violently again. This continued over and over again until Akram no longer had the strength to get up off the bathroom floor. He just lay there moaning in pain.

Sometime after seven a.m. Ralph walked down the hallway and saw that the light was on in the bathroom and the door was open. As he looked in the bathroom, he saw Akram lying on the floor curled up in the fetal position. It took a few tries to get Akram to respond to him and the responses were mostly monosyllabic.

Ralph ran back to his bedroom and in his haste to grab the phone, knocked it under the bed. Gail heard all the commotion and came out of their bathroom to find Ralph kneeling on the floor fishing for something under the bed and letting loose a stream of expletives. When Gail asked Ralph what was going on, he explained what he had just seen with Akram. Ralph finally found the phone and dialed 911.

As Ralph was making the call, Gail hurried into the bathroom to see the situation with Akram for herself. She cradled his head in her hands and spoke softly to him. She wasn't even sure if he heard her, but she wanted him to know someone was there for him and that he was not alone. In the few hours after the dirty bombs had gone off, Gail and Ralph had been watching TV as the commentators explained the symptoms of radiation poisoning.

Ralph appeared at the bathroom door and surveyed the scene with Gail and Akram. "I don't know how long it's going to take for 911 to send help. They don't seem to know. They say they're swamped with calls. But I think this poor kid has radiation poisoning from walking here. He was outside for a long time walking and exposed to the radiation. I hope he makes it."

Chapter 60

THE AUSTIN

Three days had gone by since the bombs went off and the news reports were mixed. Reporters had been able to locate where evacuees had been taken upstate. For some of the evacuees, places other than New York City were home. Those people had more than enough family and friends who were overjoyed to come to pick them up. For the evacuees who lived in New York City, they were going to stay in the trailers provided by FEMA for an indefinite period of time. FEMA had put up fencing to keep the reporters and the curious out, but by the same token no one wanted it to seem that this was a concentration camp.

People going home after having been evacuated and people living in the FEMA trailers, who were free to move around as they chose, provided almost unlimited fodder for the reporters and camera crews. The stories were many and varied and the media was eating it up. There was no containing the media and it had become a feeding frenzy.

For the people stranded in New York City, it had become a waiting game. They could see that the evacuation process was slow at best.

"Considering what we're seeing on the news, we don't have any idea how many people have actually been evacuated, but if I do the math with the number of people stuck in the city, it will probably take years to get everyone out," Paul lamented.

"We're probably in better shape than most people, because we're safe. But even if we ration the food we have, it won't last forever. What the hell are we going to do?" Valerie picked up on Paul's mood. They had congregated in Tom's apartment this time. Their gath-ering place vacillated between his apartment and Valerie's. Paul had verbalized the thoughts they had all entertained at one time or another. The mood in the room was gloomy.

"We need to ration the food even more. We're not expending that many calories sitting around, so we can survive on fewer calories. I, for one, could use to lose some weight. It's just that this wasn't the way I envisioned doing it." This was Brendan's attempt at levity.

"They will probably have to do some food drops. They will not let us starve to death," Tom countered.

Paul said, "No one has mentioned a food drop at all. I've already told David Collins to announce that he will donate a hundred thousand dollars for food and that he will spearhead a drive for the nation to donate money. Millions of dollars for food will flow in and then the city will have no other choice but to distribute it. The announcement will be made in the next two hours." Paul looked particularly pleased with himself. "I, for one, am not going to sit around while this petty bureau-crat of a mayor sits with his head up his ass."

Valerie felt her mood lighten at the thought that they wouldn't starve to death. Then reality set in and she said, "If there have been riots when they tried to evacuate people and it's going to take goddamn forever to do it, what do you think is going to happen when they try to do a food drop?"

"What do you think, Tom? You've been strangely silent."

"I really don't know what to think, but I don't think the mayor, the governor and the president are going to sit by and let the people of New York City starve to death right before their eyes and the eyes of the whole world. Even if they're not human beings with hearts, they are politicians and they won't want this blight associated with their names for all eternity when they could have done something to alleviate it."

Paul was the most animated of all of them in the discussion. "I don't know how long I want to wait and do nothing. I'm willing to sit on my hands for a few more days, but after that I'm thinking that I'm going to take matters into my own hands."

They all turned to look at him. "What does that mean?" Tom was the first to ask.

"I might not wait around much longer. I may make a break for it."

"Going outside? That's almost certain radiation poisoning if the levels haven't come down enough. You'd be risking your life. Do you understand the implications of what you'd be doing?" The concern in Tom's voice was evident.

"Paul, if you think that your candidate is going to spearhead a giant food drop, then what's the point of exposing yourself to incredible danger, when you can stay here and be safe and wait this out? No one is going to starve to death."

In truth, Paul had a plan, but he still needed to work through it in his mind to see if it was feasible. He was keeping it to himself and the four other people were not going to be part of it. He wasn't so reckless that he was just going out in the streets with radiation in the air. He had been watching the street to see if there was a discernible pattern of police activity. Paul was hoping to go out in the street when a police or National Guard patrol was passing. From there perhaps he could convince them that he was desperate, without food or water, and maybe, just maybe, they would take him to one of the evacuation centers. From there it was his ticket out!

There was a long few moments of silence in the room when it felt like a pall had descended over everyone.

Chapter 61

WALLY

Wally was more than frustrated. He had been at his computer for more than three hours using the tools and keys provided by the brotherhood. Nothing was working. Wally wiped the sweat rolling down his forehead. He got up from the desk and paced around the room several times. "Think, think" he said out loud to himself. He was trying to clear his head. He had been at this too long and he was not thinking clearly. He needed to think outside the box. Right now he felt he was trapped inside the box with no way out. There had to be a way to hack into the banks and wreak more havoc. It also meant more money for the brotherhood and, of course, for him.

The banks, the stock market and the commodities markets had all been shut down as a precaution. Wally didn't know if it should make a difference one way or the other in his ability to hack into the banks whether they were closed or not. He doubted it did, because the fire walls were certainly in effect full time.

No one in the brotherhood had to know how much money was in the master account. Wally *always* intended to send the greatest part of that money to the brotherhood, but he needed to keep a large chunk of it for himself. After all, he was the one taking the risk and it was his business which would now be ruined. He would never be able to do anything remotely related to the banking business in the United States ever again. He would have to slip across the border into Canada and from there work his way, probably to Europe first, and then to the Middle East. He needed enough money to live comfortably for years.

Now if he couldn't hack into the banks with which he did business, there would be a whole lot less money available, for him and for the brotherhood. Wally noticed that in his thinking about the possible hacked money, he had put his own interests above that of the brotherhood. Well, that was as it should be.

Wally had been at the hacking for large parts of a few days, and he was beginning to think it couldn't be done. Maybe if that weasel, Akram, had still been here, he would have had some different thoughts about how to hack in, and possibly had different and better results. If there was no hacked money from the banks, then Wally would have to send less of the money in the master account to the brotherhood.

It had been somewhat surprising to Wally that he hadn't been successful in hacking into any of the banks. He had purposely only done business with small banks and credit unions with the hope that their fire walls would not be as difficult to breach as some of the major banks, but he obviously had been wrong so far. Wally flung the pen across the room. He hoped today, and he had hoped for several days now that he was not the only one who had failed at the hacking. What it just his own wounded pride that he couldn't do this or was it something else? Perhaps fear of the brotherhood?

With a huge sigh, Wally turned his attention back to the computer. As he was about to start typing again, the lights in the room flickered, but then came back on. The computer dimmed but stayed on. There was battery power for the computer itself, but what about the internet? The lights stayed on for another ten seconds at most and then he was sitting in the darkness. The computer screen glowed, but it was now going to be useless for his purposes.

Was this the brotherhood at work trying to cripple New York City and the surrounding areas or was this just a fortuitous event for them?

Wally was waiting for word from the brotherhood about a meeting place and a means of escape from Queens. Right now everything was at a standstill in those plans until the evacuation was under control. Like everyone else, he had heard the mayor about the evacuation plans. Wally expected that he would meet up with a few people from the brotherhood once they had been evacuated to a county upstate. There were only two other people he actually knew by face and name in the brotherhood. No one at his level knew everyone or everything, so that plans could not be compromised to any great degree.

He suspected that two or three of them would meet up and then travel in small groups to the Canadian border. One of the men he knew was married and had mentioned his wife in passing. He wore a wedding ring. Wally thought that would be an even better cover to travel as a married couple for getting out of the country. The brotherhood had probably recruited a few women to pose as their sisters or wives to pass through into Canada. From there they would stay in Canada for a while and when things calmed down after the bombings, they would go to various countries in Europe and then on to the Middle East.

The one thing that Wally would refuse to do would be to have four single men with dark complexions and Muslim names appear in a car at the Canadian border trying to leave the United States. Especially in this climate, where law enforcement would be on high alert, Wally wanted to call as little attention to himself as possible. Wally's English was so good that he could very well pass for someone for whom English was his first language. He had lived and worked in Queens long enough that he could even make it sound as if he had been born there.

Wally reminded himself that he needed to be patient. This saga was coming to an end. Knowing that the bombings were coming, Wally had a supply of canned foods, water and soda in a secret cache in the building. He was bored by the lack of variety in the food, but he wasn't going to starve and he could stay put for a while if he had to. He had told the other workers, other than Akram, to leave immediately after the dirty bombs went off, saying it was for their own safety to get home as quickly as possible. He thought they all lived fairly close, and now with Akram gone, Wally was alone and bored. He again reminded himself that this was only temporary. He started thinking of all the things he would eat and the expensive wines he would drink when they reached Canada.

More important than any of these inconveniences, was that Wally had moved the money from the master account into two shell corporations' accounts. He didn't want to have to show anyone in the brotherhood the actual amounts which had been moved into the master account from the clients' money. By putting the money in two accounts of the shell corporations, he could show the transfer right after the bombings into one of the accounts. That first account was the one he would show to the brotherhood. It contained a much smaller amount than the second account. The first account couldn't be too small as to arouse any suspicion in the brotherhood. The second account contained the lion's share of the money that Wally kept for himself and his future. His money transmitter business was finished. Realistically, he was a fugitive and probably in the not too distant future, he would be on a watch list and would never be able to come back to the United States.

He thought Allah would be pleased with him, even if the split with the brotherhood wasn't fifty/fifty.

VALERIE AND TOM

The days were boring and long because they were stuck in the apartment, but with the boredom was always the underlying current of fear and dread. They were desperate for any crumbs of good news about the situation in the city. Now that people were being evacuated, the media was having a field day with interviews and, of course, speculation. The "talking heads" on television prattled on endlessly, because that was what they were being paid to do.

Surprisingly, Paul and Joel had bonded. For two people who appeared on the face of things not to have anything in common, they somehow found activities which they both liked. In the first few days, Paul continued to go downstairs to the health club and worked out, with Joel as the lookout and guard. Once they started to ration the food, Paul stopped working out, because he couldn't consume enough calories after the workouts. With all the energy Paul had, this was working a huge hardship on him, because he felt like a caged animal. Paul and Joel were now engaged in endless computer game battles which passed a lot of time.

Brendan had become downright morose. His delightful sense of humor had all but disappeared. There were still the trips and spills, but they were fewer. He had his Kindle in his briefcase when he arrived in Valerie's apartment the first day, and now he was apparently rereading the books on his Kindle, as well as the novels in Valerie's apartment. Valerie thought it was like having a statue sitting on her living room couch. At first, she tried to engage him in conversation, but his responses were brief and often monosyllabic. With all the stress, Valerie didn't have a great deal of patience with this, and didn't think it was her job to be the social director.

The only respite for Valerie was when she spent time in Tom's apartment with him. Brendan's behavior gave her the excuse to get out of the apartment to spend more time with Tom, but the truth of the matter was, Valerie was beginning to think she didn't need an excuse. After the first night they had spent having drinks together in his apartment, Valerie was interested in spending more time with him. He seemed calm and reassuring, two traits which Valerie felt a great need for at the present time, but it was more than that.

While Paul and Joel were playing video games, Tom and Valerie started doing crossword puzzles together. In the past, neither had the time or patience to finish *The New York Times* crossword puzzles, but it was fun and satisfying to work on and solve the puzzles together. They downloaded puzzles from the internet, and Tom found a book of crossword puzzles in the apartment he had forgotten about, so they had quite a supply.

All of them were hungry. They were eating two meals a day and skipping lunch entirely. The other two meals were skimpy. They all were trying to do things which would take their minds off their hunger. If they dwelt on their hunger, then it was not a difficult jump to the ever-present danger of the radiation poisoning. They were drinking quite a bit of tea and water to try to make it seem that their stomachs were full.

Tom brought out a chess set one night. Even though it was a cheap plastic set with both chess and checker men in the box, Valerie admitted she had only a passing knowledge of chess and that she would like to learn again. Tom was reasonably proficient, and he had taught the kids how to play, so it worked well and was another diversion.

Even with these distractions and trying to keep busy, the days were interminable. They were approaching three weeks after the dirty bombs went off. Valerie was used to going to client meetings, going to the office and going to court. In the course of any given day, she interacted with a good number of people, just in the office alone. There were her partners, the associates and the staff, and she was on the phone with other attorneys. All that had come to a grinding halt. Right now she was interacting with only four other people. Mostly, it was three because Brendan was becoming more and more of a recluse. Now she was stuck within the confines of the apartment itself. Some days it felt like she was a prisoner. To make matters worse, the days were getting shorter and it seemed as if it was almost always dark.

Tom felt the same way. He had spent his professional life working in teaching hospitals. He was surrounded by nurses, residents and fellows, who looked to him for guidance with the patients. Some days he wanted to scream with all the interruptions. Even with all that, Tom loved being with the patients and fighting hard to keep them alive. Some days he just wanted a little peace and quiet at the hospital. Now he thought of the adage, "Be careful what you wish for."

Tom and Valerie had another little ritual that they adhered to each night. Since the first night when they had a drink together, each night they continued that practice. The first night they were so relieved about breaking in to the restaurant, and it seemed the situation would not last that long, so between them they had consumed quite a bit of wine and scotch. Now each night they rationed the wine and liquor they had left by putting a small amount in two shot glasses and taking miniscule sips.

One afternoon Valerie appeared at Tom's door with what looked to be a small yoga mat rolled up in her hand.

"What's this? Are we going to start doing yoga?" he joked. "I don't think I can do that, because if I throw my back out, we don't have the equipment to put me in traction."

"You idiot. This would have to be the smallest yoga mat in the world and we would have to be the size of three-year-olds to use it. I would love to see you do down dog or the lotus pose. We'd probably need a crane to get you off the floor."

Tom countered, "I'd rather see you do down dog. It would be a much more delightful view." He winked at her.

Valerie, who was almost never at a loss for words, was caught off guard. She had a split second to respond. If she had had time to consider her answer, it might have been a different one. Since she didn't have time, the response was, "Well, I just might be able to accommodate you on that, and maybe something more." Now it was her turn to wink back at him.

There was an awkward silence as if Tom didn't know how he should respond to the metaphorical door he had opened. "So what is this?" he asked. It seemed as if he was changing the subject and breaking the mood.

"This is a macramé mat a friend of mine made for me with a backgammon board on it." She held up a small pouch in the other hand, which held the playing pieces. "We used to play in law school, and frankly, we were very, very good. We would play against our classmates—for money. To be candid, we used to hustle them for money."

She handed him the mat and started to close the door behind her with other hand. Tom took the mat and her hand and pulled her to him. Valerie was a little surprised by the move. She was now pressed up against his chest and looking up into his eyes. From there it was only a brief second before she leaned in closer, closed her eyes and kissed him deeply. There was no question that he kissed her back as his tongue found hers.

Chapter 63

TOM

Perhaps the most surprised person that this was turning into a real relationship, was Tom himself. After Laurie's death, it wasn't that he had purposely tried to cut himself off from other relationships, but he had been awash in grief. When that veil finally lifted, and it felt that he had come out on the other side of the tunnel, he had already thrown himself into his work. That was pretty much how it stayed. He was stuck in a rut, and it was his comfortable rut. No risks and certainly no reward. He took the job in New York for professional reasons, not expecting to find someone to date since the reputation of New York was cold and impersonal. He also was not going to put himself out there. The hour and a half drive to Yale where Amy was at school was practically nothing and their relationship had blossomed. That was how he thought things would be and he was happy about the prospect of spending time with Amy. But that was really it for his expectations.

Valerie was like a breath of fresh air. She was smart, witty and attractive. She said she was in a relationship with this guy Todd back in California, but Tom could only remember seeing him once, and as far as he knew she hadn't gone back to the coast to see him. Now that he and Valerie were spending time together, the relationship subject came up for both of them.

The irony of the situation was not lost on Tom. He wasn't looking; she wasn't looking. Yet they seemed to have found each other. When Valerie was with him in the apartment, he realized how alone he felt when she wasn't there. They were now eating dinner, if that's what you could call it, together every night. The meals were getting skimpy. Sometimes the others joined them and sometimes they didn't. Frankly, Tom didn't care who was there as long as it was Valerie. To Tom's surprise, not one of the other three was trying to take advantage of the food situation. They all grumbled, but they still were sharing and rationing.

It was certainly less morose when he and Valerie were alone. They shared their thoughts and their anxiety with each other about what was going on, but that wasn't all they spoke about. Maybe because he was hungry all the time, Tom envisioned their relationship like an artichoke. They kept peeling away the layers and there was more underneath. What was underneath was better. They had been trapped in the apartments for almost three weeks, and one day as it was turning to dusk, Tom broached the subject he dreaded. It felt like a toothache. You knew it was there and you were afraid to poke it with your tongue, because it could hurt, but you couldn't stop yourself from doing it either. "Hey, Val, I need to ask you something." Tom was looking at the rug and not at her, as if the rug were going to magically give him an answer.

"Sure, go ahead." Valerie was working on a crossword puzzle and was not looking at Tom. When he hesitated in answering her, she looked up at him and didn't like what she saw. His expression was very serious and he was still looking down at the rug.

"What do you want to ask me?" She prompted him, but suddenly her mouth was dry.

Tom continued to stare at the rug. Now Valerie was getting upset. "What?" she asked again, but with a lot less conviction in her voice.

"I know this is a tough time for all of us. We've been placed into a situation no one could ever have imagined. You and I have been spending a lot of time together. I've been out of the dating scene so long that it's laughable. I just want to be sure that I'm reading the signs correctly. I want to know if you have feelings for me or is it that we're spending time together because, because..." Here his voice trailed off.

"Is that what you think? That I'm only spending time with you out of convenience? Oh my God! I might spend time with Paul and Joel because of this lousy situation. You and I have opened our hearts to each other and we've discussed some pretty personal things that you wouldn't just discuss with anyone unless you felt there was something special with that person. I can't believe you can't see how I feel toward you." Valerie's emotions were raw and Tom's question pushed her over the edge. Valerie wiped a tear away from the corner of her eye.

When Tom saw her wipe away the tear, he flinched. He came across the room and took her in his arms as she stood up from the table. It was more of a bear hug at first and then they kissed with a longing that expressed what both of them felt.

Valerie was the first to regain her voice. "You really are a moron, you know that?" she said with a laugh. "You *have* been out of circulation way too long. Are you always this dense?"

"I guess so," he mumbled.

The mood was shattered by a knock on the door. "Oh, shit, it's Paul. What does he want now at this moment?" The frustration in his voice was evident. "We just went from the sublime to the ridiculous."

Chapter 64

THE AUSTIN

The lights flickered and went out. Then they came back on. Another five minutes went by and all seemed well. Enough to lull you into a false sense of security. The lights flickered again, and seemed to go out with a resounding blow, as if you could "hear" lights go out.

"I think I have a couple of flashlights in the kitchen." Valerie could hear Tom rummaging around in a drawer. Something dropped on the floor, but must have dropped on his foot first, because she heard him yell "shit." He bumped into something on the way back to the living room, because she heard him yell "shit" again. The beam of light from the flashlight was strong, but the rest of the room not directly in the beam, was pitch black.

"I've got two flashlights, but I think we should try to make do with just one for the time being. I hate to say it, but once again we don't know how long this is going to last."

Valerie didn't want to seem like a wimp, but she couldn't stop herself from asking. "Do you think it's just some outage, or do you think this is terrorism?" Valerie's voice sounded a little strained to herself.

"Who knows? It's been almost a couple of weeks since the bombings, so it may just be an outage. I would think that if it was connected to the terrorists that this would have happened much closer to the bombings." Tom was making this up as he went along. He had absolutely no idea of whether what he was saying was true or not. He had picked up on Valerie's trepidation, and felt anything he could say to make her feel less upset was worth it.

"Since the bombings, I feel that the fabric of civilization is becoming unraveled. Everything we have come to know as the 'normal' in our lives is being pulled apart and we seem powerless to do anything about it. We know there's been some looting and God knows what else. I'm really scared that this is going to turn into a survival of the fittest. I have this picture in my head of a blanket coming unraveled."

"I wish I could tell you definitively that you were wrong. I hope that you are wrong. All we can do now is be tough, survive and not give up hope. Not giving up hope is the most important thing."

First Valerie nodded and then she shuddered. "Is it cold in here?"

"It isn't yet, but if the power stays off, it will be. Do you want to go get your coat? It's probably not worth it for you to get chilled or get sick. C'mon, I'll go with you to get it."

Valerie started to walk down the hall with Tom and his flashlight in tow. All of a sudden, they both realized that they didn't need his flashlight. The emergency lights in the hallway were battery operated, so the hallway was fairly bright. "Ya know, I'm thinking we should take these batteries out of the hallway lights and keep them in reserve." Valerie nodded, but kept walking. She opened her apartment door, with the key. The hallway light gave them an eerie view of the living room. Brendan was reading by the light of his Kindle.

"Hey, Brendan, how's it going? You going to stay in here reading?" Tom asked.

"Hi, Tom, yeah, I'm okay. This is another pain in the ass. God I hate everything. How much more are we supposed to endure?"

Tom and Valerie both thought it was a rhetorical question, so neither answered it. Valerie told Brendan that she came to retrieve her coat.

"Brendan, I was thinking that maybe we should try to take the batteries out of the hallway lights. We might need them. I don't have a screwdriver in my apartment, and I doubt that you have one here, but I was going to see if Paul and Joel have one. We might need some help. I'll let you know."

As they left the apartment, Valerie said, "That's really a good idea, but why are you asking Brendan to help? I don't even think he knows which end of the screwdriver to hold."

Tom shrugged. "Dunno, just trying to be polite and make conversation with the guy. He seems depressed."

They walked down the hall past Tom's apartment to Paul's. Tom made sure he called out both of their names as they were getting close to the door, so as not to startle them. When he knocked on the door, Paul opened it on the first knock.

"What's up? You guys want to come in? Careful, not to trip on anything and kill yourself."

Tom explained his idea about taking out the batteries to Paul and Joel. Joel jumped up and was very enthusiastic about the idea. "We talked about leaving the apartment door open to get some light in here, but it just didn't seem safe. I've got tools in here, but I even think we might be able to unscrew the whole unit and light the apartments with them. Let's try it."

They were all excited about the idea. It was something positive to do to help themselves and it would definitely be better than sitting around in the dark with one flashlight. Joel went into the bedroom using Tom's flashlight and returned with a large red toolbox. He rummaged around in the toolbox and came out holding two wrenches and three screwdrivers. The four of them marched into the hallway with a purpose.

As they walked to the end of the hallway, Joel noticed it first. "We're not going to be able to reach without a ladder. I'll go downstairs and get one."

Paul volunteered to go with him. "Can we take your flashlight?"

"Sure, we'll wait here. It's certainly brighter here than in the apartment."

Valerie shivered even with her coat on. Tom put his arm around her. He was being protective and perhaps even chivalrous, but there was a reward for doing so. Even through her coat he could feel her body and he liked what he felt.

Joel and Paul returned in a few minutes with the ladder. Both were sweating from the walk up four flights of stairs carrying a heavy ladder, since the ladder was in the basement. Paul was a good deal taller than Joel, so he went up on the ladder first. He wouldn't have to keep his arms raised as high over his head to reach the emergency light. Even with the wrench and all his strength, it took him a few tries to get the screws and the housing to move at all. Finally, when he got something to move, he scraped the skin off his knuckles and cut his hand. "Fuck, that hurts." His hand was now bleeding.

He worked at it some more and finally got the housing off the wall and handed it down to Joel. As Paul climbed down off the ladder, Tom said to him, "Let me look at your hand. I think we can stop the bleeding with some pressure. C'mon into my apartment. Let me clean off the wound for you and we'll put a bandage on. We can't chance you're getting an infection."

After Paul climbed down the ladder, Joel climbed up. He shook his head as he looked at the light. "This is a problem. This light is hard wired. I kinda doubted that the light was just plugged into the wall. It would probably be a building code violation. We're going to have to figure out how to undo this. Let me look at this for a minute."

Tom and Paul went into Tom's apartment. Valerie stayed with Joel in the hallway as much so that he wasn't alone as because she liked being in the light.

After another few minutes of looking at the light, Joel said. "I'm not an electrician, but I'm pretty handy. Before I try to unhook this, we're going to have to kill the power. We'll have to do that tomorrow morning in the daylight in the electrical room in the basement. I won't be able to see well enough tonight with just a flashlight."

When Tom and Paul got into Tom's apartment, Tom pulled a bottle of alcohol out of the medicine cabinet in the bathroom and some cotton and bandages out of the linen closet. "This is going to hurt when I pour the alcohol on the wound. No way around it. First let me clean off the surface dirt and then I'll use the alcohol."

"It's okay, Tom. Listen, before we do this, there's something I think you should know. When we went downstairs to get the ladder, I could swear things had been disturbed in the lobby. I know it's a mess down there, but I think that things looked different. Joel doesn't agree with me, but I still think I'm right. If I am right, that could mean that people are out and scavenging and this could spell trouble.

"We have to be doubly careful of anyone getting in the building. We now have to be careful of even going between our apartments. Tomorrow Joel and I are going to try to figure out if we can program the elevator so we can control it. We don't want just anyone being able to get in the elevator and getting off on this floor. I really don't know how any of this shit works. I'm not sure Joel does either, but we can at least try."

As Tom finished bandaging Paul's hand, Valerie and Joel knocked on the door to the apartment. Joel explained about cutting off the power tomorrow and then trying to unhook the emergency lights. With that said, Paul and Joel went back to Paul's apartment.

Tom made sure he double locked the door after they left. Once the door shut, the apartment was once again dark except for the flashlight's beam. "Still cold?"

"Yeah, even with my coat on. Can you feel the temperature dropping in here? It seemed warmer in the hall."

"Probably was. The heat was trapped in the hallway. I was going to say I'd make you a hot mug of tea, but not without any power."

Valerie eyed Tom and said, "Do you have a warm quilt on the bed?"

"Yeah, should I go pull it off the bed?"

"You really are dense. Follow me. You can warm me up in the bedroom." With that, she took his hand and led him into the bedroom. It only took her a few seconds to get undressed and get under the big quilt.

"Are you going to join me or just stand there looking stupid? I could really use some warming up."

Tom didn't need to be asked twice.

Chapter 65

JOEL AND PAUL

The morning after the blackout Paul and Joel headed down to the electrical room for the building. It was much easier heading downstairs than it had been to carry the ladder up four flights of stairs. They both had a good deal of trepidation about whether they were going to be able to figure out the electrical panel. The electrical room was in the basement, so even though it was daylight, it was dark down there.

The flashlight was a huge help because they could then read what was written on the panel. There were no circuit breakers specifically marked as emergency lights. They finally decided that the best they were going to do was turn off all the circuit breakers having anything to do with the third floor. Joel was insistent that they had to write down the numbers of the circuit breakers they turned off so that they could retrace their steps and turn on the same ones when they had finished. Neither had any paper with them. After much cursing and feeling around, they were able to locate a felt marker in the loading dock one floor upstairs. Paper seemed to be in even shorter supply.

"Just write down the numbers on the wall next to the electrical panel."

They headed back upstairs hopeful that they were going to be able to pull this off without electrocuting themselves. Joel seemed to know more about this than Paul. Coupled with the fact that Paul really didn't want to die, he was more than happy to let Joel get up on the ladder to work on the emergency lights. Paul also had the excuse of the bandage on his hand.

"I don't think that we can just cut the wires because the emergency lights are sensing that the power is off. I'm not sure what the light will do if there's no signal." It took a while for Joel to undo the wires, but after a time, he was successful. Paul and Joel started cheering as Joel handed the light to Paul. That cheering brought Valerie and Tom out of Tom's apartment and it even got Brendan to open the door to the apartment.

Joel jumped down the last three steps of the ladder. He grabbed the light from Paul. "There's a switch here. Here goes nothing." With that, he flicked the switch and the light came on. All five of them cheered, clapped and high fived each other.

"There are four emergency lights on this floor. We can take them down and put one in each apartment and have a spare. Once we get them down, then Paul and I will go back downstairs and turn the circuit breakers back on." Joel grinned at how well he had done.

It took some time to complete the task of getting all the lights undone. Brendan was even willing to stand near the ladder and hand the tools up to Joel.

"While you guys are working on the lights, I think we should try to find the control panel for the elevators. Tom, would you come with me? I don't think anyone should be alone in the building."

Paul went back into his apartment and came back out with two copper pipes. He handed one to Tom. Tom was hoping that Valerie wouldn't see this happen, but she had not yet gone back into the apartment. The look on her face said it all to Tom. There was nothing for him to say. In Tom's mind, it only reinforced the conversation he had just had with her about the fabric of civilization coming unraveled.

Little did they know that their elation over their success with the emergency lights might create a never imagined problem.

Chapter 66

TOM AND PAUL

Tom and Paul headed downstairs to find the elevator control panel. "So how's the hand feeling today?"

"Throbbing, but I took some Aleve. This is a win with the emergency lights. If we have to, we can use the emergency lights from the floors they're still renovating. Hope the power comes on before we need to do that. At least we won't be miserable sitting in the dark. But with the elevator, I have no idea what we're doing. I don't think Joel does either. He never had any reason to have to deal with any elevator problems. They would just call the repair guy."

"I'm impressed that you guys were able to figure out the emergency lights. I wouldn't have had any idea of where to start. You still thinking of trying to go outside?"

Paul was not being forthcoming. "Maybe."

"Look, that's really crazy. We're not doing that badly here. A little hungry perhaps, but really not that awful. We can survive here, but if you go outside and the radiation levels are still high, you're going to kill yourself. You're not a stupid guy; I'm sure of that. Don't do something stupid."

Paul nodded but didn't answer. The silence between them was awkward. Fortunately, they found the control panel for the elevator and the subject changed automatically. Paul let out a long whistle.

"Jesus, look at this thing. This could be something NASA would put on a space shuttle. How the hell are we ever going to figure this thing out?"

"Not to be too naive, but if the power comes back on could we Google the instruction manual?"

"I can Google it on my cell, but there are going to be schematics that will be almost impossible to read on my cell. I think we'll do better if we can look at the schematics on a laptop and print the schematics to take back down here with us. Who knows if we'll understand what we're reading. Do we even know what model this elevator is? We're really behind the eight ball on this one.

"Okay, we might as well go back upstairs. This wasn't too useful a trip. We can try your Google idea tomorrow or whenever the power comes back on. Right now we're stymied."

The power didn't come back on the rest of the day, but as it started getting dark, they were all so grateful for the emergency lights. It brought back some degree of normalcy in the apartments. Tom and Valerie worked on a crossword puzzle together and Tom found it comfortable to put his hand on Valerie's while they were thinking about the answers. Her hand was cold, so it gave him an opportunity to put both of his hands around hers. By now, Tom had put his jacket on in the apartment.

They continued the ritual of their nightly drinks, but the shot glasses weren't full. They had agreed to try to do the things to which they had become accustomed, even though it was cold. The conversations wandered all over the lot, but that was the excitement of it. They thought the familiar things would partially take their minds off the cold.

When they finished their drinks, Tom said, "Last night we started another ritual, which I liked very much."

Valerie wanted to tease him a little. "Yeah, how much did you like the new ritual?"

"Very, very much. More than you can imagine."

"No, actually, I had a pretty good idea of how much you liked it."

"Well, then I think we should extend the ritual to a second night. Let's go."

Chapter 67

VALERIE AND TOM

By the beginning of the third day without power, the building and the apartment were bone-chilling cold. Everyone had on coats and gloves, and now the hats were pulled out as well. Valerie felt gross not having taken a shower, but it was simply too cold. She also didn't want to be in bed with Tom unless she felt good about herself, and now her hair was stringy and she wanted to shave her pits and legs.

Tom thought he could smell himself and he put on deodorant and used mouthwash several times a day. He had stubble, which Valerie complained was hurting her face when they kissed. Can you believe this? he thought to himself. For the first time in God knows how long, I am making love to a beautiful woman I really care about, at a time when I smell bad. Is this some sort of cruel cosmic joke?

The lights flickered on for a second, flickered off, but then came on and stayed on. Both of them looked up. "Wait, did you hear that? Oh, my God, that's the heat coming up!" Within a few minutes, they had taken off the gloves and opened their coats. Not yet time to take off their coats, but perhaps soon.

After about an hour the apartment was close to pleasant. Paul knocked on the door and when Tom opened it, Paul told them that he and Joel were going to take the elevator downstairs, instead of having to walk down the stairs, which they were very pleased about. He said he and Joel were going to take a look at the elevator controls. Both Valerie and Tom could tell from his tone of voice that he was skeptical at best. They had taken Tom's suggestion about trying to find the instruction manual on line, but there were so many models that they didn't have a clue which was the right one.

After they left, Valerie announced that she was going back to her apartment to shower, wash her hair and get into some clean clothes. Tom said he'd do the same. The thought crossed his mind about showering together, but he decided it would be better to wait until he didn't really need a shower. There would still be plenty of opportunities.

What neither Tom nor Valerie realized was that the emergency lights in the apartments stood out so brightly against an otherwise completely dark sky. This was the beacon for the man in the black hoodie, ripped jeans and sneakers. He thought that whoever has a light that shines like that, has money, food and who knows what else. I want some of that.

He didn't believe all that shit about staying inside because of the radiation. He had been outside a few times, and he felt nauseous and had puked, but he had no food and he had run out of cocaine. Those were the two most important things to him now. He had to find both and find them soon.

He went around the back of the building. The building provided additional cover. If he couldn't get in the back, he supposed he would try to get in the front of the building. He had a hammer with him, and a gun. Both would provide protection, but he hadn't run into anyone else out on the street. He smashed the hammer into a small window with something resembling chicken wire on the inside of the window. With the butt end of the hammer, he cleared the broken glass with his hand covered with the sleeve of the hoodie. He was able to squeeze through the window, but cut his hand on the broken glass on the floor.

He found his way to the lobby by the dim ceiling lights still on. And then he found the elevator. What floor did those lights come from? He guessed a few floors that were wrong. Finally, as he was about to give up, when the elevator door opened, he thought he heard noises, possibly a TV playing. Yeah, great, I found what I need.

He walked quietly down the hall to the apartment where he heard the noise. He saw the light coming from under the door. How was he going to get in? He doubted that anyone would open a door if he knocked. And then he realized that the door was slightly ajar. Valerie hadn't pulled the door of Tom's apartment completely closed when she left to take a shower.

He opened the door slightly and looked around. No one was there in the living room. Even better. He could take what he wanted and go. As he walked into the living room, Tom walked in from the bedroom. Both were completely startled. The blood drained out of Tom's face.

"Who are you?"

"Shut up. The man pulled the gun out of his pocket. "Show me the kitchen. You got any food?"

"Okay, I can give you some food, but then you gotta leave."

"You don't tell me what to do." He motioned Tom ahead of him with the gun. "Open the refrigerator. Get a bag and put this stuff in a bag. Hurry up."

Tom really didn't know what to do. He wanted to stall to see if he could figure out a way to get the gun away from him. If he gave up what food he had, they would be in serious trouble. On the other hand, this guy could be some kind of nut who would shoot him no matter what. He also didn't want Valerie to come back to the apartment and walk in on a man with a gun.

Tom pulled a brown paper bag out of the closet. He took his time filling it with cans. He turned to the guy and said, "This bag is getting heavy. If I put more in it, it's going to rip and you won't be able to carry it."

"So take out a second one." There were only two bags in the closet and as Tom turned to pick up the second bag, the guy spotted the bottle of scotch on the counter from their evening ritual, and his eyes lit up. "Put the bottle in there, too."

Tom decided to make his move. He picked up the bottle of scotch and spun around and hit the guy flush in the face with the bottle. As he did, the gun went off and hit Tom in the chest right below the shoulder. The guy was bleeding from the face and appeared to be somewhat dazed, but he was still holding the gun. Tom had fallen to the floor and was bleeding profusely.

Valerie came back to the apartment to find the door open and a man's voice she didn't recognize talking to Tom. She stopped dead in her tracks and listened. Fear gripped her as she heard the exchange between Tom and the stranger.

Valerie grabbed the copper piping Paul had given Tom, which had been sitting in the corner of the room. She cautiously approached the kitchen, being as quiet as possible. Just as she got to the entrance to the kitchen, she heard the gun go off and then saw Tom fall to the floor bleeding. Valerie didn't think about anything. She swung the copper piping and hit the man in the back of the head. The pipe hitting against his head made a sickening cracking sound. His body hesitated for a second, his knees buckled and then hit the floor face first.

Valerie screamed. Then she ran over to Tom, who spoke to her. "Call 911. I don't know if they'll come, but I need help." He looked pale and as if he was going into shock.

Chapter 68

VALERIE

Valerie felt her own heart rate go into overdrive as her adrenaline kicked in. Valerie grabbed the first thing she could get her hands on, which was the kitchen towel. She wadded it up and applied pressure to the wound.

"Okay, I'll get help." She didn't know what to do first, call 911 or find more towels to apply to the wound. She raced into the hallway, yanked open the door to the linen closet, and grabbed as many towels as she could. As she returned to the kitchen, she could see that the kitchen towel was turning red. She had to step over the body of the intruder to get to Tom. She pressed the new towel onto the wound and put Tom's own hand on it. "Hold this. I'm calling 911."

Again, she stepped over the prone body of the intruder and ran into the bedroom. She grabbed the phone and dialed 911.

"911, what's your emergency?" Answered a female voice.

Valerie was so breathless from fear and adrenaline that she almost couldn't talk. "We had an intruder come into the apartment and he shot the owner. His name is Dr. Amendola."

"Is Dr. Amendola still alive?"

"Yes, but he's badly injured. He needs help NOW."

"Okay, what's the address?" The disembodied voice seemed just one step away from being mechanical.

Valerie screamed the address into the phone. She repeated the apartment number twice.

"Is he conscious? Can he talk to you?"

"Yes, I'm applying pressure, but he's bleeding pretty badly. Stop asking me these questions. Just send HELP!"

"Okay, ma'am, I've already dispatched a unit. Are you hurt or is anyone else hurt?"

That question finally penetrated Valerie's brain, which had somehow managed to block out that she had hit the intruder with a copper pipe.

"Yes, the intruder is hurt, too."

"Alright, I will tell EMS that there's a second injury. How badly is the intruder hurt?"

Valerie was rapidly becoming hysterical and it was evident in her voice. "I don't know. I don't know." Now she was screaming into the phone.

"Alright, try to stay calm. I've sent EMS."

"Okay, hurry." Valerie hung up and raced back into the kitchen. Tom was lying on the floor and he was still conscious. "I called 911 and EMS is on the way."

For the first time, Valerie looked at the intruder and saw an increasing pool of blood on the floor near his body. Valerie gagged, but caught herself.

She applied more pressure to Tom's wound. Her hand had blood on it, as did Tom's. "Is he still alive?" Tom asked.

"I dunno. I'm not touching him, but there's a lot of blood on the floor near him."

"What happened to him?"

"I hit him with the copper pipe after he shot you."

Another thought jumped into Valerie's mind. This was the first rational thought and not driven by adrenaline, that had come into her mind. "Shit, how is EMS going to get in the building? The front door is locked. Let me get someone to open the door."

Valerie dashed out of the apartment. She hesitated for a second out in the hall. She didn't know if Paul and Joel had come back upstairs yet. Her best hope was Brendan. She ran to her apartment yelling his name. He opened the door a crack and Valerie pushed her way in.

Brendan looked terrified. He had heard what he thought was a gunshot and a scream. In a torrent of words, she told him what had happened and that she needed him to open the front door for EMS. "When you get downstairs, start screaming for Paul and Joel and send them up here. Go! EMS will be here any minute."

Valerie went back to Tom. She changed the blood soaked towel and now she applied a lot of pressure. Tom groaned in pain. After a few minutes of really leaning on the wound, she thought the bleeding was letting up a little. Then she heard banging on the front door and Paul was calling her name. She jumped up, ran through the apartment and opened the door. Paul followed her into the kitchen as she explained briefly what happened. He told her Joel stayed at the front door with Brendan.

As Paul walked into the kitchen and looked at the bloody scene, he said, "Crap, what happened in here? It looks like something out of *Helter Skelter*.

"I already told you."

"Yeah, you said you hit the guy, but he's dead."

"Shut up and help me with Tom."

Paul bent over Tom and started applying pressure. Valerie took a step back and now surveyed the bloody scene. It was gruesome. She retched and ran into the bathroom.

When she returned to the kitchen, she said to Tom, "Just hang in there. EMS will be here."

Tom looked up at her and nodded, but he didn't say anything. His breathing was shallow.

"How long has it been since you called them?" Paul asked.

"Shit, it has been well over a half hour. Where the hell are they?"

"I guess they're not responding as quickly as they would have before the bombings."

In reality, NYPD, FDNY, and the National Guard more than had their hands full. They were trying to do the evacuations as quickly as possible, but it was a task of monumental proportions under extremely difficult decisions. By the same token, they didn't want anarchy to prevail, because they thought that anarchy would beget more anarchy. There were a small number of units still assigned to answer emergency calls. Tom was lucky in that there was a unit close to completing a call not too far from the apartment.

The EMS workers and the two police officers arrived outside the building in hazmat suits. They shed them in the lobby so that they could walk and work on the injured more efficiently. However, getting out of the hazmat suits added to their response time and precious seconds were lost to Tom, in addition to what seemed like forever in response time to Tom and Valerie.

Shortly thereafter, there was banging on the door and two EMS workers came in with two NYPD officers. Brendan and Joel followed them in. They stayed in the living room.

It was tight in the kitchen with Tom, Valerie, Paul, the dead body and two EMS workers. Paul gave way to one EMS worker and ushered Valerie to the entrance to the kitchen where the two NYPD officers were standing. The other EMS worker bent over the intruder and felt for a pulse. He looked up and shook his head no. Then he went over to help with Tom.

The older of the two cops got the message from the shake of the head from the EMS worker. He looked at Paul and Valerie and said, "What happened here?"

Valerie shrugged, since she was having trouble putting words together. As she pushed her hair away from her face, her hand was shaking visibly. The cop looked at Paul standing in the doorway to the kitchen as well. The cop turned to Paul and pointedly asked the same question, "What happened here?"

Even though Paul had never witnessed a crime scene before, and he was unnerved, he had not been the prime actor in this horrific drama, and the rational side of his brain was working much better than Valerie's. He was hoping to divert some of the attention away from Valerie and perhaps give her some time for her to think and not just run on adrenaline. "I dunno. The dead guy somehow broke into the apartment and shot Tom."

One of the EMS workers said that they were ready to move Tom. Paul moved Valerie out of the doorway and squeezed her hand hard to get her attention. He was standing close to Valerie and mumbled under his breath to her, "Keep your mouth shut with the cop."

The two EMS workers finally had Tom on a gurney and were beginning to try to wheel him out of the kitchen. They had taken his vital signs, as well as putting on pressure bandages and an oxygen mask. He looked ashen and his eyes were closed. As they walked through the living room, Valerie took his hand and called his name. He opened his eyes with some difficulty, smiled at her and closed his eyes again.

"I want to go with him. Where are you taking him?"

The cop blocked her way. "Hold up. You're not going anywhere. No one has answered my question about what happened. We have a dead body lying on the kitchen floor. We have a piece of copper piping next to the body with blood on it and we have a gun. Someone's fingerprints are going to be on the gun and the copper piping. You two are being taken into custody and we'll let the Assistant D.A. in charge of intake sort this out."

"What, are you crazy?" Valerie asked. Paul poked her in the back again. The cop couldn't see Paul do it. For his entire adult life, Paul had been about Paul. Everything he did and said was calculated to push his career forward, become successful and make a lot of money. He could have thrown Valerie under the bus with the cop and tell him what he had seen when he came into the apartment and what she told him. But he didn't. He made a calculated decision to put himself in jeopardy to help Valerie. Despite the tragedy in New York City and the tragedy in this very apartment, and maybe because of these, Paul did one of the first selfless acts of his life. Paul let himself be arrested with Valerie, in part to stay with her and be able to help keep her calm, and in part to create some reasonable doubt as to what had happened, which he thought would work in Valerie's favor.

The older cop told the other officer to call in the crime and secure the crime scene. "Stay with the body until the medical examiner arrives, and don't let anyone touch the gun and the copper pipe until the crime scene unit arrives." The copper pipe was in plain sight, as was the blood on it.

Valerie still looked dazed, but some of the adrenaline high was wearing off and Paul's admonition to her was finally sinking in, as was her training as an attorney.

As the cops put handcuffs on Valerie and Paul, the older one recited the now familiar Miranda warnings. "You have the right to remain silent. If you give up the right to remain silent, anything you say can and will be used against you in a court of law. You have the right to an attorney. If you can't afford an attorney, one will be appointed for you by the court. Do you understand these rights?"

Valerie still couldn't think clearly. She tried, but her brain wasn't working the way it was supposed to.

Brendan, who had been virtually useless since the bombings, now stepped up to the plate big time. "I'm coming with you. I'm Brendan Stewart and I'm their attorney."

"Yeah, right," said the cop. He eyed Brendan up and down. Brendan looked more like a homeless person than an attorney.

Brendan drew himself up to his full height and puffed out his chest like a Ball Park Frank. "Officer, I am more than happy to show you my card." With that Brendan reached into his wallet and handed his business card to the cop. For good measure, he also handed the cop his Secure Pass, with his picture on it. This was the card attorneys used to be able to bypass security and metal detection in the courthouses.

The cop looked at the two cards and then back at Brendan, whose hair was a mess and needed a shave. His clothes were rumpled. The picture of Brendan on the Secure Pass was a far cry from the man who was standing before the cop. He handed the two cards back to Brendan, and shrugged. "Okay."

The seriousness of the situation finally dawned on Valerie. It was as if the blanket of fog in her brain was lifting. She asked the cops if she could have a minute with her attorney. The two cops stepped back.

Valerie leaned forward and whispered to Brendan. "Do you know what you're doing? Do you have any experience in criminal law?"

He whispered back, "Absolutely none. I only know the Miranda warnings from television. But I'm all you've got right now."

Was this the second cosmic joke for Valerie? The first being that she and Tom found each other amidst a disaster of epic proportions. People were dying and New York City might never come back, yet she seemed to have found real happiness with Tom. She prayed he would pull through. Now she might be ripped away from Tom if she was convicted of manslaughter or some other felony. If she was a convicted felon, she would go to jail, be disbarred and her career would be a smoking pile of ashes. Her whole life as she had come to know it, might be over.

Chapter 69

VALERIE

Sometimes after the fates have been cruel, they smile on the victims. It appeared that was what happened with Tom. His choice to be able to walk to the hospital from his apartment was now about to work to his benefit. Matthews Memorial was the closest hospital, so that was where EMS took him.

As the adrenaline wore off a little and the flight or fight instinct receded, Valerie was starting to return to her old self. As they were taking Tom out of the apartment, Valerie asked where they were taking him. The answer of Matthews Memorial was a ray of hope. She said to the EMS workers, "Dr. Amendola is an attending at Matthews Memorial; he's a transplant surgeon. Make sure they realize who he is when you bring him in to the ER."

The EMS workers looked a little surprised considering the mess the apartment was in, but said that they would definitely tell the doctors in the ER. That made Valerie feel a little better, knowing Tom would get special care.

Now that her head was a little clearer, she also said to Brendan, "Call Randy Cunningham." He was one of their partners who had done a lot of criminal work as a young lawyer. "His contact info is on my phone. Pull it out of my pocket and call him NOW! Tell him I need him to represent Paul and me."

Brendan nodded and did as he was told. Those two pieces of information, the one about where Tom was being taken, and calling Randy, would ultimately make a tremendous difference for Valerie.

Under normal circumstances, Brendan would never have been allowed to ride in the police van with Valerie and Paul, but the circumstances in New York were still anything but ordinary. The other bonus was that it was going to take some time to get everyone into hazmat suits to be transported. Especially in Tom's condition, this suiting up was going to be a tremendous challenge. While this process was taking place in the lobby, Brendan called Randy.

Randy answered his cell phone thinking from the name on the screen that it was Valerie, so he was surprised that it was Brendan. As Brendan gave him the gist of what had transpired, the surprise for Randy gave way to incredulity. He had been in Westchester for a court appearance when the dirty bombs went off, and he was stranded there because his apartment was in Manhattan. He asked to speak to Valerie and although she was handcuffed and seated on one of the chairs in the lobby, the suiting up was taking enough time, which allowed her to speak to Randy as Brendan held the phone to her ear.

"Valerie, are you okay? Are you hurt?" Once Randy had ascertained that, he said, "Shut up and listen to me. Remember that now you are not an attorney. You may well be a defendant in a criminal case. You DO NOT talk to the police or the D.A. Tell Paul the same thing. It seems that Brendan is going to be able to go with you and that's a plus. At least we'll know where you'll be. I'm stuck in Westchester and I can't get back into the city. I have no idea how they are going to be handling arraignments because no attorneys can get into the city or get to court from anywhere else in the city. I'm guessing that this is going to have to be done on the phone. Memorize my phone number so you can call me, because you're going to have to give Brendan your phone or it will be confiscated since you are in custody. If I have to relay what to do to Brendan on the phone, I will, but I would rather talk to the D.A. I think the D.A. is going to make the decision to charge you with a crime or not, and if so, what to charge you with.

"Now listen really carefully. This case is going to come down to timing. It's going to be really important that there was virtually no time between when you and Tom thought you were threatened by an intruder with a gun who shot Tom, and you tried to defend yourself and Tom, and when you actually hit him with the pipe. Do you understand what I'm telling you? This is going to turn on the issue of self-defense. You got it?"

As the shock of what had just happened wore off, Valerie was able to understand the nuance. If she hit the intruder in self-defense, that was one thing, but if she hit him after a period of time after he shot Tom, that was something else. "Okay, got it. Randy, I'm so scared. This last hour has made the horror of what we've been living through after the dirty bombs even more of a nightmare. I'm really scared." With that Valerie choked up and the tears ran down her face.

"Valerie, it's okay. I'm going to help you, but you've got to get a grip on yourself. I'll be doing the heavy lifting. Just hold it together and keep your mouth shut." Just as Randy finished his sentence, the cop came over to take Valerie and Brendan took the phone away from her ear.

Brendan told Randy that they were taking her and he was going to get into a hazmat suit. Randy was adamant when he responded. "Calm her down and keep her quiet. Those are your two major jobs now. Let me know when you get to the jail or wherever they take her and what the procedure will be. I'll be waiting with the phone in hand. Don't mess up, Brendan. You can do this."

Chapter 70

VALERIE

When they got to the holding center for the court, it was bedlam. Despite the pleas from the mayor and from NYPD, some people had still ventured out. People had been arrested for an assortment of crimes, including assault, looting, robbery and many of the other crimes in the Penal Code. Those who had been arrested were being put in holding cells and were milling around in the holding cells waiting for their cases to be called. Valerie slumped down in a corner of the room, and tried go over the events in her head. She was physically and emotionally exhausted.

After people were brought in to the holding center, they were processed according to whether the person was being accused of a felony or misdemeanor. That proved to be a good thing for Valerie and Paul, because an Assistant D.A. was screening the people accused of a felony to determine exactly what crime to charge them with. If they were going to be charged, they would then be arraigned by one judge, and the people charged with a misdemeanor before another judge. There were at least triple the number of people to be arraigned on misdemeanors. When Valerie and Paul were brought in to speak to the Assistant D.A., he was surprised that there was an attorney on site for them. In reality, if Brendan really knew anything about criminal law, he could have had a thriving practice from all the jailed people who wanted him to represent them. While Brendan was waiting for Valerie and Paul's case to be called, he had ample time to go over everything again on the phone with Randy, since it was a good four or five hours before their case was called.

At first, the D.A. was skeptical about the fact that Brendan was really an attorney based on his appearance, so once again he had to show his business card as well as his Secure Pass with his picture on it. As they sat in the room with the D.A., Brendan then put Randy on the speaker phone with the D.A. to hash out the case. With the sheer volume of cases facing a very short staff of D.A.s., Randy was able to make the case for self-defense, which seemed more reasonable than many of the other outrageous stories the D.A. was being told. Perhaps in a different time before the dirty bombs, the D.A. might have wanted to split legal hairs over the timing and the self-defense issue, but now he was only going to be able to prosecute the clearer cases, those with nothing muddying the waters.

Once the D.A. determined that he wasn't going to charge Valerie and Paul, they and Brendan were escorted to another staging area, where they were once again going to be put in hazmat suits and transported to one of a number of centers to be checked out physically. If they were not ill, they would be transported out of the city as part of the mayor's evacuation plan.

While they were waiting, they were first ushered to a cafeteria where turkey, ham, tuna fish and peanut butter and jelly sandwiches were piled high and had never looked so good. There were huge kettles of chicken soup and tomato soup, which smelled wonderful. Before Valerie went in to the cafeteria, she hung back and called Randy. "How can I ever thank you for what you've done?" She had held it together for so long and now with that simple question, the tears started to flow again. She wasn't just crying that the case was over, but also because this part of the long nightmare was coming to a close.

Randy felt such a sense of satisfaction over what he had accomplished for Valerie. He hadn't felt this good over any case in a very long time and most of his cases were much larger than this. "Hey, Valerie, we make a very good team. You get arrested and I get you off. All kidding aside, I can't tell you how happy I am that you thought to call me, and that I was able to help you. I hope those are tears of joy I hear."

Valerie was wiping her eyes on her sleeve and weeping unabashedly. "Randy, I owe you so much. My whole life could have been over if I was charged with murder or manslaughter. You're the best partner and friend a person could have."

Randy was more than pleased to hear this. He had liked Valerie from when she first came to the New York office, but he felt that it would be tacky to start dating his partner. They had lunch together fairly often, but with some of their other partners. Randy had not been able to figure out a graceful way to ask her out, without her seeing it as a date.

"I'm stranded in Westchester. I rented an apartment, so you can feel free to come here if you want to, when they transport you out of the city, until you get your bearings about what you want to do."

"Thanks for the offer. It's probably premature until I know where we're going, but I may very well accept your offer. Let me go now, since I think there's some food in the cafeteria calling my name. I'm not sure anymore when I last ate and even then, we were rationing food. I'll call you when I know something. I memorized your cell phone number as you told me to do, so I won't forget to call. Thanks so much again, Randy. Bye."

As Valerie headed into the cafeteria, her head was swirling with all that had gone on, and she badly needed something to eat. She thought that in fifteen minutes with something in her stomach and perhaps a little clearer head, she could then try to figure out how to find out about Tom.

Chapter 71

VALERIE, PAUL AND BRENDAN

As they sat in the cafeteria, Paul thought that chicken soup had never smelled so good. He already had consumed two bowls of the steaming soup, and now he was working on a turkey sandwich. Valerie found Brendan and Paul sitting at a table after she chose tomato soup and a ham sandwich.

"I need to thank both of you for all you did. Paul, thanks for not throwing me under the bus with the cops and for making me keep my mouth shut. I was in shock and my brain just was not working."

Paul smiled. "You know, Valerie, after the dirty bombs first went off, I thought you were a royal pain in the ass, but I have grown to really like you. In spite of myself. Hey, when do I get to drive the forklift?"

Valerie then turned to Brendan. "I need to thank you too, Brendan. You stepped up at the moment I needed you. You probably have a promising career as a defense attorney." She said that with a smirk on her face.

"I would have had a heart attack if I really had to face a judge on this case. It's so good that you thought to call Randy. As I said to you, my knowledge of criminal law is limited to one course many years ago in law school, and the Miranda warnings from watching *Law & Order* on TV."

"Especially because of that, you were brave to step up."

Before Brendan could reply, Paul said, "As bad as this whole situation has been, maybe we all learned something about courage when it was needed from each of us. That was a pretty amazing thing that you did to save Tom from that dirt bag. Somebody else might have just frozen in place. You stepped up too and you might have paid a terrible price for it."

At the mention of Tom's name, Valerie's face clouded over. "I need to find out how he's doing, but I have no idea how to find him at Matthews Memorial. I certainly can't go there, but I need to know his condition." She couldn't bring herself to say the words, "if he made it" out loud.

"Hey, wait a sec. Tom has a daughter who goes to Yale. I met her one weekend when she came to visit him. I met her in the gym with him." This information from Paul jogged Valerie's memory.

"Of course, it's Amy. Shows my brain still isn't working properly. He called her from his land line a bunch of times. But how are we going to get into his apartment to retrieve the number?" Valerie's tone had now turned to upset.

"Paul to the rescue again. I forgot to tell you that when I got my cell phone back after we were released, there was a call from Joel. The poor guy was beside himself when we all left the apartment in various stages of 'bad and worse.' I called him back and told him the good news, but he was so unhappy to be left alone in the apartment. Maybe he can get into Tom's apartment and get the number off the phone."

Brendan asked, "Don't all the doors lock behind them as they close?"

"Apparently not or the intruder wouldn't have gotten in to Tom's apartment." Valerie's tone had sarcasm dripping all over it. "I must not have pulled the door shut when I left his apartment. This mess was my fault.

But I guess the door closes if you pull it with enough force."

"Wait a minute. Oh my God, this might be it! One day as we were in Tom's apartment, he was too lazy to walk into the bedroom to use the land line. After a while the cell phones were working most of the time, so he grabbed my cell phone and called her. I should have the number. Please, please, please, let me not have deleted it."

As Valerie was saying this, she was scrolling down the numbers on her phone. "Here it is! I'm calling her now."

If Amy had not answered her phone, Valerie would have jumped out of her skin. As Amy answered, Valerie launched into one long run-on sentence about who she was and what had happened. Amy knew who Valerie was and gave Valerie the answers she hoped to hear. Her father was in stable condition after surgery to remove the bullet. He had lost a lot of blood and was quite weak, but was expected to pull through.

Tom's residents had come through for him. When he was brought into the ER by EMS, not only did his residents recognize him, but they had also been fighting over who would be the one to treat him. He was lucid enough after surgery to ask them to call Amy and tell her what had happened and that he was okay. His residents made sure Karen Gallagher, the hospital administrator, knew what happened and "miraculously" she had him brought to the Transplant Unit to recover away from the chaos of the rest of the hospital. Amy told Valerie Tom was very concerned about what happened to her and wanted Amy to find out. Amy had no idea how to get in touch with Valerie or where she was, which was very upsetting to her father. Tom's cell phone was back at the apartment and Amy couldn't remember Valerie's last name.

"Here's his phone number in his room. I spoke to him and he sounds weak, but he definitely wants to talk to you. I guess when he's released from the hospital, he'll be able to get out of New York City. I will be so glad to see him. I told him he has to walk me down the aisle when I get married, and now I feel better that he will be able to keep that promise." Amy's voice quivered with that last sentence.

Valerie gave a thumbs up to Paul and Brendan as she spoke to Amy. She walked out of the cafeteria to have some quiet and privacy to talk to Tom.

A very weak voice answered the phone. Valerie said, "Hey, it's me. I am so glad to talk to you and that you're okay." Now Valerie's voice quivered.

Tom perked up a little as he heard Valerie's voice. "Where are you? What the hell happened? I think you saved my life."

"I think I probably got you shot. I was sick with worry that you weren't going to make it."

"But I did make it. Tell me what happened. I remember seeing you handcuffed, but not much after that," came the tired voice.

"Tom, I'll get to the whole story, but first I need to tell you something. I love you. I want us to be together. That was the hardest part these past few hours, not knowing if you were going to make it and if I was charged with a crime, that we couldn't be together. We made it through to the other side of this horrendous situation because of each other. I see how precious time is. I don't want to waste any of it, unless you and I waste it together." The tears were rolling down her cheeks.

While Tom couldn't hear the tears, he did hear a stifled sob and the crack in her voice. "I love you, too and we will be together. Hard to believe all that's happened to us. I've always believed in karma. Maybe the good karma is being returned to me for the work I've done for my patients. I think you might be the good karma.

"I want to take you to a really expensive restaurant where we can finally eat a good meal. Right now all they'll let me have is Jell-O, so I'm still hungry. I want to do some more crossword puzzles together and lose to you at backgammon."

Valerie laughed through the tears. "And I want us to continue BOTH of our nightly rituals."

Chapter 72

THE MAYOR

Shortly after Valerie and Tom's phone call, Paul, Valerie and Brendan left the cafeteria and were taken to a staging area where for a second time, they were put into hazmat suits and driven to a site near NYU Medical Center. There a makeshift clinic had been set up where they were going to be screened for any symptoms of radiation poisoning. If they displayed no signs of radiation poisoning or sickness, they would walk through what looked like a long tunnel, where the helicopters were waiting at the helipad on the East River to evacuate them out of the city and out of their long nightmare.

For the three of them, the nightmare was coming to a close, but what would be the fate of New York City, the self-proclaimed "greatest city in the world?"

The mayor hadn't been home at all since the dirty bombs went off. He slept on the couch in his office and probably hadn't had more than four hours of sleep in any given night. His wife had sent several changes of clothes that were washed by whoever was washing the uniforms of the emergency workers. He had absolutely no idea who that was. He hadn't eaten a meal that didn't consist of soup and/or sandwiches. This past morning he had eaten cream of celery soup for breakfast because the truck delivering the food to the command center broke down. At least it was something hot.

He was exhausted and stressed to the limit. If he could have, Ryan Bernard would have put on a hazmat suit himself and gone out to evacuate people. Anything to make this disaster better. He had received e-mails from virtually all the world leaders offering help and sympathy for the people of the city. Clergy from all faiths had told him of their concern and prayers. In the past week, he had received his second set of personal handwritten letters of encouragement from the Pope, the Archbishop of Canterbury, and the chief rabbi in Jerusalem. His response to each of them was to thank them for their concern and ask them to pray for strength for the emergency workers to continue to do their jobs against incredibly daunting odds. At the end of each message to the three clergymen, he wrote a personal note asking them to pray for him to make the right choices for the people of New York and if possible, to ask God to let this blight pass and pass quickly.

They were, however, starting to see good progress in the evacuation of the city. Well over one hundred fifty thousand people had been evacuated. As exhilarating as that was to him, it made him profoundly sad to see the city he loved, almost disintegrating before his eyes. The parts of the city which had been evacuated looked like a ghost town. One of his aides made a joke that they might see soon tumbleweed blowing down some of the streets. Ryan spun around and physically grabbed the aide. He told the aide to get the hell out of the room if he thought this was a joke. The rest of the people in the room were shocked by the mayor's violent reaction. However, that comment haunted him partially because there was some truth to it. Having his city becoming a ghost town was the last thing that Ryan wanted, yet he could not visualize any other way to deal with this disaster.

As the city got a handle on the evacuations, they then started an elaborate plan of bringing high protein food and bottled water to stranded people. The workers started calling themselves the Pod Squad, a take-off on the names of the *Mod Squad*, a TV show of the Sixties, and the God Squad, a priest and Rabbi talking to groups in the Nineties. The Pod Squad worked the opposite ends of the quadrants from the National Guard doing the evacuations, since it was still going to be some time before these people were evacuated. It had taken quite a few moving parts for the Pod Squad to come together. It came about when of the mayor's aides said his elderly mother was a recipient of Meals on Wheels and that idea should be able to be translated to the city's needs. After the mayor's aides scouted around, a company in Dutchess County that manufactured plastic containers offered to make the containers for the city. The company had to retool to make the new pods. The quantity of food to be put in the pods was staggering. The food was prepackaged and inserted into the pods. The pods looked like takeout containers from restaurants, so they were self-contained, not very heavy and easy to maneuver. The Pod Squad could bring in hundreds of these containers and distribute them quickly to any place, and be gone in a few minutes. Trucks and vans could be loaded with thousands of these pods.

The radiation levels had come down somewhat, but not enough to allow people to go outside safely. The scientists from DEA in the City continued to talk to the scientists at the Department of Defense several times a day about the scrubbings. They had tried fourteen different combinations and variations in the composition in the scrubbing material. They continued to spray different parts of the city with different formulas of the scrubbing, carefully monitoring each area to identify any better results. The results so far had been modest, but nowhere near good enough.

Ryan had just finished another briefing with the governor and Jordan Reid, the Director of Homeland Security, and when the flat screen went dark, he stood up, crumpled the five pages comprising the notes for today's briefing into a ball, and flung it with a vengeance into the wastepaper basket. He then sat back down, put his elbows on the table and put his head in his hands.

Two of the three aides who were with him during the briefing quietly left the room without saying a word. The third aide, Russell, didn't know what to do. He wanted to say something appropriate or comforting to the mayor, but he didn't know if the mayor wanted to hear some words of consolation or if he just wanted to be alone. He was afraid the mayor would start yelling at him if he said anything that would appear to the mayor to be empty, pious platitudes. So he just stayed exactly where he was standing in the room near the door, but staying completely quiet, hoping he was showing support, albeit quiet support to the mayor.

All of a sudden the door to the conference room flung open with a bang and the chief scientist from DEA, James Petrone, almost knocked the aide down. "Mr. Mayor," he screamed and the mayor jolted out of his chair. The mayor's back had been to the door. Before the mayor could say anything or ask what else could go wrong, a torrent of words came from James. "Number 14 worked! It worked! We sprayed the West 57th Street area early this morning, and by noon, the radiation levels came down seventy-five percent!"

"You what?" came the response from the mayor. "Are you sure?"

"Yes, the numbers came down. We've barely been moving the needle with the other products. We're going to spray three other areas right now and check the

levels in four hours and again in five hours. If the results are the same, DOD can reproduce Number 14.
This would make it safe to bring people out in closed
vehicles for now without hazmat suits. If we can in-
crease the efficacy some more, then we might be able to
clean the air and people can stay in the city. It's going to
take some refinement, but I think we can do it. The
greatest city in the world will be back."

Ryan hugged James and Russell at the same time.
When they finished the group hug, Ryan didn't have
any words, but his pulse had definitely increased, as he
hoped the pulse of New York City would.

Epilogue

Mohammed had never understood the meaning of a broken heart. Maybe he had been too young or didn't have enough life experience, but now he finally did understand. Sometimes he felt as if he couldn't breathe because the grief felt like a vise on his chest. He had struggled with whether he should send Akram's body back to Saudi Arabia or have him buried here. Finally, he had acquiesced to his aunt and uncle's pleas to return their son to them.

Akram was more of a brother to him than Mohammed's own brothers. Mohammed was now faced with the horrible task of going through Akram's personal belongings in their apartment. Their great adventure of going to America together was beginning to work out well, but it had been snuffed out by the dirty bombs. There were several things which Mohammed puzzled over and how they should be handled.

Mohammed had retrieved Akram's cell phone, keys and clothes from a central location set up by the city. Before Akram died, he apparently was lucid enough to sign a form giving Mohammed the right to claim his body and the possessions on his person. Mohammed had felt yet another stab in his heart when he thought of Akram dying alone in a hospital.

After Mohammed had charged Akram's cell phone, he found pictures of him with a beautiful woman with dark hair and a winning smile. As he scrolled down through the contacts in the phone, he saw the name Holly. Mohammed was trying to muster up enough courage to call her and tell her what had happened to Akram. She probably had called him after the dirty bombs, but he never returned the calls. Mohammed didn't know the password, so he couldn't check the messages, but he felt fairly certain that she must have called him and with no return call, she must have been frantic.

The next item among Akram's belongings was the flash drive. Mohammed had inserted it in his computer and saw that it contained financial information on accounts from Wally's customers. If Akram had downloaded this information onto a flash drive and took it with him, then it must be important. Mohammed knew that Akram was desperate enough to risk his life to get away from Wally and go out into the radiation, so this flash drive must be important. Mohammed was now debating if he should go the police with this information.

Wally had been in Toronto for about two months. Once the radiation levels had come down, New York City and the surrounding boroughs started to come back to life. As annoying as it was to remain in Queens after the dirty bombs, Wally was more bored than anything else. Although he was restless waiting around, Wally kept his boredom in check, and didn't want to call attention to himself by being one of the first people to try to leave the country. The brotherhood provided Wally with an attractive woman to be his travelling companion to cross the border into Canada and they seemed like husband and wife and didn't arouse any suspicions.

Wally's original intention was to go to Canada and let the heat die down even more. After a period of time when Wally felt it was safe, then he would probably go to London and from there go to the Middle East.

So far it hadn't been a bad winter, and Wally liked the cultural diversity in Toronto. There were all kinds of restaurants with great food. He was considering possibly staying here and maybe opening a new money transmitter business or some other related business. He had made good money in the money transmitter business even before the dirty bombs. After he had the customers' money moved into his master account, he was well fixed financially. He probably would take on a new identity. He had always liked the names Troy or Derrick. Those sounded much more American than Wally.

Joel had been beside himself that Tom had been stabbed and Valerie and Paul had been taken away in handcuffs. He was so unhappy that he was the only one left of the five of them who had braved the aftermath of the dirty bombs together.

As the radiation levels came down to acceptable levels, Joel was finally able to go home to his wife and son. He had been so terrified that something would happen to them and he would never see them again. In what was one of the more improbable friendships, Paul and Joel stayed in touch. They spoke twice a day until Joel was finally able to leave the apartment and go home. Joel always liked Valerie and felt she was such a down-to-earth person. She also made a point to call him and check on him while he was stuck alone in the apartments, and that meant a lot to him.

After Joel's small foray into electrical work taking down the light fixtures in the hallways, he realized he had an interest in working in a trade. He wanted to get his electrician's license. Paul had gone to Florida to continue work on David's campaign right after he was able to leave the city. Paul didn't want to admit it out loud to anyone, but he wanted nothing further to do with New York City. Right now it was easier to work on the campaign from Florida, and Paul had no interest in going back to New York anytime soon. David felt responsible that Paul was in New York when the dirty bombs went off, so he was more than willing to accede to Paul's request for a favor.

Paul asked David if he could give Joel a job at one of his properties in Florida and get him into the program to earn his electrician's license. So Joel and his family were moving to Florida courtesy of Paul and David.

The aftermath following the dirty bombs had not been kind to Brendan. He had retreated into himself while he was staying in Valerie's apartment. He tried his best to stave off his overpowering fear by throwing himself into the novels on his Kindle. When Brendan heard what he thought was a scream and a shot, he was paralyzed. He remembered bits and pieces of what happened. He had a vague recollection of Valerie screaming his name, and then coming into Tom's apartment with the police and the EMS workers. He couldn't remember anything in between.

He almost felt he couldn't take a breath when he saw Tom being wheeled out on a gurney with an oxygen mask on his face. Valerie and Paul told him he had stepped forward with the police to be their attorney, but that was a blur in his mind.

Brendan was having panic attacks and the medication was only partially helping. He was seeing a psychiatrist, who said between the therapy and the medicine, he would do better, but right now it didn't feel that way. He was afraid to get on the train, he was afraid to go to the city and some days he was afraid to even venture out of the house. He knew his wife was worried about him, and in truth, so was he. He secretly been researching bomb shelters and buying property away from the New York area. He hadn't told his wife about any of these plans.

Randy Cunningham had put on the full court press to get Valerie to come stay with him in his apartment in White Plains right after she left the city. In another life, Valerie might have agreed with not too much thought, but she got the vibes that Randy had another agenda. Her life had been turned upside down as it was, without complicating it any further.

Todd had wanted her to come back to L.A. for a few weeks, if not for good. Valerie didn't want to break up with Todd on the phone; she thought it was just plain mean, but when he pushed her and wasn't picking up on her cues, they had that conversation. Valerie felt bad for Todd, but her heart was with Tom. Of that she was absolutely certain. She knew it was easier being the one doing the dumping. After their conversation, she wasn't sure if Todd had even realized how far apart they had drifted.

Tom felt like the mythological phoenix that rose from the ashes. It especially seemed that way after the stabbing. His life had taken so many unexpected turns over the past few months. He felt it was merciful that no one knows the future. All he had planned to do was take a position in New York City for maybe as little as one year. It was a career move. It should have been no big deal.

The irony was not lost on him. He had never truly realized how precious each day was. His sickest patients seemed to have realized that, but maybe he never quite got it deep down. Valerie had said when she first called him in the hospital that whatever time they had left, she wanted to spend it with him.

Sometimes the end is the beginning and the beginning is the end.

About the Author
Noël F. Caraccio

Noël F. Caraccio is a full-time practicing attorney in Westchester County with a concentration in Real Estate, Trusts and Estates, and Credit Union law. She has served on the Board of Directors of a number of not-for-profit corporations, including School of the Holy Child, Bonnie Briar Country Club and WARC Properties. She is a member of the New York State Bar Association and the Westchester County Bar Association, where she was also a member of the Grievance Committee for many years. At the present time, she serves on the Board of Directors of Marian Woods, a not-for-profit adult residence in Hartsdale, New York. She is an avid golfer, having won the Club Championship at Bonnie Briar Country Club in Larchmont, New York.

Shattered City is her second novel, which emerged from the idea of how New York City would react to a catastrophic event and whether people had the ability to rise above their own self-interest. She is also the co-author of the novel *Secrets Change Everything*.

CPSIA information can be obtained
at www.ICGtesting.com
Printed in the USA
BVHW03s1658050418
512448BV00029B/6/P